B. Catling

HOLLOW

B. Catling is a Royal Academician, poet, sculptor, painter, and performance artist. He is professor emeritus at the Ruskin School of Art and emeritus fellow at Linacre College, University of Oxford. The author of the Vorrh Trilogy, Catling makes installations and paints imagined portraits of cyclopes and landscapes in tempera. He has had solo shows at Serpentine Gallery, London; Arnolfini in Bristol, England; the Suermondt-Ludwig Museum in Aachen, Germany; Hordaland Kunstsenter in Bergen and Museet for Samtidskunst in Oslo, Norway; Project Gallery in Leipzig, Germany; and Modern Art Oxford. Additionally, he is the creator of six large-scale installations/durational performances for Matt's Gallery in London.

HOLLOW

B. Catling

VINTAGE BOOKS
A DIVISION OF PENGUIN RANDOM HOUSE LLC
NEW YORK

A VINTAGE BOOKS ORIGINAL, JUNE 2021

Library of Congress Cataloging-in-Publication Data
Name: Catling, B. (Brian), author.
Title: Hollow / B. Catling.
Description: A Vintage Books original edition. |
New York : Vintage Books, a Division of
Penguin Random House LLC, 2021.
Identifiers: LCCN 2020038391
Subjects: GSAFD: Fantasy fiction.
Classification: LCC PR6053.A848 H66 2021 |
DDC 823/.914—dc23
LC record available at https://lccn.loc.gov/2020038391

Vintage Books Trade Paperback ISBN: 978-0-593-08115-0
eBook ISBN: 978-0-593-08116-7

Book design by Nicholas Alguire

www.vintagebooks.com

Printed in the United States of America
10 9 8 7 6 5 4 3 2 1

For Caroline, with me on the spiral
between the bittern and the lark

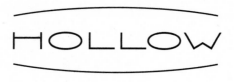

HOLLOW

DOG-HEADED MEN

"Saint Christopher is a dog-headed man."

The Oracle, bound in wet blankets, spoke for the first time with a voice to silence the angels. The eight men and their horses stood silently, paying close attention, while turning away from a ninth man, who hung in the tree above them, his face frozen in twisted pain. Scriven had been executed by the leader of this savage pack for the crime of writing.

Barry Follett would have let his victim stay where his lance had dropped him, but being eaten by wolves was considered a terrible fate, even if postmortem, so the men agreed he should be put out of the reach of wild animals. None of them cared enough to go through the motions of a real burial, and no one ever wanted to talk about the dead man again. So they strung him up in the branches of the nearest tree. The dense forests of sixteenth-century Europe were saturated with wolf packs. They had no fear of men, especially in the higher elevations and ragged mountains.

No one understood why Follett's intolerance of writing had led him to kill this man, and now he had forbidden any discussion about what had occurred. Not that conversation had been rampant thus far in their journey. The snow and cold blighted all communication. No one had time for small talk or cared to hear what the others had to say. Only the strange words of the Oracle, which seemed instigated by the sudden violence, were worth heeding— and the men listened carefully before the wind snatched its words away, whisking their sound and their mystery into the eternal fury that squalled above.

The group had made it to the hard granite of the upper sierras, and its cracked, narrow paths were tighter and less forgiving than Barry Follett's treacherous fist of a heart. Their leader sat alone on a bare rock above the gathering, silhouetted by a bright cold sun that stared down from the steel-blue dome of the sky. He was cleaning the head of his lance for a second time, while planning the route his seven ironshod pilgrims would take. He had hoped the first words the Oracle uttered would reveal his path; he was not expecting the inexplicable statement about a saint.

Follett had recruited his crew of mercenaries only months earlier, shortly after accepting the task to deliver the sacred Oracle to the Monastery of the Eastern Gate. His employers were the highest members of the High Church. They had summoned him, and he had consented only after being reassured that his potential employer had nothing to do with the Inquisition. Three solemn priests questioned him for more than an hour before nodding their agreement. One, an Ethiopian from a Coptic order, had been holding a small object during their meeting. He stood and held the precious thing so Follett could see it. It was a miniature, painted on ivory, showing a distant view of a vast mountain-like structure and its surroundings.

The oldest priest declared, "This is a depiction of your destination when it was known as the Tower of Babel."

The black finger of the priest standing over Follett pointed at the tower, and he said, " 'Tis now called Das Kagel."

A vast structure of spiraling balconies and stacked archways reached up to penetrate the clouds. A great movement of the popu-lace speckled the enormous tower, while villages and townships crowded around its base, all balanced against a calm sea support-ing a swarm of ships. The finger moved a fraction of an inch over the tiny painting to point more exactly at something that could not be seen.

"This is where you will find the monastery, and I should tell you the tower is changed beyond recognition. But you will know it by its profile and by the populace that infest the base. The Blessed One must be inside the monastery gates by Shrovetide, before the liturgical season of Lent closes the world and opens the mirror of Heaven."

Follett cared little for Heaven and had never been near the East-ern Gate; few had. It was a shunned place that most men would avoid. Only a savage gristle of a man like Barry Follett would, for a price, undertake what needed to be done.

The priest abruptly palmed the miniature, and the conversa-tion moved on to the details of Follett's responsibility, payment, and duty.

When the terms were accepted, the black priest described the abnormal and difficult qualities of Follett's "cargo," especially the feeding instructions.

"The Blessed Oracle has little attachment to this world. Its withered limbs make it incapable of survival without close support. You must appoint a man to watch it night and day and to supervise its cleaning. It eats little, but its sustenance is specific: it eats only the marrow of bones, and those bones must be treated, prepared, by the speech of sinners."

The other two priests paid great attention to Follett, gauging and weighing the confusion and disgust in his eyes.

"Your choice of the right men to join you in this mission will be crucial. They must have committed heinous crimes, and they must have memories of those deeds that they are willing to confess. You will encourage or force them to speak those confessions directly into the box of bones; the bone marrow will absorb the essence of their words. This ritual is called a Steeping, and it is at the core of your duties. The marrow will then be fed to the Blessed Oracle in the manner of an infant's repast. Do I make myself clear?"

Follett nodded.

"Once the Oracle becomes accustomed to you, and when it needs to, it will speak."

"Secretly? Just to me?" asked Follett.

"No, out loud. It has nothing to do with conspiracy or secrecy. The Oracle speaks only the truth. Much of what it says will make no sense to you because it often speaks out of time, giving the answer long before the question is asked or even considered. Its words should be carefully examined, especially if it is guiding you through unknown lands."

A long silence filled the room.

"Do you have any questions for us?" asked the eldest priest.

Follett had only one question.

"What animal should be used for the preferred bones?"

A wave of unease elbowed aside the earlier composure.

"*Preferred* is a little difficult," answered the black priest.

"You mean anything we can get on our journey?"

"Yes. Well, in part."

"Part?"

"We cannot tell you what you already know in your heart."

"Man bones?"

"We cannot say."

"Human bones?"

Follett grinned to himself while maintaining a countenance of grim, shocked consideration. After allowing them to dangle from his hook, he changed the subject back to how the Oracle would bless and guide his journey and how he should speak to it. Thus, he indicated to his new masters that they had selected the right man to provide safe passage for the precious cargo. They gave him brief, broad answers and finished the interview with the pious conviction that their part in this transaction had been satisfactorily concluded. All other details were left to him. He had carte blanche in the "sacred" assignment.

Follett needed men who would obey without question, who had stomachs of iron and souls of leather. Men who would take a life on command and give their last breath for him and, on this particular mission, have no terror of the unknown or veneration of the abnormal. They would also have to have committed violent crimes that, if proven, would consign them to the pyre and the pit. The first two of his chosen company he had worked with before; the other five were strangers recommended to him.

Alvarez was his oldest acquaintance; they had nearly died together on four occasions. Without doubt, Alvarez would be the chosen guardian and servant of their precious cargo. Follett demanded that Alvarez accompany him to take charge of the delicate creature.

The Oracle had traveled from Brocken in the Harz Mountains. Alvarez and Follett were to collect it from a forest crossroads three miles from a tavern in the Oker region, a sullen valley dominated by the vast mountain range. On the third day, it arrived, escorted by two silent, heavily armed women and a tiny, birdlike priest. The soldiers placed the handmade crate, lined with chamois leather and silk, between them, and the priest again explained the complexities of the Oracle's needs—the details of its feeding, travel, and preternatural appetites. He delivered his instructions three times in an eerie high-pitched singsong so that the tones, rhythms, and resonances insinuated themselves into the deepest folds of the men's memories. Every particle of instruction, every nuance of requirement lodged there, keeping their disgust at what they had been told to do from ever touching them. They were simply caring for a rare thing that would direct them on their journey.

Alvarez took his charge seriously. He would protect and mother this abnormality, even against the other men in Follett's chosen pack, if necessary. He was able to dredge up a kind of respect for the contents of the box, which helped dissipate his rising gorge every time he undid the catches and lifted the lid.

Pearlbinder was a bounty hunter and paid assassin, if the price was high enough. He was the biggest man in the pack, and the long riding coat he wore over his tanned fringed jacket suggested a bulk that resembled a bear. His speed, lightness of foot, and untrimmed beard added to the impression. He also owned the most weapons, including a Persian rifle that had belonged to his father. He carried many memories of his homeland and wore his mixed blood loudly and with unchallengeable pride, but his use of weapons was more an act of pleasure than an application of skill. Follett had known Pearlbinder for fifteen years and always tried to recruit him for the more hazardous expeditions.

Tarrant had the concealed ferocity of a badger entwined with a righteous determination, qualities that might be invaluable in this mission. He also spoke frequently of a family that he must get back to, so the payment at the end of this expedition would see his future solved. Thus, Follett would never have to lay eyes on him again—a conclusion that he relished with most men.

The Irishman O'Reilly was a renegade, wanted by the authorities in at least three countries. He was a ruthless man who needed isolation and a quick reward. In Ireland, he had been part of a marauding criminal family, most of whom found their way to the gallows before the age of thirty. He had been on the run all his life, and his slippery footfall had separated him from reality. Brave and foolish men might say it had turned him a bit softheaded, but they never said it to his face. Some of his stories seemed fanciful, especially when he spoke of times that were different from the ones they were all living in now.

Then there was Nickels, the bastard of one of Follett's dead friends. He was fast, strong, and ambitious for all the wrong things. Skinny and serpentine, with a quick mouth and an even quicker knife hand, he was also the youngest, so they called him "the Kid."

Follett knew he needed men experienced with the terrain, and the Calca brothers were perfect. They had grown up as mountain men and had traveled these lands before. Although they looked like twins, Abna was two years older than his brother, Owen. They were not identical, but they had learned to be alike, to think and act as one in defense against their brutal father and against the harshness of the nature that had no respect or interest in singularity. They were strongest by putting aside the need for any traces of individuality, opinions, or desires. They were bland, incomprehensible, and solid, the perfect slaves for Follett, who told them what to do and what to think. The Calcas obeyed him without question and mostly remained mute, except for a weird sibilant whisper that occasionally passed between them and sounded like a rabid deer dancing in a husk-filled field.

Lastly, there had been Scriven, who proved to be a grievous mistake. He had come highly recommended for his skill as a tracker and a bowman. Follett had taken him without suspecting that he was an avid practitioner of the worst form of blasphemy that the old warrior could image, and one that he would never tolerate in his company. But nobody saw Scriven's demise coming, especially the man himself. Better that such errors are exposed early before they turn inward and slyly contaminate the pack. Scriven had been found spying on the other men and making written copies of their confessional Steepings. He had been caught listening and scribing Follett's own gnarled words. Pearlbinder grabbed him and held him against a tree by his long hair. He pushed his sharp knife against the man's jugular vein, allowing just enough space for his larynx to work and for him to attempt to talk his way out of his fate. He was midway through when Follett unsheathed his lance and pushed three feet of it through Scriven's abdomen. Written words had condemned Follett before. Words written by others that he could not read. Ink keys that had locked him in a Spanish cell for three years. He had always distrusted written words, and now he despised them.

"Get it warm," shouted Follett. Alvarez started to unpeel the stiffening bedding and clear the Oracle's nose and mouth of frosted water. Dry blankets were unpacked from the mules and quickly bound around the small blue body.

"Choir," bellowed Follett, and all of the men except Pearlbinder made a tight scrum around the diminutive bundle, forcing the little body heat they had toward their shivering cargo. This was the part they all hated, except Tarrant, who was always first to press close to the Oracle. Proximity to the otherworldly thing made the rest of the men ill and turned what was left of their souls inward and septic. But they had all agreed to be part of the ritual. It was in their contract. The balance of gold to horror was a much gentler bargain than many of them had made before. Their heat and guilt were needed, and they were balanced by the bliss emanating from the Oracle.

"I now know it lives. It only lives when it speaks or makes that sound of words," said the Kid. "Behold, the rest of the time, it is dead."

"Verily, it is not dead," said Pearlbinder from the other side of the men. "Make no mistake, it sees and understands more of this world than thee ever will."

The Kid's smirking sneer was instantly quelled by Pearlbinder's next words.

"It sees all and knows the ins and outs of thy soul. It remembers every stain of thy thinking and watches every act we commit. It will engrave a map of thy rotten heart on a scroll of its own flesh."

Any talk of scrolls or books made the men alert and anxious. All knew such talk was impossible after what had just happened, but Pearlbinder was clever and could speak around things that no other dare even think.

"Take great note of what thee speaks, for it is remembering."

The Kid spat, and nobody spoke again.

There was a gnawing silence as their breath plumed in the air, and each thought back on the words about animals and men and men who were animals. Something about the obscure statement that the Oracle had said seemed familiar and kept the bile of that day's events at bay.

The landscape and the clouding-over sky had begun to close around them. Snow had left the growing wind and ice slivered into its place.

"Move out," shouted Follett. "Tie Scriven's horse on behind. We have four hours before dark."

Everything was packed away, and the men were in their saddles and moving. Their leader stayed behind, mounted beneath the tree. When they were out of sight, he lifted his twelve-foot lance and pushed it high above his head and to one side so that its blade nestled and writhed among the ropes that held the frozen man to the swaying wood. The wolves would feed that night, a good time after he, and those he trusted, had passed beyond this place.

CYST

Inside the cloister of the Monastery of the Eastern Gate, Friar Dominic stood in a vacant posture, a thin young monk trapped somewhere between dither and doubt, his arm outstretched toward a dirty black rope that hung on the outer wall of the church. He yanked at the rope without ever looking at it, and the smallest bell in the tower clattered out. "The bell with the wooden tongue" they called it, because it was cracked and gave a poorly defined sound capable of carrying across only a small distance. Still, the bell gave him courage because it would bring others.

Friar Dominic had been passing though the cloister when he heard a voice in the Cyst, which had once been the nest of the Oracle Quiet Testiyont, who was now dead. Still, a few of the brotherhood had reported hearing a faint utterance in the last month. The Cyst was a hollow built into the wall—too small to be called a room and too big to be called a recess—with a small aperture that allowed in a minimum of daylight and air and for the prophecies of the Oracle to be heard. In many ways, it was a typical anchorite dwelling. There was just enough space to be walled in alive and still manage to exist, and more important, to be separate from the world out-side. Over the years, its dimensions had changed to accommodate the different shapes and sizes of the beings who formed the long, unbroken chain of oracular occupation. Now it was a remnant, the Cyst cracked open and the Oracle's body gone. The ragged hole was waiting for a new sacred body to be sealed inside.

The rules stated that the person closest to the voice in the wall must approach and record its sayings, before calling others to wit-ness. But nobody ever wanted to be the first participant in this phenomenon, and most avoided that corner of the cloister. Espe-cially after the Oracle died. The piece of charcoal that hung on a string near the Cyst to record such divine grace was damp and faded. Unused. Now Friar Dominic's hand was reaching out for it.

The Monastery of the Eastern Gate sat in deep seclusion. For centu-ries, it had guarded one of Earth's darkest secrets. Every monk there knew the function of their home. Some embraced it; some ignored it, giving themselves over to other duties of prayer and dedication. A few had been turned mad or inverted, but most just got on with their allotted tasks and pushed the vast abnormality, which was in the daily care of the monastery, to the back of their minds.

Each novice who wanted to be admitted to the abbey had to witness what made it unique. Afterward, many ran away and never returned. In a few, the sight planted a seed of insanity deep in the putty of their minds that would slowly grow to infest their souls. Most saw it only once, but a few demanded an annual exposure. Dominic had been taken there by the ancient Friar Cecil when he was thirteen years old.

"Beyond this gate lies a great walled enclosure that sections off a portion of landscape down to the sea's very edge. Three square miles of confined isolation in which rages a perpetual war between the living and the dead." Friar Cecil watched the boy closely as he spoke, searching for signs of terror or disbelief.

He had performed this ritual chore many times and thought he knew every conceivable consequence of what he was about to divulge.

"What you must understand is that what you witness is not a manifestation of evil but the workings of the mind of God."

He had said these sentences so many times before that the words seemed to have lost their vitality and meaning, in the way that over-washed patterns of color maintain only a pale impression of what they must have been.

Friar Cecil waited a moment for the young man to absorb his words. When he saw the flinch of acceptance, he placed the vast iron key that he was holding into the lock of the iron gate. As he turned the key, he explained, "For the living, this is the only way in and out of the enclosure."

Before them stretched a dismal road lined with trees of oak and ash. Beyond this rose a gray, featureless wall that went on for miles. Dominic stopped to look about himself and then back at the abbey, which seemed to have shrunk disproportionately to the small distance they had walked.

"There are no windows on this side of the abbey," commented the boy.

"It is better that way. Nothing to distract us from our duties."

"But there is another door, a small one. There, at the base of that towerlike structure." He pointed to a newish windowless door in the ancient stone.

Friar Cecil ignored him and did not look around.

"That is for the abbot's use and does not concern you."

They walked silently for a while in the unkempt field that seemed a terrible waste of land to the boy. They reached a hump in the field that enabled them to see what lay below. Sounds and a wafting stench arose from nowhere, making the boy shudder, and the smoke smeared the dense air, burning his eyes.

"Brace thyself."

As the old monk spoke, the view unzipped into growing focus and accumulating detail, revealing a great battle, where thousands of bodies clashed in ferocious turmoil. Grim reaper armies struggled against citizens of the undead, or those who did not know which they were. The volume increased as the scene became clearer.

Dominic watched grinning skeletons hack apart men, women, and children. They fell, rolled over, and were frozen stiff for a moment, before struggling to their knees, dragging their separated parts together, and rising to fight again.

"It's always the same," shouted Cecil over the racket. "The same victims are forever punished and butchered, and then arise, pulling back together their hacked limbs and picking up their dented, rusted weapons to push back against the always-triumphant troops of bone and savagery."

Dominic was frozen to the spot, watching the skeletal army's ruthless, impassive joy as they executed and tortured all who attempted to stay alive.

"This is the Glandula Misericordia," shouted Cecil. "The Gland of Mercy. In the real world, it forms a balance and an expectancy of the day-to-day existence of death. This is the Mercy that God has given us, and as long as this epic tableau continues, humankind will be protected from facing the horror and numbing reality of the pointlessness of life, and therefore the futility of faith and the belief in the Almighty."

The young Dominic aged as he witnessed the perpetual Mercy. His innocence was being stripped away with every disgusting sight that assailed his childhood ideas about the glory of God.

Friar Cecil saw how transfixed Dominic had become and tugged at his arm. "I think you have seen enough for one day, or for a lifetime." Cecil tried to break the spell and move the boy away, but Dominic would not budge. Only his head moved as he scanned every detail below.

"You must not become enraptured here. They will see you and want you to join them."

The resonant echo of a hurdy-gurdy joined in with the screams and the sound of crackling flames.

"You have seen enough."

Dominic turned to Friar Cecil as if only just remembering he was still there. "There is a king down there in a spillage of gold coins."

The bright, shocked vacancy of his words moved the old monk.

"All the world is there, my son. And it is our duty at times to bring the world here to see. His Holiness in Rome has sent many kings and potentates here."

"Some are laughing and playing at dice."

Friar Cecil had no reply for such incongruity and confusion.

"Who is the naked man who sits so alone?" Dominic continued to question.

These words jolted Cecil, who looked from Dominic's face into the writhing field of conflict.

"Where?" he asked.

The novice pointed toward a dark, broken archway. In its shadow stood a white naked man with his eyes closed. Cecil turned away, grabbing Dominic's arm.

"You have seen too much," the monk said, and steered the novice back toward the retreating path.

The sound and stench drained away, and the boy asked, "How can all this be kept secluded, hidden from the world?"

"It is not hidden; it is unseen," answered Cecil. "You can feel the influence of the wind without seeing it. Very few have actually seen this place, but all have benefited from its existence. Its power blows through our monastery and across into the villages, the cities, and the world. And those in power know it is the abbot and monks of this abbey who possess a direct relationship with, if not actual control of, the Gland. And the Oracle embedded in its walls is the focus of that conjunction." They finally reached the gate. "The Oracle known as Quiet Testiyont is the most famous in living memory, which stretches back into centuries of forgetfulness. If you survive today, you will be allowed near his presence."

Dominic did indeed survive the ordeal of witnessing the Gland, and during the next seven years, he had been present on several occasions when the voice in the wall spoke. But now the Quiet had passed, and there were whispers among the Brotherhood that what possessed the Cyst might be a ghost or worse. Abbot Clementine refused to discuss the matter and had little tolerance for any who did. He used his faithful Friar Cecil to keep an eye on the rest of the monastery and report his findings.

Cecil was not known for being the sharpest knife in the box. Prior to Clementine's arrival, he had never been given any position or task of responsibility, leaving his inherent desire for sly servitude unrealized. The new abbot recognized something in Cecil that he could use and instantly proclaimed him as the Gatekeeper, the only monk who could take novices to see what existed beyond the Eastern Gate. This had been a wise decision, indeed. Cecil's lack of imagination and intelligence meant that the horrors found in the Gland did not disturb him, so the novices felt safe, clinging to his unemotional indifference as if it were strength or faith. It also made him a devoted slave to the abbot, satisfying his every whim and his need to know everything that was going on in the abbey . . . which, at the moment, appeared to be nothing.

Then the whispers started again.

Dominic heard the impossible and knew what he was supposed to do. He grabbed the charcoal and scrawled what he thought he heard onto the lumpen plasterwork. As he scratched, Dominic looked around, hoping to see another person somewhere in the cloister—someone to share the moment with or, better still, someone to pass the moment to—but the cloister was deserted.

The sound came again, and something in its muffled insistence forced him to lean even closer, almost putting his nose into the ragged gash and peering timidly inside. There was an unease that shivered between the need and the consequence of that intimacy. He stooped there a long while, listening for any sound that did not belong to the open courtyard or to the busy world outside. Dominic let go of the distractions and was about to concentrate on the wall when the tiny sound of a skylark, far beyond all human noise, distracted him. Its constant velocity dipped and spun. For a moment, he was there with it, soaring above the abbey, removed from the endeavors of man, weightless, bobbing in the sunlit air.

Then what was in the Cyst bellowed, and Dominic fell back into darkness.

MARROW

Three days after the murder of Scriven, the group came to an unmarked crossroads. Follett asked the Calcas if they knew or could divine which path they should take. After some hushed mumbling, they declared they did not. The other riders looked at one another and at the confusion of paths. They had been traveling in the high country for just less than a month, which was enough time for almost all of them to gauge and weigh the contours and gullies of each other's personalities and woeful talents.

"We will make camp here and ask the Blessed One," said Follett, who then called to Alvarez. "Get it ready."

Alvarez dismounted and unpacked three soiled blankets from the mules. Throwing the blankets into a snowdrift, he kicked and stamped them until they were sodden. Then he lifted the Oracle's crate off the pony.

Follett put some snow into a bucket and added tepid water, which he kept in a leather and canvas bottle close to his horse's neck; the warmth and movement of the animal was just enough to keep the water from freezing. Once the snow had softened, he plastered the blankets with the icy paste. The Oracle started to shiver, and its stumpy teeth began to chatter and bite into the thick cloth. Then Follett applied the slush to its head. This process had been simpler on the plains, where water was plentiful and the warmth of the day allowed the men to rest while they waited for the Oracle to speak. There, the fast-running streams also added a lively sound to the grim ritual, concealing some of the Oracle's noises, which hadn't been words then.

But up here every sound was brittle, and so everybody listened; the waiting time seemed endless in the crisp air. The only advantage was that the cold brought on the fever more quickly, and in the fever, there might be words.

The rest of the men made camp under a great sheltering oak. They all sat around a small fire to eat their meager rations. Follett stood up and walked to the panniers and returned with the Oracle's fodder, the box of bones, which, in the old tongue, they called a Pyx.

"O'Reilly, it is thy session to charge the bones."

Follett carried the Pyx into the gathering with great solemnity. Everyone had known it was O'Reilly's turn and assessed where they were in the rotation.

The Pyx was full of femurs and humeri: sawn sections of long bones heavy with marrow.

O'Reilly came forth, took up the box, and retreated among the trees. Each man conducted the act in his own way, but all chose solitude in which to perform the ritual. O'Reilly crouched against a vast rock and perched the box on his knees. After a time of consideration, and maybe joyful expectation, he unwrapped a green silk cloth and draped the fabric over his head and the box, much in the way a patient with congested lungs inhales warm vapors from a bowl of boiled herbs. Once his head and the box were under the smooth containment, he twisted the latch, lifted the lid, and began his confession.

"This time I will speak of a burning that I caused at the age of nine. In the homeland it was, the western shores. I have little memory of the

doing of it now. It ain't much, not like the slayings that I offered before, this one's thinner than fly piss, but it's all I have left to say.

"*It was the first time I had been inside a* house. *My da had broken in and hammered the Occupiers to a pulp. He had taken me and my two cousins with him on a raid for the first time. Some of the Occupiers had run away inside the* house, *hiding in the distance and tallness of It.*

" '*Twas difficult for me to understand. We lived in one room at home, and here there were many rooms stacked upon each without tumbling, all joined together so there was no outside between them, so that you could walk inside them, one to the next without ever leaving. Even the lavs was inside so that the stars and wind could not see ya. And the ice cudna whiff and nip at ya when ya's took a dump. Everything in the world was inside. So I went running in all of them, trying to spy where the prey had fled. I stopped every then and now to listen for footfalls. But cudna. I stood there, stopped dead, and looked about in this endless place of polished wood, not knowing which was before and after. I knew there was another soul close by and thought that they had stopped running, too. Holding their breath and muscles when I stopped to listen, but still giving off tiny little wee inflictions. Bits of their existence ricocheted and reflected about like spots of light to illuminate the stillness of the place.*

"*It was in one of those that I saw the walls more clearly, like in a shudder of candle. I touched that spot and saw that the wall was made of lots of smaller parts all stacked in rows like the neatest turf or peat you've ever seen and on its side, like. I picked at one and it came loose, kinda slid into my hands. It was like a small block of wood or hard peat or the sort of cake that Ma makes only at Christmas. But it felt like hide. The tanned skin of a beast, a fine beast. Then it fell apart in my hands—not all the way, mind, half of it fell open and just hung there, showing its innards. Which flapped like a breeze and were made of something else. Another dried skin, I think it was, thin as a dried leaf, but with a touch on it that I cudna understand. I held it close to my face and smelt its strangeness, then I sees it's been infested, eaten all over by some kinda bug. I've seen this kinda thing before in old wood. Fair nibbled all over, every part of it. I puts my finger on it to feel the squiggles and tiny wee notches. But they ain't there. So I put my eye right up agin' it and just about sees that the squiggles are not hollows but stains, made in a pattern of lines. Then I remember I seen a smaller one of these blocks before. The priest of the parish had it. Bible, 'twas named.*

"Then I hear a sound deep inside the house *and realize that my da and my kin are far-off. Then it came to me: I had lost my direction, a-gawping at this thing, and misplaced my comings and goings. Lost, I was lost. I had lost whence I had come without a moon or a tree or a fire to guide me. I was just about to holla when I heard a new sound close by. I gripped my cudgel, dropped the maggoty block, and spindled about. The sound came from a tall wooden box, a long thin one standing up on its end, farther off in the distant shadows. Like a coffin it was, but taller, as if made for a tall thin man. It was echoing inside, the noise of the creature in its nest. Atop the box was fixed a plate on its side that looked like the moon with more squiggles chasing each other all in its circle. Then I sees that the front of the box has got a long skinny door in it with a key. So I pulls on it and the thin door opens. Inside are things dangling down and amid them is a wee brat. The brat of this* house, *hiding. 'That's a shit place to hide,' says I, and the brat squeaks out between sobbings, ' 'Tis my grandfather's cock.' ' 'Tis it now,' says I, and shut the door and turn the key and nicked it for myself. It was dense with wealth and sat heavy in my worn-out pocket agin' my bare skin. The noise inside the box changed. Just then my cousin Mik came along and I was joyed to greet him. He's a-grinnin' and stinkin' of smoke and oil, a big flagon of which he's got in his hand.*

" 'I's got one in 'ere,' *says I.*

"Mik *kicks the box with his foot, and it jangles like a church bell playing itself. So he puts the flagon down and wraps his arms around the box and gives it a big shake, like in a wrestling match. Then the top falls off and all manner of tiny wheels and hatpins and bits of insect and husk jump out, all made of clever metal.*

"We ain't seen nothing like it before, or since, because there ain't nothing like it back here in these bygone times. Mik *stamped his boot down hard on all of them bits skittering across the floor . . . just in case, like. Something inside the box is a-slithering about, and quick as a magpie* Mik *lifts the flagon high above his head and pours oil down into its innards. It starts to leak from underneath like Granni O'Shaughnessy; it's also juddering and pecking about the floor, also like Granni O'Shaughnessy.*

"'Like Granni O'Shaughnessy,' says Mik, 'let's put a spark in her bloomers.'

"And so he sets a flame to the little legs under her and whoomp up she goes, with most of the flames kept inside the box and shooting out its neck.

"''Tis a fuckin volkino,' laughs Mik.

"'Or a chimney,' says I.

"Then there is a sound farther inside the house.

"'Will that be ya da?' asks Mik.

"'Dunno, could be another runaway,' says I.

"'I'll see,' he says, and scoots off into the other darkness.

"There's a bit of spluttering, and some screams in the box now, and the wood of it is very hot to touch. Steam has come out of the keyhole, so I don't think it no good to use the key; instead I drag a wealthy chair over to it so I can climb up high to peer down into its burnt guts. It stinks bad and the only sounds and movements now are crispy and snapping. It's very dark and smoky in there. And then I sees 'im, or maybe her, can't tell with all the hair burnt off, looking more like me, about the same size, looking straight up the chimney with smoke coming out the empty holes where the eyes should be. That's when I started laughin', nearly fell off the chair, I did. Was still laughin' when Da dragged me home and said that I mustn't tell anyone, ever, about that . . . and I did not. Not until now. Now it's box to box like, which I hope is accepted.

"Amen."

When he finished, he closed the Pyx softly and took his head out of the silk cloth, grinning. As he returned to the other men, they all smelled the musk of his dark past, and some of them thought they had heard laughter in his confession. That should not have been possible. O'Reilly had peculiar ways, and some of the things he spoke made no sense, but laughing while in the Pyx could be dangerous for them all. Some glanced at Follett to see if he had heard or had an opinion, but he did not, as all his attention was focused on the next day of the journey. O'Reilly handed the Pyx over to Alvarez.

Follett looked up from his planning and ordered the allowance.

"Two catches per."

Each man retrieved his tin cup and approached their leader who had unsheathed the whiskey. Alvarez was first because he had important and disgusting work to do; the powerful shot would help him in this endeavor. O'Reilly staggered in toward the back of the queue and Follett saw him.

"Not thee; not tonight. Thou knowest the Laws."

It had only been O'Reilly's second session of Steeping, and in truth, he had forgotten that nothing strong was allowed for a day after the act.

"But, Captain, I used a telling from my other times, from the before or after of it, not from now." The Irishman was wide-eyed and ruddy as he spoke quietly to Follett.

"Are thee spinning yarns again? More ghost stories and lies about other centuries?" Follett was obviously annoyed by this new conversation.

"But, Captain, it's like that in my homelands; the befores and the afters get mixed up and cross-streamed in the everydayness of it all."

"This ain't your country, and you obey the times we ride in and the path that I ordain. None other!"

The conversation was closed, and so was the supply of whiskey, which Follett yanked back into his saddlebag and went to join the company of horses.

Alvarez had already taken charge of the Pyx and removed a truncated bone from it. This he held in his left hand, and in his right was a long metal spoon with a delicate pointed bowl; between his knees was clamped the head of the Oracle. With great deliberation, he dug the lip of the spoon deep into the marrow of the bone and rotated it to core out a section. He gingerly retrieved the contents and fed them to the lolling mouth before him. As it ate, the creature brightened, a radiance blooming under its colorless skin. It became agitated and tried to look around in the darkness, squirming against Alvarez's grip as if a new set of muscles had developed deep inside its shapeless body. Suddenly it pushed hard against Alvarez's groin and pistoned up its head. The light from the campfire flickered across its face. Marrow was smeared all around its open grinning mouth that seemed to be trying to kiss Alvarez. Very few things had ever made the old warrior back off until now. He sprang away from the Oracle, letting it tumble into the stained snow. Follett heard his companion's cursing and rushed to his side, while waving at the other men to stay where they were.

"That fucking thing is disgusting."

Follett stared at Alvarez in disbelief.

"Let's get it back in its box," he said and leaned down into the snow to retrieve it.

As he did so, the Oracle rolled over on its back and said, "The cloven road awaits. It can only be seen in the dark of now."

Follett hesitated and then commanded Alvarez to help him carry the Oracle to the crossroads. It was pitch-black and they stumbled twice, finally placing their burden in the middle of the paths. It sat still as a rock for a moment, then shuddered, turned its body, and pointed its only vestigial limb toward one of the tracks. Follett found a small boulder and marked the direction.

While they were away, the men talked quietly and built up their fire. The drink and the meager amount of thick, hot food they ate had a soporific effect on them all. A brief splutter of conversation burbled among them, mostly insignificant, until the Kid said, "I have never seen a man killed with a lance before."

All sunk deeper into what was left of their drinks, looking around to make sure that Follett was out of earshot.

"He made the mistake of crossing the captain," said Pearlbinder.

"I know that, but it's a bad way to die," said the Kid.

"He had his moment to repent before Follett unsheathed his blade, but he forsook it. We all knew that once that steel was uncovered, there was no going back. Follett was a cavalryman before being cast out; he can use a lance like most men use a sword, and he enjoys it."

"But Scriven's crime was nothing!" said the Kid.

"Not to the captain, it weren't. Captain hates books and writing. 'Twas statements taken that way that condemned him," said Tarrant. "Writing had lied about what the captain had said, and wormed it black and permanent against the white paper skin."

"That's what Scriven did: he listened to the captain's confession to the bones, and then wrote it down," explained Pearlbinder.

"But why? What would he do with it?" asked the Kid.

"That we will never know," said Tarrant.

A hush hung like fog around the men.

Then O'Reilly chirped up. "He could have had mine if he wanted. 'Twas a real juicy one, would make good writings."

The Kid laughed; the other men groaned and turned away. The flickering light of the fire sealed the conversation, all remaining questions and answers joining the pale smoke as it swirled up into the dark branches and the clear cold sky above. The men pulled their sleeping sacks closer to the fire and started to crawl their way into earthly oblivion.

DULL GRET

The lands at the base of Das Kagel were undergoing a change that nobody understood. It had begun two years after the Spanish arrived, dominating everything and exporting much wealth and produce to their impoverished lands. Then their church entered into a new phase of intolerance, as the Inquisition took control of civic matters and found punishable heresies in all things. This church enforced rules and laws in the Lowlands without any respect for national or local traditions and politics. Only the festivals that matched the Inquisition's delight at bloodshed were encouraged.

The same veins of corruption, the same arteries of cruelty, were used by the plague as it swept through the land. Once it had taken its toll and moved on, the abnormalities and the visions began. Omens and sacrifices followed, and odd creatures and unknown animals that nobody could explain began to appear. They were being seen more frequently. The peasants called them Woebegots and Filthlings because they were even lower on the food chain.

Meg Verstraeten would surprisingly become the most famous of the peasants. Born into the ranks of near–slave labor hired by land-owning farmers, Meg's prospects were slight, and she was expected to snuff out by her early fifties. But she had reached a sallow maturity, having never yet complained about the hard work and abuses of her first forty-six years. Meg had gotten lucky with her late marriage to the appalling Rynch Cluvmux, a slow, dim man who had once had money and prospects.

The only things they shared were anger, frustration, and loneliness. Meg withered with determined indifference to fit the derogatory name "Dull Gret." She began to wear her grown-in ugliness out loud, as a physical manifestation of her egregiously cankered soul. She was gaunt, bony, and tall. Her profound melancholia came from long-term abuse and isolation, which had soured a unique child into a demi-hag, fueled by the ill-tempered, black bile of the gallbladder and infected by the increasing rankness of her marriage.

Meg brooded and talked to herself about all the injustices of the world of men. Men were foolish, wasting time and lucre in idleness and bigmouthed prick-loutary. Cluvmux was a perfect example, a worthless apology of a man whose only half-achieved purpose in life had been to sire their son, Dircx. The boy had grown up watching his father piss away his trade and its lucrative consistency. Now they were broke.

Cluvmux was the third son of a third son, in swine butchery with a special skill in the cutting and curing of belly draft. But the sweet fat had turned bitter with a drunken botch-up of the family recipe and the loss of two fingers. The boy had seen everything around him fall away or had been slapped senseless for no apparent reason.

On his sixteenth birthday, Dircx ran away from home, but with his father's hereditary foolishness, he did it during the closure of the curfew bell: when no citizen was allowed out of their home, let alone on the open road. He had traveled no more than a couple of miles from the town gate when the Caballistas del Camino found him, tied him by the heels to their horses, and dragged him back to their prison keep, his poor head and face meeting every rock and dent on the dusty road and every brick and chiseled scroll on the bridge along the way.

Cluvmux was far too afeard to approach them and beg for leniency for his son's transgression, so Meg had to go; she had to do it.

No one was sure if the colonization of the Lowlands had anything to do with the arrival of the first Woebegots and Filthlings, but they came around the same time. The creatures began to swim toward the villages in the thick brown waters of the rivers. Some crawled onto land to seek nutriment at the town gate; some were found sheltering in barns and stables. At first they were quickly slain, being feeble, slow-witted, and friendly. But as the years passed, they grew tougher and began to understand their surroundings and to build a nervous resistance, which had the flavor of retaliation.

And now they were multiplying and becoming more robust in appearance and size. But most alarming was that they were starting to master language and communicate among themselves. The reason for their evolution, their increase in numbers, and some of the other more startling circumstances that were happening under the shadow of Das Kagel was unknown. Only the abbot of the Monastery of the Eastern Gate feared a possible cause and effect. The death of Quiet Testiyont had not been announced to the outside world, and the absence of a working Oracle coincided with many of the abnormalities that were being seen, reported, and dreamed.

There were two Woebegots on the bridge the day that Meg decided to beg for the release of her son, and they watched her very carefully as she traipsed across. One resembled a large black newt but with a crested head and a pinched face, looking like a burned leaf folded to give a near-human expression. It hung close to the parapet in a stain of water. Trying to clamber up onto the road from the side of the bridge, it had fallen back into the river again and again. Finally it heaved itself up and over the edge and sat in mud and exhaustion.

The other one was thinner and looked like a stretched rat, or some sort of weasel or mink. She could not see its face because its entire head was hidden under a child's sunhat, which it had stolen from a pram somewhere in town. The hat was pale yellow and floppy. The Woebegots liked hats, but the ones they acquired were always too large. The most disturbing thing about this creature was its hands, which, unlike its clawed back feet, were curiously human and the same color as the hat. It tilted its head sideways to look at Meg. She could see its soft eyes under the shade of the brim. It watched her carefully as it moved, crablike, toward her feet. She thought it was totally harmless and estimated that she could kick it over the side of the bridge or stomp it to death if she so chose. Also her good fletching knife was tucked in the neck of one of her black canvas boots with the wooden soles.

"Gercha," she hissed at the creature as it flattened its long furry body into an eellike shadow, only the hat staying jaunty.

On the other side of the bridge, Meg found the outer shed where the caballistas and their horses loitered. With her best servile manner, she approached, wringing her apron in her big red hands and explaining about her son and the mistake he had made. The guards laughed at her when she asked to have her son back and apologized for his youth. They explained that if and when he recovered from his "collection," he would be locked in one of the great wheels of the treadmill until they remembered to let him go.

"But what of his trial?" she asked, and the men stopped smirking.

"Thars won't be nun."

"But he's innocent, just a boy's folly; he deserves a trial."

"Dersefs! He dersefs nufin and is lucky to be alive."

"I wish to speak to your commander," she said primly, holding back her tears of fear and impotent rage. One of the soldiers standing at the back came forth and looked closely at her face. He took off his helmet. A laurel of green metal leaves had been added to the helm, a sign he had achieved some valor.

"Begone, yoos will make it wurst for the brat."

Meg flinched from his face and his words, but she held her ground. "He should have a trial."

The soldier came closer.

"If he was myn, I would beg that he goes to the wheel. Tribunals is run by priesthood. The wheel is a gentle maid compared to them and what they will give to him."

His words silenced her, and she and the men were quiet until the last speaker bellowed.

"Begone!"

On her way home, she pledged revenge for her son with what was left of her life and for everything that had ever been stolen from her. Another Woebegot had found its way onto the bridge and made a beeline for her clanking ankles. She stopped and looked down at it, another minor outrage to her person. The thing rubbed against her like a cat made of boxwood, lifting its flattened face admiringly up to hers, its long, hairless legs indecently female. It had no arms and was dressed in rags, but its eyes were like expensive Antwerp beads, and they glimmered and beseeched her exhausted orbs. Meg meant to say a word to it, but she was caught between intentions, her maternal feelings having been so recently scorned. She did not know whether to give it prospect or the back of her tongue, and while she hesitated, her insulted emotions tugged at the black twine of her gut. She hoisted the heavy knife out of her boot and into her angry hand. The creature instantly ceded, dimmed its eyes, and shrugged its shoulders up to where its ears should have been in a tiny gesture of defeated resignation; an act it had copied by shyly watching humans, aligning the sequence of their actions in its memory.

Meg bent down in one movement and cut the gesture in half, wiping the blade clean on the bottom corner of her apron before striding home, weeping and determined to change her life and everything else around her.

TRANCE

"It's some kind of trance," said the blur.

"He's not the only one to have fainted in that corner of the cloister," commented the second blur, whose voice was becoming recognizable.

Dominic tried to turn his head to hold a detail in his vacant eyes.

"You should have that place torn down and exorcized. There is nothing good in there now," suggested the second blur, whose features were sliding and compressing into the shape of Friar Cuthbert.

"He awakes. Dominic! Dominic?" called the first blur, who had turned into Pittancer Johbert.

Cuthbert lifted the prone man's head and looked more closely into his rolling eyes, then put a steadying arm around Dominic's shoulders.

"Can you see me, boy? Can you hear me?"

Dominic's throat and tongue made the appropriate shapes. He drew air up past them, but no words came out. The sound that escaped him made the others quell and nearly drop him. It was not unlike the call of a bittern: a low, flat modified honk, a boom. Dominic's eyes were now wild but focused; he gulped air and forced himself to utter more sensible sounds. But the bittern spoke again, this time louder and more urgent.

"Don't agitate yourself so! Try not to speak, you must have hurt your larynx in the fall," said Johbert to the panting and confused young monk, who was now gripping his own throat in terrible anxiety, trying to massage or squeeze his voice to make more human sounds.

By nightfall, it was clear to all the brothers who examined Dominic that his human speech had vanished, or been stolen. The unfortunate novice became quite distraught when Friar Benedict asked him to explain the charcoal script written on the wall of the Cyst. It had been Benedict who first insisted on the charcoal being placed there months before, when the Quiet had begun to change. He wanted a true record of everything that took place within the cloistered wall.

Benedict was a grizzled old man whose life had been marred by a deformity of his mouth, which warped his speech and twisted his upper lip into a permanent snarl. He spent most of his time in the scriptorium, clarifying histories and cataloging the useful elements of the known world: compiling the consuetudinary for future generations of monks. His iron will had formed no rust over the years, and his irascible, dogmatic temperament was legendary. He would have interrogated Christ himself had Christ ever dared step inside the monastery that had always been Benedict's home.

"Pay attention, child, and tell me exactly what you heard," the old man demanded, his hand already on Dominic's shoulders, as though ready to shake out the words, if necessary. "Your writing on the wall was clumsy. I can't quite make out all the words. It would be unforgivable if we never understood your meaning after such a valiant and distressing attempt to chronicle the miracle."

The word *miracle* produced different reactions among the

brethren, but they were nothing compared to Dominic's paroxysm of violent gesticulation and the series of resounding booms that followed.

Suddenly he was out of bed and shambling across the room in the general direction of the door. With care, the pittancer tried to restrain Dominic, but he was rudely pushed aside. By the time Dominic was across the cloister and approaching the offending wall, a quarter of the monks were behind him. Even in the dimming blue light, the novice could see the charcoal scrawl. He staggered toward it and slowed as the words came into view. Some of the monks tried to read the passage again. Dominic recognized the swirls of his own hand. His signature in the letters of a sentence that he had never seen before . . . in a language he understood as Latin but which he could not read or write. He wanted to scream that he had not written this message, but some treacherous doubt was hiding in the black space behind his lost voice.

"You see it? The second and fifth words are unclear," pressed Friar Benedict, oblivious to the poor youth's plight. "It makes no sense in its present form; it looks like it says something about a dog?"

"What dog?" demanded Abbot Clementine, who had appeared behind the posse of monks.

Dominic turned and boomed at the abbot until the Father Superior had to cover his ears with his hands. This allowed Friar Benedict to take charge, sending the boy back to his bed and dismissing everyone else so he could speak to the abbot alone.

"What ails the youth so?"

"A voice was heard again, here by the empty Cyst, and it shouted at the poor child."

"Who witnessed this?"

"Only he who was so grievously afflicted by it."

"A sore throat is hardly grievous."

"It is not just a sore throat. His voice suddenly vanished, and it's made the boy deeply disturbed."

Abbot Clementine barely concealed his contempt and harshly said, "I think you are making too much of this."

"*Father Superior*, I make of it what I am told and what I see with my own eyes, and what I have chronicled about events here since the Testiyont disappeared."

"The Testiyont did not disappear; it simply got old and died, as we all will. How many times do I have to repeat myself to waylay these morbid fears and fishwives' rumors?"

Benedict felt the sting, but he would not let himself show emotion or allow his rage to lead him into the arguments he was so famous for having. So he ignored the slight completely and continued.

"If *we* had been informed of the Oracle's place of burial, then the anxiety about its soul's being at peace could have been taken out of the equation, on the evidence of the phenomena attached to its Cyst."

"Equation! Evidence! What are you talking about? Nothing is happening here, you old fool. It is you and the few others with too much time on their lazy hands who are causing so much doubt and spreading wicked rumors about the fate of the Testiyont. I have told you everything you need to know. And *I will not have my authority questioned again!*"

Abbot Clementine was a strong, powerful man, and during this speech, he had closed on the diminutive Friar Benedict, spitting the last words down on his wrinkled brow before shrugging violently, marching over to the faint words, and rubbing them out with such violence that the plaster beneath crumbled under his censorship.

That night they inclined Dominic with a potent tincture of valerian. The roof drifted away and he started to sink into a hollow of darkness. Just before the work of the warm hebetude was complete, there was an irony of birds. The far-distant warbling lark and the low-wading bittern sang together: one fluttering in the clouds, the other skulking cautiously among the reeds, their unique songs and the extremes of their gravity shared, like the shy invisibility that kept them hidden and alive. The somnambulant Dominic looked deep into the marshes, hoping to see more, but the condensed darkness refused him. Then a vague luminescence started to grow, looking as if it wanted to form into a face—a white man's face, with eyes shut tight. Mercifully Dominic's dream lifted its sight away, soaring upward to find the flutter in the high blue skies. But halfway up, it became entangled in the snow-covered paths of a distant mountain, and there, in the blinding whiteness, another shadow was forming that was not a man. Dominic's sleep finally overcame his racing mind. He did not see that both sets of closed eyes were trying to see each other, or that soon they would.

PEDILAVIUM

In his high room in the fortified tower of the ancient monastery, Abbot Clementine was trying to read a transcription from the library addressing the agency of prayer on the delay of physical decay, but the wind was distracting him. He had made this room his own, refusing the grander chamber in the north wall. This aerial cell gave him more privacy and the distance he needed to carry out his own personal research. He had built the dividing wall in its modest proportion to create a private chapel. No one dared question him about his holy cupboard, which was just about big enough for a kneeling man and an altar. No one had helped him build it. This he had done by his own hand, a hand well used to the art of masonry before he had taken his vows. He had also built the small door in the base of the spiral stone staircase that led to his room. He had the only key. No one needed to know about it, and he would not allow anyone to question him on it.

Clementine had grown strong here over the years: directing the condition and sanctity of the monastery; making sure that the troublesome, cantankerous army of monks followed his doctrines, rules, and attitude; and keeping the machinery of protection constantly running in this cursed corner of the world.

He looked at his hands, which had gently constructed the nest that sat on his private altar. He saw their restraint and strength. In his fifty-second year, he was poised and ready to take on new powers and determinations. He had done his time in the wilderness, proved his command and responsibility to all those above him who had tested his mettle in this place of crucial isolation. All this was known about the good abbot. What was not known was the real purpose of the enclave he had constructed, which remained permanently locked when he was absent.

He had been seeking the lost thirteen Hymns of Orphic Separation, those that dealt with the actual manipulations in rituals of the other eighty-nine. Many learned men believed those fragments were the stuff of legends, but he had found six hymns in scraps of translation and scholars' notations, enough to allow him to experiment.

Distractions continually demanded his attention, and he was losing patience with them. The snooping, overly inquisitive monks and the growing number of reports of unknown animals with disturbing human elements, the likes of which had never existed before, were only part of the problem. Far greater was his suspicion that since no living thing occupied the Oracle's Cyst in the crumbling wall, a degeneration in the integrity of the Gland of Mercy was occurring. There were more frequent reports of smells and sounds emanating from that field of horror. People were beginning to ask questions.

The first sign of slippage in the centuries-old balance of realities had begun at the same time Clementine started drawing energy from the Quiet Testiyont to fuel his own rituals. He had realized years ago that the best place to conduct the rites was in a church or a monastery, so that the power of prayer might be diverted, stolen to give vigor to more singular needs. When he first started, he had not known that he was also drawing directly from the wealth in the Cyst. It was only after his astonishing success that he saw the change in the Testiyont: a weakening, a fading, a speculative hesitation in the being that had never shown doubt. What distinguished this Oracle from all the previous ones of its kind was the veracity of its implantation. No other had adhered or taken root with such intensity and determination, which helped explain the clarity of its cogent predictions. Just before the Testiyont began showing signs of frailty, it had told of another that was coming to be its replacement and explained how it would be stronger in all that it knew. It would answer demands and specific questions, debate with a chosen monk, and give him one, many, or all the keys to the Kingdoms. This prophecy had tempted the abbot to confiscate such predictions from any other ear in the abbey and to find out more details for himself, making certain that he would be the chosen one.

As the Baptist had enraged those savage kings into believing that the One coming after him would change the world, Clementine thought this might be a sign that the most famous Oracle was about to give up the ghost. The abbot knew this phase was one in which powers and influences could be interchanged, or learned, and he had no intention of sharing this information with the brothers. The Gland of Mercy had been constant and stable for decades. This was his moment to discover exactly how that worked, to gain as much knowledge from the fading Oracle as possible before it was gone. No human had ever dared such a thing. So he told no one of the Testiyont's condition, and in the dead of night, the abbot broke open the wall of the Cyst and, a few minutes later, carried out its occupant in a bedsheet.

Days later, Clementine delivered the sad news that Quiet Testiyont had died peacefully and that he and Friar Cecil had considered it best to conduct a service and bury the remains quickly, because of the condition of the Blessing's physical body. Friar Cecil gave a stern nodding agreement to everything the abbot uttered.

But a small group of monks were outraged, and argued that their own rites of prayer should be permitted at the grave. Friar Benedict had been the most verbal and demanding. The abbot would hear nothing of them, simply repeating that the disturbing and noxious condition of the remains demanded an expedient response and that all the necessary prayers were conducted with grace and sensitivity. The abbot also insisted, "under the circumstances," on imposing a rule of silence and containment for the next month or until he deemed fit.

A great blanket of gloom descended on the silent monastery; the forced retreat of contemplation hushed even prayer until the abbot was satisfied.

Clementine knew his iron will was keeping secret the fact that the Quiet was still living, installed in his own tower room. But something more was maintaining the thin shadow of life in the Quiet's fading body, while the abbot continued to extract its last few febrile words. In their last conversation, the Quiet's remains were almost spent, its wisps of being moving only slightly. There was a murky translucence that had the slumping, gruff unpredictability of a sleeper caught in the cobwebbed depths of a dream.

"Blessings be upon you," whispered the abbot, his voice dry, his mouth cemented in an emulsion of awe, pity, and dread.

The despairing remnant made an unpredictable motion, an utterance thinner than silence that choked all ambient sound.

Eventually and with great dread, Clementine said, "One of your kind is on its long journey to join us."

He heard his words glisten in the still air, as the thing in the nest started to make a deep pulsing noise that insinuated itself into every fiber of the ancient building and into the abbot's weakening bladder.

Then it spoke in a voice it had never possessed before. "We are the weird of what is going and what will come, and this is the last utterance we will make. The years of dissolving here have layered the silt of that which has become and that which will occur within these walls. The becoming will be much greater than the departing and will cleave to one here within, after they sing as one, binding a heart whose ink shall write a path unknown to us."

The soft nest that sat upon the altar was silent and empty. Clementine did not mourn for the Quiet, but for the conversation that had remained unfinished. He wanted it to speak again and unconsciously listened for a sound in the chapel. Even the wind, which had halted his reading, mimicked the Oracle. That is what those fools had heard below. The abbot's rule of silence and containment had eliminated all human noise, allowing natural sounds to take a more prominent place in the courtyards, cloisters, and stables. Without the noise of men, everyone could hear more clearly, and it was this greater ability that made some brethren think they heard voices where there were none. This had been his reply to the note pushed under his door declaring that "abnormal voices" were coming from the broken Cyst and that some of the brethren feared it might be the unquiet spirit of the Quiet.

He was certain that his sensible explanation would be ignored or derided. And the monks, for much poorer reasons, were also listening for the ghost of Quiet Testiyont to return with new prophecies from the other side of its hidden, forlorn grave.

"More distractions," the abbot said to himself.

A sound of light scratching and panting shifted his attention across the room.

Abbot Clementine slid out of his high scholar's chair and crept over to the door, listening intently for the sound of an eavesdropper outside. He grabbed the latch and wrenched it open with colossal force, expecting to terrify the dim, furtive spy who was skulking there, but the landing was unoccupied. He looked down the empty spiral stair and then returned, shutting the door with loud contempt.

The resonance of the crash caused the inner door to his chapel to creak open. Perched on the altar next to the nest, he saw, to his disgust, one of the unnameable vermin. It stared straight back at him without a shadow of fear. It looked like a polecat with tiny yellow claws that mimicked human hands, one of which was holding a scrunched-up yellow hat. The creature grinned at him in an insolent manner. It gestured at the nest, shook its head, and put the yellow hat over its eyes like a mask. The abbot knew exactly what it was saying, and a great wrath came over him. He stood next to a low bureau that held two heavy pewter candlesticks flanking a dense pewter cross. He grabbed one of the candlesticks and advanced into the chapel, taking a wild swing at the obscene intruder. But it was much too fast for him and fled before he had brought the great blow crashing down onto the gently made nest.

"Vanished!" the creature called as it descended the tight stone corkscrew of stairs, its shrill tones echoing in the spiral. This was a voice that was unique and totally its own.

When it reached the base of the stairs next to the secret door, it screamed "Vanished!" over and over again. Shredding the imposed vow of silence. Making sure everybody in the abbey, and a few outside, heard its declaration, which sounded much more like an accusation.

Abbot Clementine was breathing heavily, his anger congealing to failure as he confronted the mangled last home of the Sacred Quiet Testiyont. The bent candlestick in his fist had transformed into the cross, which he had grabbed by mistake in his rage, and the pewter was now buckled into something that would never again be a cross. He dropped it, stood back in shock, and confronted the wrecked nest. He remembered how the Oracle had diminished while in his solitary care; the memory had sustained him until that vermin, almost casually, gnawed its reality into doubt. He hid himself away and ignored the knocking at his bolted door. He had to understand what was going wrong.

The imposed silence had not yet reached its allotted time of four weeks. Abbot Clementine knew he must be the one to rescind this penance; it could not end because of the circumstance. Especially after the demon's uproar had desecrated all that had been achieved in the holy quietude. He would give permission for all the tongues to celebrate before they began to wag. He dressed in a garment of heavy irritant cloth that made his flesh creep as it rubbed against him. It was a robe of penitence, and it was his time to wear it. He then prepared to wash the feet of every friar in the monastery. This was his monthly duty—although he had not fulfilled it for a quarter of the year—to lower himself, demonstrating that his humble soul and his position of power and authority were merely an illusion in the eyes of God. The obedient Friar Cecil had carried out the abbot's commands, announcing to all the brethren that the restrictions of speech had been lifted and that there would be a general assembly that afternoon. His words were loud and oiled with enthusiasm, the first to be heard for far too long. He enjoyed these tasks that declared him to be in the confidence of the Father Superior.

The dark-robed figures filled the refectory like a gloat of shadows. Some of the elderly monks were also speaking in whispers and groans as they seated themselves at the long communal table.

The abbot was already speaking as he strode into his congregation. He held out his arms dramatically, somewhere between embrace and crucifixion.

"Simpering idiot," Benedict mumbled as he trundled along in the line of gathered monks.

"My brethren, it pleases me greatly to gather you all here today and to thank you for your stoic solemnity during our period of quiet reflection." The abbot's voice was clear and bold.

"We have much to be grateful for, and our prayers this evening, I am sure, will reflect that."

Benedict raised his eyes, and both the abbot and Friar Cecil saw the flicker of contempt in them.

"We must also give thanks for the soon and safe arrival of our new Blessing."

There was a noticeable movement, a bodily reaction in the flock.

"Even as I speak, it approaches, somewhere on Das Kagel with its entourage, descending to be in our midst."

After a second of hesitation, most of the monks began to talk to one another. The abbot's proclamation had been a success. A growing wave of curiosity and anticipation filled the elemental hearts of the majority of the brothers. And while they babbled, tubs of water were brought forth. Friar Cecil reappeared carrying a towel, which he unfolded and placed on the long bench. He clapped his hands above his head for attention and then pulled his cassock up to his knees. Perching himself at the end of the bench, next to the towel, his legs facing outward, he forced the others to turn and see what he was doing.

"Idiot," Benedict snarled faintly.

The abbot was ready, with rolled-up sleeves, to begin his humble task. On his knees, he held each foot of the brothers he had controlled so ruthlessly. He felt their weight as a cherished relic and washed each with care. Some internal part of him actually enjoyed the touch of another human being, the substantiality of its existence after the harrowing presence of something that was not really there. The water, loam, and grime became a blessing that healed any guilt that Satan or his demons might cause to rise within him. But they were dainty adversaries compared to the next-but-one friar, whom he was gradually approaching with his tub of increasingly murky water.

Those who had been cleansed were allowed to leave the assembly. Most did so with genial expressions, some even with a beatific glow. Abbot Clementine had moved along the line and now held two small, gnarled feet that had been thoroughly washed and scrubbed clean. Without looking up, he felt the bone notch, he felt the sinews tighten against his touch, and he knew who owned those rigid extremities.

Benedict wrenched his gargoyle stare away from the abbot and cast its fearful glance upward and over one shoulder. Like a listener suddenly hearing an urgent far-off cry.

CATARACT

It was a quiet night that slivered into dawn. No wind breathed, no snow fell. Swathes of the early sun's shifting white light refracted in the sparkling crystals. They had been on the road for an hour and were still sleepy. They were climbing steadily higher, following the edge of frozen land that would lead to the great mass of the glacier. Its smooth, unearthly silver gleam already dominated the distant horizon, suggesting both a land of unreachable celestial perfection and a brooding monster best left in perpetual slumber. It was from there, looking down and beyond, that they got their first glimpse of the Von Lyrehnbok ravine.

The Oracle started to shudder, its small yapping sounds rattling its crate and causing the old mule that bore it to flinch and step out of its own dream, stumbling slightly on the icy path. The presence of the glacier excited the Oracle, something about the draining starlight ricocheting off its surface, the touch, the tinder of it. The nearest lip of the glacier sprawled eighty miles north of the ravine and sent millions of tons of meltwater cascading through it. In quiet times like these, you could sometimes hear the glacier sigh, groan, or explode, sending the profundity of its voice echoing beneath all other sounds and substance. A crack or a boom from the interior of its restless motion sounded like the Author of All Things speaking to the land in a language older than time.

It was a long, intense ride that morning. The old bones of the men, mules, and horses warmed up only after an hour or so. They crept along the high ridge and eventually joined the rim of fast water.

"How far do we have to go before we sight Das Kagel?" asked Pearlbinder, drawing his horse up behind Follett.

"Truth is, I don't really know. Somewhere after we cross another mountain beyond the cataract. I have only been given stages along this journey. We must trust in the Blessed One to steer us between them."

Pearlbinder made a noise in his throat that could have been dulcet agreement or a growl of disdain. At this early hour, it was impossible to distinguish between the two.

The great Brow waterfall grew in voice and dominance with each careful step. One side of the narrow track looked straight down into the rock gulley, which tumbled and gushed with the tons of water cascading from the massive waterfall. Each man held the reins of his mount in a vicelike grip, keeping all their attention on the next step. There were contrasts of the natural world here that many of the party had never seen; water crashing in tons of violent fluidity next to water locked into frozen braids, signs of its agitation still visible, like carved marble.

The nervous trees that clung to the edge of the waterfall and the path were patchy and torn. Great lumps had been ripped out by the torrent. The men saw fragments of the skeletal remains of bridges that had been erected to cross the maelstrom at its thinnest path and when the water was at its lowest. The wreckage was proof enough that this was the only way they were going to get across and then down the mountain. Follett waved the party forward, and the reluctant horses and mules needed strict guidance to do anything other than turn and flee. So they were made to bleed and smart, to move on along the ledge, the tilted land around the roaring power of the great cataract.

Strange white protuberances flocked along the sides of the thin, slippery path. They had been normal plants at one time, but the constant mist from the crashing waters had frozen them again and again, so the leaves and stems had become smothered and stilled into vague fingerlike forms of uniform white, an army of sea anemones locked in a long seasonal stasis. Frozen claws of ice came up to grab them. Each man's life flickered into silence under the roar of this world.

To avoid eternity, they had to work together against the moment, to shout at one another as they dismounted and pulled the animals toward more substantial land and the shelter of the thicket. The hair on their heads and on the horses' manes and tails was beginning to stand up, and some of their metallic possessions were becoming animated in air full of virulent static electricity generated by the water's speed and the land's resistance. They ducked their heads and dragged their mounts into the trees, where some of the Brow's power lessened and the magnetism faded.

They stood dripping and unsure of what to do next when a giant stepped out from behind a massive tree.

He was over nine feet tall and dressed in the way of prophets: animal skins over an ancient, threadbare robe. He carried a menacing staff and spoke in a voice that filled the trees. "Do you seek cleansing or passage?"

O'Reilly unsheathed his sword, ready to kill the monstrous man. The giant shot out his hand like a piston and a rock flew forward, hitting O'Reilly in the chest, cracking his sternum and nearly dividing his rib cage. The expression on his face was beyond description.

"*Weapons are forbidden here!*" boomed the giant.

Pearlbinder had been slowly easing his large-bore Safavid rifle out of its ornate scabbard when Follett gripped his arm and strangled the motion.

"Don't!" he commanded.

The giant's head was entirely swathed in bandages; their woven delineation covered something that was not even vaguely human in shape, being more horizontal than vertical.

Pearlbinder moved forward. The others were locked in an overpowering sense of awe; even the animals hung their heads and looked away from the towering apparition. Pearlbinder stepped closer, a genuine respect welling up in him. The words arose through his learning and his hunger at the gates of bewilderment: "Sir, Master, I believe thou be of the *Cercopithecidae,* a bloodline of—"

"No! *I am a man,*" the giant cried. "As a man cursed with the plague of leper, I tie my head in this way to contain its flesh and spare any trespasser the sight of its malignancy."

"But, Brother!"

"I am not your brother. I am he who was born wild, whose hand is turned against all men. And all men's hands turneth against me."

Pearlbinder was silenced but kept slowly moving toward the giant. He needed to witness his existence up close, to be in the proximity of a being from another world, even if the being did not understand its own meaning. The air was disturbed by O'Reilly's falling from his horse and screaming on the iced ground.

"Put away thy weapons and he will be healed," the booming voice declared.

Follett got off his horse and walked over to his fallen man. He gave the order to sheath and stash all weapons. In three strides, the giant crossed through them and knelt by his victim, placing his hand on his chest.

After a long while, he pulled more of the same bandages that covered his head out of a satchel, making a long, twisted sheet between his hands. He then lifted his pointed head, gargled, and heaved up a great wad of phlegm, glutinous and colorless in consistency, which he spat into the cloth through a gap in his bandaged head. He wound the steaming folds tightly around the wounded man. He then lifted O'Reilly as if he were no more than a bundle of dry twigs. Pain and horror made O'Reilly turn gray, edged in blue. The giant carried the poor man off into the thicket, to a place where a vivid shaft of sunlight had penetrated the cold. He put O'Reilly down in its unexpected warmth, watching as the pain vanished and the rag solidified and shrank. The shock made his patient pass out. The sullen loops of the bandage came undone and were caught up by the great magnetism. Their ends rose and floated slowly about in the bright air, becoming weightless and balletic in their motion.

The men watched, entranced. The giant turned and made his way back through the trees. "Art thou going over?" he queried as he approached Follett.

"We seeketh a way to Das Kagel," he answered. "How do we cross?"

"I carry thee across the waters."

"But the horses?"

"I carry thee on them."

"And the tariff for your work?"

"A companion."

"Companion?"

"Leave someone just for me."

Follett looked around to see if the men could hear this conversation.

"I will take the damaged one; he is of no use to thee."

"But O'Reilly is our . . ."

Then he stopped and weighed the words he was about to speak.

"If thou taketh him, he will die," the giant pressed.

Follett agreed to leave O'Reilly. "We will take his horse with us."

"No, we will need it," said the giant.

"For what?"

"To eat."

Follett quickly changed the subject to their crossing, pointing to the water and turning all eyes away from the glowing rags in the beam of sunlight deep in the trees.

"Now," said the giant, "tie everything down and I will take thee."

They followed him along a winding path close to the edge of the raging waters, eventually stopping at a place where the trail widened, giving the water a larger, shallower space. Boulders and polished slabs of stone stuck out of the speeding torrent and shone against the sun. The giant pointed and gave directions to the riders. A terrible fear hovered over them.

Pearlbinder broke the spell by edging Sophia, his trusted mount, forward and announcing, "I shall go first, Great Master."

"So be it," said the giant, pointing to a flat stone in the water where the crossing would begin.

Pearlbinder blindfolded Sophia and whispered in her ear, then rode her onto the slippery rock. The giant discarded his rags and his staff before wading into the water. He came up like a mer-king on the other side of the rock, beneath the horse, his thick arms grasping her legs, his neck and shoulders bearing the animal's belly as he lifted beast and rider in one solid action.

Pearlbinder hung on tight, flattening his body along the line of the horse as the giant turned and made his way from one rock to another. The monstrous river seemed to divide against his power. None of the men had ever seen anything like this. The giant's strength was amazing, his practiced footfall sturdy and without doubt. He placed Pearlbinder and Sophia delicately on the other side before returning for the next man. Midstream, he seemed to glow magnificently in arches of rainbowing mist and gleaming ice. The only disconcerting thing was that his bandaged head had become wet in the process and its shape could now be more clearly defined. A huge canine profile shone under a halo of spume and flying spray.

"It is as it was spoken," quoth Follett.

The giant made nine trips in all. When all the men were safely on the other side, he returned for the mules, carrying one under each arm. The third he treated with more reverence than anything else he had lifted that day.

Surely he was exhausted, surely he was slowing from fatigue— but no. The care he took in carrying his last, precious cargo was deliberate. This being knew what was in that box and how it was more precious than all the lives around it. But how? Follett had said nothing about the crate that housed the Oracle, and none of the other men, except Pearlbinder, even dared look at the giant. Having been so close to him in the crossing, feeling his power and protection, Pearlbinder was beginning to balance it against his terrible strangeness.

The giant cradled the third mule and its tethered crate, holding it tight against his chest with his staff laced beneath, like a mother carrying a child on the seat of a cross. He strode across the water toward them.

Now that they had crossed, Alvarez became impatient to move on, wanting to leave the memory of this place and the incident far behind him. His twitchiness infected his horse, causing it to shy and step backward, toward the water, just as the giant gave up his precious burden. The mule smelled the horse and started skidding on the wet rocks. The giant's hands descended, clamping the mule and the crated Oracle back in place. But the Pyx of confessional bones tipped out of Alvarez's saddlebag, emptying its contents into the water.

Alvarez cursed as Follett slid off his soaked horse and made a dash for the floating bones. The Oracle let out a cry from inside its crate, stopping everyone dead in their tracks. The voice found the bones that eddied and jostled, as if trying to escape into the open water. The sound hissed, sung, and attached itself to each fragment, like so many tiny sails unfurling as pennants, or like those convoluted scrolls of speech in medieval paintings, often called banderoles. All the men saw this, and Alvarez held his swiveling head and sight line steady on the bones as his nervous horse pirouetted in a full circle. It looked like words were illuminating and flickering there. Or was the spectrum of mist and sun lying?

Follett was on his knees, groveling in the fast shallows, pushing aside the frozen plants, splashing in the water, and catching the bobbing bones, his wet hands quivering. Suddenly the giant, who had released the now-stable mule and moved back out into the stream, swung his long staff and struck a submerged stone twenty feet out in the flood. It shifted and changed the dynamic of the current, which unbound the eddies that had kept the bones contained. They lurched forward, beyond Follett's desperate reach, and entered the unstoppable waters.

Leaning on his staff, the giant looked back at Follett splashing to shore, crushing the dwarf forest of frozen plants, and burst into a deep and rolling laugh. It could be heard still above the roar of the Brow as he crossed the water. It still boomed and echoed when he reached the other side, entered the shivering trees of the copse, picked up O'Reilly and his horse, and disappeared.

OL' KLOOTZAK'S PLOT

One of Meg Verstraeten's small gifts was growing plants, flowers, and herbs alongside the turnips and cabbages that kept her family alive when the coins were scarce. The stony dirt patch that she gently called her garden was a twenty-minute walk from her married home and outside the town walls. She liked being there, away from the stupidity and noise that held everything together in the shortsighted daily life of her husband's family and friends. Out here in the fields, she could see for miles across the water-laced landscape.

This morning was bright and even, with a frosty crispness that sharpened the smells and the details of the land. Meg looked up at Das Kagel and let its magnitude fill her eyes until only its bulk existed outside her tired pain. She often did this when the drudgery of her life honed its pointlessness on the loose side of her complex soul. She looked higher and saw the tiny birds, which she knew must be gigantic, their shadows flapping against the blinding snow.

She had never seen anything so pure. Today, in the cleansing cold, she recognized a frozen heaven. So far away that she could not hear the birds cry in the silent wind that buffeted their flight.

She wanted to be with them, high above the tree line where only the blue shadows and the majestic gray clouds spun and melted into one another. She had never been more than a few miles up its ragged, lonely path that was said to spiral to the summit. What treasures must lie there? But none would let her go. Her father would have agreed with her husband about that. It would be wasting her time, and it was dangerous. Best stay close to the kitchen and the animals. They were right; they were always right, even when she knew they were wrong. But they were back there, and she stood tall in this garden and dared to breathe the height and width of the mountain into the remnants of her imagination, which had been so rich when she was a child.

A sudden recall of that time strengthened her reverie and then plunged Meg into sadness, still tasting the reflection of her innocence before it was knotted by labor and scrubbed dull by abuse. She could even dream then, before the men undressed and snuffed it out into a nightmare. Their tallow, in the darkness, muzzling her screams, burgling her home.

The wind was making her eyes run, but she still kept the mountain in her head, where the untouched places were, the hollows that would always remain unknown to her. The spaces as bright as flowers and as secret as seeds. She had heard old people talk about such places in Das Kagel and understood that they were speaking about her. For in her childhood, everybody had recognized them in her.

Now she spoke to those spaces, but only out here, where nobody could hear her or see her lips move.

"'Tain't the insults. 'Tain't the cruelty toward all that is dear and kind. 'Tis the wrath that swells in all my hollows, filling them so there is no space for anything else to nest and thrive in. I have no family now. Only the other women who suffer the same as me."

Meg walked to the far end of her garden without ever taking her eyes off the cloud-covered peak. Stopping, she stared down at a weed-covered section of earth, the only patch that was left to grow wild. The place where she had buried her uncle Jacob after poisoning him with carefully selected mushrooms.

As she left the garden with a small basket full of her tenderly grown potatoes, Meg decided to stop and visit Willeke Dijkstra, one of her oldest friends. Willeke was the only person alive who knew of the punishment Meg had exacted on the old man in her vegetable field decades before. She had also been a victim of Jacob Verstraeten's lechery and cruelty, and she had been happy to help her friend, following her instructions about which of the wild fungi to pick and prepare.

Meg had let the old villain know that she and her companion would be having a picnic that day, somewhere out in the fields. When the old man turned up and told them that he had told nobody of his visit, they feigned surprise and did not complain when he helped himself to most of their repast. He had been unbuckling his belt when the first pain hit.

The girls stood up and stepped back from the old blanket, which they had so daintily set to serve as their table and seating. The second pain took away any actions old Jacob could control, and his eyes widened in bilious comprehension. He kicked and rucked up the blanket in his agony, folding himself into its scruffy irregular symmetry. It found its final composition an hour later, and the girls dragged it and its soiled weight across to the pit that they had dug.

The kitchen table, where they now sat, was sturdy, spotless, and covered with half the contents of Meg's basket. Willeke examined the vegetables and smiled at their quality.

"They didna come from the ol' Klootzak's plot?" she asked in such a deadpan voice that Meg would have taken her seriously, had she not heard the question a countless times before.

"Ney, Mother, theys comes from the sun-end near the apple trees. Which I think will be a goodly crop this year."

"Are there signs already?"

"The closer leaves are curled, making a tighter base of the flowers." Willeke grinned and nodded at Meg's good news and brought out two small glasses and a stone bottle of gin.

They had been friends from childhood, their families working the land and marrying across its seasons. Willeke had refused to join the clans when they made Meg an outcast. There was no proof that she had committed any crime, though the coincidence of her quiet, terse gaiety and the vanishing of Uncle Jacob seemed to have a balance that many considered might be cause and effect. But it was never spoken of by those who also remained silent about all Jacob's other dealings with the children.

Meg didn't solicit sympathy or ever ask for help. She'd never had, nor developed, a curved approach to life. She did not practice the skills of dissembling canniness that help lubricate daily confrontations and exchange. Meg was blunt and direct, a trait that she rarely found in others and greatly admired when she did. Many said that this trait and her lack of womanly wiles were why she had become so distanced from her family. Hadn't the same thing happened in her marriage and turned her husband to drink and her son to waywardness?

And these traits had made her dangerous friends. Not like the meek Willeke Dijkstra, who always sat in Meg's shadow, but more like Grietje van der Elzen, who was burned at the stake six months earlier. Both Meg and Grietje had a knowledge of childbirth beyond the basic mechanics—and both understood the powers and persuasions of certain plants and their applications; many of these plants grew in Meg's garden. Meg had had a closeness to Grietje, which became a perilous involvement the moment Grietje was arrested by the caballistas, accused of witchcraft, and found guilty.

The women had all pushed their way into the town square on the day their friend was turned into smoke, cinders, and ash. Their menfolk had gotten there early to make sure they had the best view of the spectacle. So the women had to jostle and stand on tiptoe to watch. But they did not have to strain to hear Grietje's words, which she shouted loudly. She had been offered a crucifix to hear her redemption, but instead she bellowed out the name of every demon in the book, and a few that had never been written. The men automatically took steps backward and trod on the toes of the women behind, some of whom had covered their ears. Meg did not. She strained to understand the meaning of this roll call. Had her friend gone insane? Or was it just an insult spat out to confound her torturers?

Near her end, when the words bubbled with smoke, a sudden

new force came with them, and just before they roasted in her skull, Grietje turned her eyes to the crowd, seeking someone. She found Meg and screamed again, the sound giving Meg a prodigious slap. The percussion of their meaning dislodged years of subservience and made her head ring with vibrant certainty. Meg stumbled back and crossed her arms over her bosom in defiance and to keep the clarity and power of Grietje's last breath inside her forever. None of the men saw this because they had moved forward again and could not take their eyes off the woman being stripped by the flames.

All the women turned away in shame, but they'd witnessed everything and knew a transformation had taken place. They moved in a reserved mass, turning their backs on the spluttering cinders, and closed in around Meg, lifting her up and away. Nothing happened after that, but all were waiting, and nothing was said.

"Have you seen any other signs?" asked Willeke, who poured more gin and then went back to nervously fondling one of the potatoes.

"Only those verminous ones, the painter's birthlings that Grietje named."

"Filthlings?"

"Aye, there be so many now, even in the city, in the homes, and they're changing in some ways, losing their strangeness."

"Are they really the same ones that Grietje assigned that terrible day?"

"They must be the same. What else? But they are changed now."

"Changed?"

"Yes, they have learnt to talk."

Willeke became cross, put down the potato, and said, "In a devious, lying blasphemy, no doubt."

"No, that's what's so strange. They sound honest, direct, and true."

Willeke was out of her depth, so she changed the subject to regain her position in the conversation. "So you say! But, more important, have you heard any more about poor Dircx?"

The question banjaxed Meg's train of thought completely, and the vacuum it made started to fill with unexpected emotion, because for a short while, her speculations had replaced her hurt. She looked across the table at Willeke, tears forming in her eyes, and her mouth spoke for her: "We have heard nothing, and Rynch says we never will."

She hadn't thought about her son and husband for a long while, and their names sounded odd on her tongue.

"I doubt Rynch knows much about what he says. And what 'as he done to find out?"

Willeke was becoming defensive for her friend, who had just shown her vulnerability. She poured more gin and asked and answered her own questions. "Did he go and plead for Dircx? Did he do anything? *No!* You did it all!"

Meg was now fondling the same potato and limply some old part of her said, "Rynch has been busy."

"*Busy doing what?*" exploded Willeke. "Where is he now?"

"Preparing for Carnival."

"*Ah!* Carnival."

"He is playing one of the central characters in the mock battle between Carnival and Lent. He is practicing for the part again."

"Practicing for getting pissed out of his head again, spending money you don't have, and trying to get his leg over any doxy stupid enough to come anywhere near him."

Meg looked very glum at the truth of her friend's tirade, until an inch of giggle unzipped part of her mouth.

Willeke didn't see this and was in full flow. "Every Shrovetide we go through this ridiculous ritual. The entire town, the entire country goes mad. Spending weeks preparing, so that for three days they can wear masks and debauch themselves in the palaces and the taverns, in the gardens and the gutters. And mostly we stay at home cooking and slaving so this can happen. And all the loose women that our husbands make looser give whelp to a tribe of scurvy bastards next autumn. Three days in which anything can happen, and it all does.

"I dread to think what will happen this year with even more foreigners, beggars, and lepers coming in from the countryside, more criminals and actors befouling the streets. And *your* unholy

Filthlings with their 'new ways' jabbering and fornicating over the foodstuffs and children. And who will stop them when it ends and the bell rings in the hardship of Lent that is imposed on us all? *Who* will explain to them that the beast must be caged and the bottle stoppered and that all holiness return? God is in His Heaven, and all sin is wrapped in hangovers and lardered away for another year. And . . ."

Willeke paused to regain her breath and fill their glasses and then looked up to see the beaming countenance of her friend wiping a flock of very different tears away from her face with the back of her wrinkled hand. The potato was rolling across the floor.

PUMPKIN

Friar Benedict was on his way to further examine the remains of the Cyst where the voice had come from when he was interrupted by a novice who nervously told him that Friar Ludo wanted him in the kitchen.

"The kitchen?" asked Benedict in his best irritated voice. "Why?"

"There is a thing there that nobody knows."

"What kind of thing?"

"What the peasants call a Woebegot, we think."

Little from the outside world was worthy of Benedict's observation and speculation. He had long since given up the trivia beyond the abbey walls. But the rumors of these new creatures had alerted his curiosity. The proliferation of new animals excited his imagination and its taste for the arcane. He knew such things no longer existed in the modern world. Nothing of this nature had been heard of since he was a snotty-nosed child during the passage of the Archimandrites. No, these new rumors must be species of unknown creatures driven to his door by a famine or by a deformed seasonal migration from a different curve of the world. At least that's what he thought when he entered the kitchen.

A village oaf and his son had gathered the nerve to rap on the World Gate of the monastery and ask if they might speak to a learned man. Benedict was known and respected by all the monks as a wise and distinguished scholar. The abbot, however, had a different opinion, believing that any such qualities were ruined by Benedict's irascible and petulant personality. In the past, Benedict was to be approached or indeed summoned only if something was deemed worthy enough to dislodge him from his books. There had been strict instructions that all incidents of the abnormal were to be reported to him, so that he, and only he, could examine and pass judgment on the odd and unexpected. But the abbot had recently proclaimed that Benedict should be released of such worrying duties and be allowed to pursue his studies without interruption. And that he, Abbot Clementine, would now take on the mantle of any such investigations.

But Friar Ludo made his own decision on who to call when the peasants and their sack were shooed into the rich odors of the monastery's kitchen. This was about as deep into the holy brothers' home as any outsider was allowed. The gormless duo stood with Friar Ludo around one of the enormous scarred wooden tables that dominated the room. On it they placed a hessian sack.

"These good folks have brought us a specimen of an animal that nobody has ever seen before," said Ludo, poking the sack with a set of long-handled iron tongs.

"Wees never seen the like of this un," said the farmer to the monks, his head swinging from one to the other, seeking signs of approval or interest. He got neither.

"Very well, let's see it," said Benedict, and Ludo gingerly held the corner of the sack and opened it roughly with the tongs. He then pulled the sack upward with a shaking motion and in a theatrical manner, which Benedict thought inappropriate to the circumstances. What fell out made both monks step away from the table and then step closer in a single unbroken motion.

"Never'd seen its like," said the farmer.

It looked like a melon or a pumpkin or some other species of overgrown gourd that had been skewered with an elaborate spit of the same color: a bright, sickly orange. Benedict took the trembling tongs from Ludo and turned the thing over. Ludo put his hands over his mouth and stepped backward. On what had been its underside was a face, or at least a travesty of one: A long gash with a downward turn appeared to be a mouth. Above sat two shallow depressions in which orbs seemed to float. No sign of personality or character could be seen in them; they looked more like ancient, flaccid pickled onions than the windows to any kind of soul. The turning also revealed the nature of the "skewer"; each end of the creature unfolded into a three-fingered hand, which made it clear that these were in fact slender arms outstretched from the lumpen head or body of the thing. There was no sign of legs.

"Is it dead?" asked Ludo from the back of the kitchen.

"Shod be, I 'ad it with the muck-fork a dizen times or more," said the farmer.

"Did you now?" said Benedict, turning the body again and stretching one of the arms out to its fullest length. He thought it was almost elegant in its odd proportion, like a muscular female child.

"Aye, I gave it a right trolluxing." The farmer sharply elbowed his son to get his instant agreement.

"Then where are the wounds?" asked Benedict, without raising his eyes to confront the man.

The man looked from the creature, to his accuser, to his son, and back again, several times, without a single word of understanding.

"We need to dissect this thing. I suspect foul play, or blasphemy, or worse. Brother Ludo, please call the gentlemen of the watch."

"Nay, nay," said the son. "We'd meant no harm by it. Pa killed it because it were in our barn."

"Don't talk nonsense, child!"

Benedict had become furious in his manner and his speech, something he was much famed for when having to address novices about minor misdemeanors. His outrage also made his crippled lip stick above his teeth on the left side.

"Do you not understand? Your fafer nefer killed thif becausfe *thif* thing never livfed."

He tugged at his mouth and continued, which made him even angrier.

"You must think us foolfish, bringing such nonsensth here. It's bad enough that you or your kindred have constructed this outrage, with fruif of field and other matter. But to use the limbf of the dead is sacrilege. Defecrating recent graves of children for your own folly is a criminal offense."

The old monk was holding the three-fingered hand in his own as he spat these words, and was about to erupt with more details of their just punishment, when the fingers twisted, gripped, and held his own.

His shriek was heard throughout the cloister.

Friar Cuthbert dropped his hoe and ran from the garden to confront whatever was occurring in the kitchen. The sight that met him confounded all possible responses, and left him with only the ability to cackle behind his nervous hand.

The miserable Friar Benedict was dancing with a hideous puppet and screaming "Get it off. *Get it off!*" at the top of his voice.

Three other white-faced witnesses were frozen to the spot, including Dominic, who'd been drawn to the commotion from his bed in the adjoining infirmary. It was the most convincing mummery the young monk had ever seen. True, the pumpkin-headed monster was poorly made, but the way the slit flapped open as a giant mouth and the apparent strength in its arms as it propelled about the room were amazing. However, it was the old monk's acting that gave the whole thing a terrifying reality—especially his staring eyes, his squawks, and the way he bent his hand so it looked as if the puppet was twisting his fingers and forcing him to dance with the pain of it.

The monk and the puppet were hopping and falling around the kitchen table. Every so often, the puppet seemed to lunge with its free hand toward a dirty sack on the tabletop. On the third insane circuit, it clambered up the old monk's body and grabbed something from the lip of the sack. It was most convincing. Friar Benedict's great shudders of revulsion were almost believable. The puppet grabbed the object and brought it clattering to the floor. It was a dented saucepot. Letting go of the monk's hand and quickly balancing the pot on its fat head, the puppet ran off on its hands like a great demented bird.

Benedict sat with his hands over his eyes and mouth, sobbing. The others did nothing until the farmer's son said, "It's what it was a-wearing when Pa killed it, that crock on its head . . . a-wearing it then, as it be a-wearing it again now."

Nobody needed to argue with the boy's stoic assertion.

DRIFT

They were two hours above the tree line when the weather changed. They knew their passage through the mountains was going to be harsh and fierce, but they could never have expected the savagery of the cold that was about to descend on them. A dry, freezing bitterness crept toward the men. Gradually a different tincture of wind cleated the air, grew into a shudder, and then unfurled, cutting them like a frozen razor. Everything in its path cringed and withered; tons of settled snow bellowed into the ravines. Freezing gusts screamed through them. It was clear to Follett that the tents would be ravaged in seconds.

They needed shelter. Follett gave the command and they dispersed, leaving Alvarez to tend to the Oracle. The Calca brothers, who had traveled these lands, knew there were caves hidden beneath the drifts of snow. Follett sent them in advance, seeking signs of a possible entrance. The other riders dismounted, turned their horses' heads away from the driving wind, and placed themselves behind the beasts' bodies.

An hour or so later, Abna Calca appeared and waved to everyone to follow him. Heads down, they obeyed and grimly plodded on until they reached Owen Calca, who was digging into the compressed face of ice and snow under an overhang of bare black rock. The men formed a line before the vertical stone wall and began to break the ice and shift the snow as the brothers directed. Once Owen and the others were working, Abna Calca continued farther around the track to search for more signs of entry under the snow.

On a blind patch of the mountain, he found a crack in the ice and hacked it open with his spade, stabbing his way through the snow-filled artery. He emerged into a ventricle that he estimated to be large enough to house the party. All he had to do now was find another way in for the horses. He sniffed the air in the cave and knew one must exist. A sliver of frost light followed him but faltered against the blackness of the interior. He listened for a curve in the hush of the hollow, a sealed-up hole whose density wasn't stone. He could see nothing but felt for the cold where the snow formed part of the wall. In total darkness, he began to claw and hack at its surface with his spade.

After forty minutes, the black became lighter, and he knew it was the gray illumination of day trying to find its way in from the outside world. He kept digging, his teeth clenched and his heart pounding, the spade shaving away the solid night.

Outside, the men had stopped only once in their clearing of ice and snow, when they found the remnant of a wooden sledge. Alvarez saw it as God's providence. Follett saw it as a curse, having expected to find the remains of its last owner frozen and grinning up at them, but they did not. The rest of the men hastily broke the sled into kindling and then continued to hack and shovel their way forward.

Suddenly Owen Calca signaled the men to stop working. He put his unshaven face hard against the wall of snow and closed his eyes. He moved his head several times before finally finding a place to settle. He stayed there a while and then quickly took up a spade and swung it against the glistening depression that bore the lines of his beard. A faint light bloomed in the cave as the brothers dug toward each other, carrying brightness and salvation into the mountain.

The men opened the fissure and squeezed through. Once inside, they lit a dim fire of rags, animal fat, and shaved slivers of wood from the sledge. Owen explained that the sledge was of great antiquity and had long since refused to house moisture from the current climate. They were all exhausted. Getting the horses into the cave had not been easy, and Pearlbinder's big roan mare was still not inside. Her breadth and height were greater than the cavern's entrance. They had even greased her sides and pushed and pulled, but to no avail. On the last attempt, she had become lodged there, much to Pearlbinder's horror. He spoke softly to Sophia through her anxiety—and to the Kid and Tarrant, who were left outside in the hammering sleet.

"You will have to go back around to the other entrance," instructed Follett, and Tarrant reluctantly agreed.

"Fuck that," said the Kid, who fell to his knees and, sliding over onto his back, began to push his way between the big horse's legs. "Keep the fucking thing still."

He yelped as he slid along, keeping a cautious eye on the mare's movements. Her fetlocks shivered and her hooves dug into the permafrost. No horse liked things slithering under their belly.

Seeing Sophia's reaction, Pearlbinder said, "Comes from the time of Paradise. The dread of snakes." A man of some education, he was the only one of the group who could read, now that Scriven was gone, and the only one to record everything the Oracle said, deep in his memory. He was wise enough not to use pen and paper.

The Kid possessed the flexibility and speed of a serpent, an asset in the physicality of this predicament but a positive disadvantage to the horse's understanding of his identity and intention. Realizing his dilemma, the Kid kept talking all the while, broadcasting the greatest feature that made humans apparently superior to beasts and the masters of horses: a voice without a hiss. When he had slithered, unscathed, to the other side of the horse, he complimented Pearlbinder on his training and the mare's good behavior. Then the horse's saliva dripped on the Kid's head, and he saw

Pearlbinder's hand in the mare's mouth. He had been steadfastly holding on to her tongue while he watched the Kid's progress.

"Thank thee," said the Kid, gaining his feet and brushing earth and snow from his breeches. "I didn't want to gut such a fine beast."

"Nor I thou," said Pearlbinder, sheathing the ground-thin hunting knife that he held concealed in his other hand.

The Oracle began to call out, its shrieks bouncing against the stone walls. It had heard the resonance in the cave and was playing with the length and shudder it gave its voice; its chattering jaws snapping the edges of the flickering light, like flint. It needed to be dried out quickly, and more wrecked wood was brought to the fire. The ragged ceiling danced and shuddered as the smoke rose.

"We shall be wanting more wood," said Alvarez, who was holding the Oracle close to the fire. As its keeper for the journey, he was the only one who knew when to ask the questions that would guide the party's quest. Follett trusted his skill and his decisions as much as he trusted those traits in any man. He looked hard at Alvarez and his shivering charge.

"There are no trees up here. Nothing to burn," he said.

All the men paid close attention, because they knew what was coming next.

"Then thou must send someone down to glean," Alvarez said in the most convincing tone he could muster without sounding like a challenge to Follett's leadership.

"Vespers approaches," said Follett, the muted glow of the last remaining flames etching every line of his worn and sinful face. Alvarez moved the Oracle, and it sent a new whimper through the cave.

"It will not sustain."

Follett stared long and hard into Alvarez's face and then said, "Calcas, fetch wood, and be soon."

The brothers turned without saying a word and showed no signs of disquiet about what they had to do.

"And taketh Pearlbinder's horse. It ain't going to get in here."

———

Samuel Kahn Pearlbinder was not the kind of man who would normally be told what to do or think. A few had tried and been met with grievous injury or instant demise. Pearlbinder had owned the same mount for five years and had given her the name Sophia. He didn't love much, but he loved Sophia. Five years was a long time in his trade.

He was still standing by her when he heard the command and saw the Calcas approaching. His hands moved away from the animal and curled toward his sword.

"She will depart this life," commanded Follett. Everybody stopped moving and turned toward him.

"We can't get her in, and she will die outside. If she stayeth where she is, jammed in there, she'll half freeze and block us in; we will be forced to hack her apart where she stands."

There was sense in his words.

"Sam, you can take Scriven's horse until I get thee another."

Only Follett could control Pearlbinder, and he would do it calmly and with common sense. It was the only thing that slowed the burning fuse of Pearlbinder's anger. If a man dared mouth their opinion on the matter, Pearlbinder would likely slaughter him and anyone else who offended him or his horse.

The low fire hissed and cracked in the silence, which was now profound. Then, without a word, Pearlbinder turned back to the horse and started to push against her neck, while stroking her sides close to where her ribs were wedged against the cold rock.

"Better to be free one last time," he muttered to her, leaning his entire weight against her. Gradually the horse understood and started to back up into the freezing light outside.

The Calcas looked at Follett and he nodded that that they should proceed. Outside, Pearlbinder gave the reins to the brothers and turned away, not wanting to see the departure.

Follett directed Pearlbinder to the Pyx.

"Give it your anger. We need all we can get with the little we have left."

Pearlbinder hated this ritual and could not believe that Follett had so comfortably agreed to its condition as part of their expedition. The captain and he were sensible men; they avoided all talk of demons and angels even though they knew they existed. Now these voodoo rituals were written into their contract of blood and gold, without any obvious purpose. There were few crimes that he had not committed and a few unique ones that he had sired. If he must take part in this ungodly bullshit, he would do it with more gusto than any of the others. He would dredge up the foulest acts of depravity to plague the rotting bones' jellied cores.

Pearlbinder strode across the cave, unbuckling his weapons and letting them fall in clashing, dark heaps. He tore off his clothing until he was totally naked and then snatched up the Pyx containing the few remaining bones that they had managed to save from the rapids. But instead of seeking seclusion, he carried it next to the fire and prepared to speak. The openness of his actions silenced everyone, even Follett. Pearlbinder sat for a long time, the yellow and white flames sending up ghost tongues to lick at the contours of his rigid, pensive face and at the constellations of scars on his body. Then he let go with a loud oath that spat phlegm and ectoplasm into the cringing box. His voice boomed and confounded the ragged dark space. The horses pressed against one another and away from the firelight. The Kid stopped smirking after the first five minutes and pushed his dirty fingers into his dirty ears. All the men were shocked senseless except Tarrant, who gradually moved closer to watch more intently something he had never seen before.

Pearlbinder was hoarse when he abruptly finished and snapped shut the lid of the Pyx. Without looking up, he croaked, "Alvarez, get your spoon."

FA/T AWAKE

Sluggishly asleep, churned by too much gin and a shouting match with her drunken husband before bed, Meg was dreaming. A nightmare was riding her hard under a red, scratched sky. She was marching in a great seething tumult of locked bodies. A mixture of known faces and unknown creatures waddled into one another and attacked. The bridge was thick with their conflict, but this was normal compared to the giants who roamed about so slowly, performing rudimentary tasks that had no name or purpose. Things of great beauty lived here alongside horrible travesties, and Meg moved among them, equally large and slow. In the far corner, masked by bare trees and contained within broken walls, was the huge gaping mouth of Hell itself, stupid and built of bricks and plaster. The gigantic Meg shrugged at its presence, knowing she could defeat all the horrid weak demons spewing out in a tide of brown bilge. She looked about, uncertain, not understanding where she belonged or what she should fear.

Her sleepy, tired wonder gloved her disgust until a sound turned it inside out. Behind her a bent, rubbery man in a lewd pink gown was sitting astride the roof of what looked like Der Linden bakery. On his head he carried a boat of squabbling old men, who were throwing giant pearls and plates of food over the side, as if to lighten the craft and save themselves from a catastrophic shipwreck. Instead of a sail, a fragment of a thin glass ball perched above them, and nearby bells rang furiously. Was this some kind of disgusting priest? Then Meg saw what he was actually busy doing: With great deliberation, he was spooning something from a hole behind his back where his arse should be. The hole was bigger than his head, and it was full of sticky black night soil, which he ladled onto plates held up by a crowd of women standing below. One of the most enthusiastic to receive his bounty was Willeke Dijkstra.

A terrible sound and a loud stench awoke her from her nightmare. The dream slid back into the darkness of the bedroom as Cluvmux snored and farted at the same time. Meg pulled the bedsheet up to her face, covering her wet nose. Her husband was not known for his delicacy of manner or his grace of favor, but this was beyond his grossest bedtime insults.

The day had been one of many practice jousts for Cluvmux and his cronies. An excellent excuse to drink all day long, though he needed no excuse; he would have done so anyway. Meg guessed just a little extra might have been imbibed, judging by the condition of his noxious bowels. She twisted out of their small wooden box bed and slid her cold feet onto the colder floor, while he continued to snore, sitting up in his usual sleeping position, oblivious to his odious crimes.

In her kitchen, the night was quieter and cleaner. Meg made herself a drink of milk and fennel. She topped it off with warm water from the kettle, which always hung above the cinders of the stove. Bits of the dream stayed and tried to find a place where they might fit snug in her trench of a memory. But all those spaces were occupied by watery thoughts and unfocused pictures of her lost son. These were her daily nightmares. What business did this other glaringly vivid dream have there? Its colors and events found

Hollow 71

sympathy with her husband's stench. She opened one of the shutters for more air and looked at the starlit sky as an owl passed through the frosty trees. The yards and houses out there were the same as those in her dream, or was it a nightmare? It had retreated so far that she could not tell.

A small movement drew her attention to something at the base of the fence—a rat, she thought—and then it made a sound like speaking. She leaned farther out, feeling a chill run along her spine. The sound was becoming clearer, and a child's small, floppy hat was pushing toward her out of the shadows. She could not see its color under the stars but thought it might be yellow. Then she knew it was the creature she had hissed at on the bridge. The one she hadn't cut in half. A great and peculiar pity cupped her, and the motion of it worked like a key in an unseen lock, which the being understood and which allowed it to communicate.

" 'Tain't like before, Missis, we shan't come near."

"Better not," said Meg, without knowing why.

" 'Tis just to say that soms of us b'longs you."

Meg whispered harshly into the shadows, "Show yourself."

The small, floppy hat shook from side to side, like someone shaking their yellow head.

" 'Tain't wise," the voice in the shadows said. "Our difference gives stigma and malice to your kind."

"I won't hurt you," said Meg, surprised at the emotion of her commitment.

"Can't be known," said the shadows.

"What did you mean, 'belongs'?"

"Soms of us b'longs you."

"How is that possible?"

"Atachyments, and we will be telling all the other mothers on this night."

"Telling what?"

"That they must flock together around you as they did on the day of Lady Grietje's cooking."

"You knew Grietje?"

"I and others were her family. Now we are yours."

"Family?"

"You called us that."

"Never family."

The voice quieted and said, "You say *'vertraut.'*"

Meg gradually understood. "You are saying *Hexen vertraut* in German. You speak German? Is that where you are from?"

"No, Missis, not there. I am here, in your family."

"But what you said doesn't mean family."

The small hat was slowly drawn into the shadows, and the starlit yard felt the loss of understanding as it waited for Meg to explain.

"You are a familiar, not family."

"What is the difference?"

Meg carefully explained to the best of her ability. There was a long, quiet pause while, in the trees, the owls listened to the disappointment below. A small sound of creaking wood announced that the pale yellow hat in the shadows had left through a crack in the yard's fenced enclosure.

Confused and overwhelmed, Meg returned to the familiarity of her snoring bedroom. She climbed back into her side of the crated bed and used the weight of the pungent air to stop being too fast awake, trying to understand what had just happened and anticipating the next morning.

VOICE

Dominic was woken by the memory of his own voice speaking clearly again. He was confused about where he was: this narrow room wasn't his cell; the window was in the wrong place. Where was he now? What had happened? Maybe his voice was trying to tell him. There was a great calm in the room, sunlight shafted across the floor, and motes of dust floated languidly in the undisturbed air. There were five beds, but four were empty.

What had his voice been trying to say? He was just about to ask when his mother spoke to him.

"Domi, you are so good at sleeping, always have been."

He looked down and saw himself sleeping under a gray blanket; nobody else was in the room.

"Where are you, Mumma? I can't see you."

"Here, my boy, by the stove, next to Anna."

Dominic moved his head from side to side, but the body in the bed did not. He realized he was on the ceiling looking down.

"I can't see the stove, just some beds. I think I am in one of them."

As he looked closer, the left arm of the sleeping body began to shake violently.

"Wake up, Domi, you are having a bad dream. Please wake up and help us find your father."

The arm went limp and the body in the bed opened its eyes and looked at its mother. It tried to speak but could not.

"His voice has been stolen, too."

The floating Dominic heard his voice out loud for the first time.

"Get dressed! We must start a search beyond the farm. We have looked everywhere. I can't think where he is; all the horses are here."

His mother pulled the blanket off the bed; the Dominic there was trembling and much younger.

"But, Mumma, Poppa is here no more. He is in Heaven with little Anna."

"What are you saying, you cruel boy?" Her voice began to falter, the words coming apart as their sound gained a different weight. "What are you saying?"

"The great illness that swept over this land saw them both away last winter."

"No . . . noo . . . nooo!" she wailed and looked anxiously around the room.

"I slept through it all, and when I awoke, it was just you and me. We tended the farm by ourselves until it came back for you. When I woke up the second time, you had gone to join them. I found your poor dead body."

The old woman walked backward away from the bed, one arm outstretched, ready to find the door handle and escape. As she did so, she looked up and saw the floating Dominic talking to her.

"Save me," she whimpered as she opened the door and disappeared.

Dominic would have found none of this surprising in his old home, in those years when he had to look after the farm by himself. The plague had little interest in the animals, and those that survived starvation multiplied and grew. He'd managed to keep half the crops going, and the chickens were abundant with eggs. For two years he fed and watered them and himself every day, until people began to drift back into the depopulated lands. He had experienced death at close range, and its trauma had been replaced by a numbing fear that transformed into dense acceptance of the dead, who visited him to ask where they were. That was when his voice faded away and he had nothing to say.

When the priest and the three nuns found the silent child, they'd quickly taken him under the protection and care of the church. They also took the farm and all its troubles off his hands. By the time he entered the Monastery of the Eastern Gate, Dominic was speaking again, shyly and with much hesitation. The ritual initiation of visiting the Gland of Mercy appeared to have had no real effect on him. Friar Cecil reported the novice's lack of reaction to Friar Benedict, who had a great curiosity about the interface of innocence and corruption in the human soul. But Benedict had absolutely no tolerance for obsequiousness, stupidity, and laziness—the three qualities Friar Cecil possessed in abundance. Detecting Cecil's disappointment in the novice's response to the Gland made Benedict even more contemptuous of the abbot's favorite lapdog and twitched a bead of interest on Benedict's long rosary of curiosity.

His terseness weakened and gave way to sympathy when he met Dominic and heard of the boy's experiences and attitude. He took him under his spiky wing, a place most novices would have shunned.

The boy had grown strong and tall, and his voice had remained intact until now. Whatever had shouted at him from within the Cyst had caused him to regress. The return of his mother to the room in which he had been recuperating was a vexing and disturbing occurrence. The part of his consciousness that identified the sleeping body on the bed seemed able to talk, even if only to a ghost.

"What will become of me?" Dominic asked himself, and the body in the bed turned to look directly at him. They stared into themselves until an answer came.

"Vanished!" a high shrill voice cried in a space outside the somnambulist's realm.

"Vanished!" it screamed again beyond the valerian-coaxed separation, which instantly dissolved.

"Vanished!" it yelled, over and over again, and Dominic knew this was a memory inside a dream. The first time he had heard it, it had had nothing to do with him. But now that he had dreamed it again, he knew that his voice had not been permanently stolen; it had just been rudely borrowed.

THE ORACLE

Outside the cave, the wind was rising with the darkness, its eerie whistle matching the Oracle's warbling chants. The men heard a jagged rustle at the entrance. It was the sound of Abna Calca pushing one of the heavily laden mules through the hole. His brother dragged the other. Both carried bundles of wood. All the men, except Pearlbinder, were instantly on their feet. The Kid blew on the ashes, sending cinders back into his own face.

"Be at ease with this bounty. We know not how long we'll be imprisoned here," Tarrant called out before Follett had a chance.

The Calcas let go of the animals and tried to move their arms in their frozen coats, which cracked with frost. Then they silently walked over to Pearlbinder.

Abna took off his hat with some difficulty and said softly, "We let Sophia go in sight of the tree line, where we found this wood. There were some signs of recent habitation nearby."

Pearlbinder nodded and stared into the flickering fire and at the frenzied activities around it.

"There was even a broken hutch," said Owen, his eyes fixed on his shoes.

"Bind the tents together and seal that gap," shouted Follett.

The men worked frantically for an hour, stitching the heavy, dense material and tying it with strips of leather. When they were finished, it looked like the flayed skin of some mythical beast.

"Looks like a sunfish," said Tarrant.

"A what?" asked the Kid.

"Sunfish. I seen one from the deep sea beached on the isle of Ghawdex."

"What the fuck does thee talk about fish and sons?"

"I say there is a semblance here."

"I says thee talks shit." The Kid laughed.

"Enough of this, get that freezing breech sealed!" bellowed Follett. And all the men took an edge of the heavy canvas mass and dragged it toward the gap in the stone. They forced it into the crevice until the wind was gagged and the cold held its breath. The damp wood was now blazing, and the flames gave forth a generous glow. The men unpacked pots and slabs of dried meats and began preparing the first hot meal they had had in days. A tide of well-being rose in the cave; even Tarrant and the Kid's animosity had declined.

The flickering light of the fire sealed the conversation, washing away all remaining questions and answers. The men pulled their sleeping sacks close to one another, in a circle around the blaze, and started to crawl their way into sleep. Outside, the wind reached a new pitch, the heavy loose snow flinging up into a stampeding whiteout that seemed a million miles away.

Days passed without time, the flickering hours recorded only by the expenditure of firewood and victuals. Months and hours slid through each other without any sensible exchange. The storm outside continued, seemingly gaining momentum.

The Oracle had remained mute or drooling, but, charged and swollen with Pearlbinder's sins, it began to fill the cave with its unbidden voice. No longer in random outbursts of oblique messages but in a song, or something close to one. It sang with the wind, matching its timbre and pulse, swaying between the bass of its hopeless moan and the crescendo of its sustained unearthly whining. It sang in union and descant, and all the men fell into a fathomless sleep and dreamed a dream that did not exist. The Oracle sang all through what must have been the third night, because when it was over, day existed again outside. There were tiny holes in the high ceiling that let in spider-thin threads of light, which slivered in the eerie intermittent glow and swam above the dismal slumberers. The fire had finally died out in the freezing cave; the still air was full of chilled, static smoke and weak illumination. The men gradually awoke to this vision and to the cold and to the ebbing of the Oracle's voice. The storm had blown itself out. Follett was first to grab hold of the canvas, quickly followed by the others, who wanted to breathe clean air again. They tugged at the frozen shape, which refused to move; the mass had frozen solid, ice and snow rammed into every space behind it. The Calcas brought their axes and tried to cut it into pieces. But the iron-hard bung ignored their might and their blades, sounding like a sullen bell when their axes skidded off its unyielding rigidity.

"Check the other vent," shouted Follett. Tarrant picked up a shovel and went to the other side of the cave.

"It must have been an ice blizzard," said Owen Calca.

"How long will it take to thaw?" asked Alvarez.

"It won't" came the answer nobody wanted to hear. "Not until the spring. The wind must have changed direction and became vicious. Must have been cascading against that entrance night and day."

"Cascading and freezing," added the other Calca.

Tarrant returned with a dented shovel, shaking his head.

"We are all fucked!" said the Kid.

And Pearlbinder began picking up the few remaining bits of wood and discarded twigs.

"How much food do we have?" Follett asked Alvarez.

"Less than a day's worth of heavy rations."

Then the spidery beams of light went out as the storm returned.

———

Inside the cave, the temperature had dropped below zero, and only one lamp was burning, its whale-oil stink giving off impossible recollections of the sea. The contradictions disturbed even the violent equilibrium of Follett's savage band. Nobody spoke; they were saving their energy, and besides, no one had anything to say. The angel of death was nearby and made of ice. Then a scratching started somewhere at the back of the cave in the total darkness. The men tried to look at one another and saw only the shadows that hollowed each man's features. Everyone was present in the tight group, which meant the noise was being made by someone, something else. Pearlbinder unsheathed his scimitar, and Tarrant lifted the lamp higher. The Oracle's crate was open and lying on its side. It was empty.

Follett snatched the lamp from Tarrant's hand and rushed toward the scratching, almost running into the solidity of the cave wall's leaping shadows.

"Find it!" he bellowed.

Three of the men followed him more slowly. Follett now had his face and the lamp hard against the stone.

"It's coming from inside," he whispered.

"It can't," said Pearlbinder. "It's a solid mass. I saw that days ago, when we had some daylight and the fire."

"Listen, man," said Follett, stepping back to allow the others to witness the truth of what he had just said.

"It is. It's in there," said the Kid.

Then the wall giggled.

"It's the fucking horror. It's got inside."

From a stick, rags, and oil, Tarrant quickly made a flaming torch, which he brought to the perplexed men. The giggling was growing more intense, and echoing. Alvarez started hammering on the stone with the blunt end of an ax, the sound announcing a great hollowness on the other side. All the men started pounding and hammering the stone wall, until, with his fifth blow, the Kid fell through. Tarrant thrust his spluttering torch into the devouring space.

"It's a door. There is a door in the rock."

Tarrant pushed against it, causing the door to fall inward with a resounding echo, illuminating the space within. The sound seemed to go on forever, climbing inside the dark hollow, which appeared to be a featureless passage once the dust and reverberations settled.

The corridor was ten feet high and as wide as three men standing next to one another. It had a slight upward gradient, and at the farthest point touched by the flickering light, they could see the Oracle rocking back and forth, laughing at the gawping men.

"How did it get here? It can't walk," said Alvarez. "And that slab of a door was closed."

The questions traveled up the corridor, past the small dust-covered figure. Then it snuffed out all their queries as it sang, " 'Tis the road to light. A star road made for thee."

Follett ordered his men to retrieve all their possessions and saddle their horses. The riders gathered in single file behind Tarrant, who was already in the tunnel, holding his torch up and away from his horse's head, ready to lead the expedition into the unknown. Pearlbinder put his saddle, swords, guns, and bags on Scriven's mount.

"The dead man's horse looks a bit bowed under your size and all that junk," commented the Kid.

Pearlbinder ignored him.

"I wouldn't ride no skewered man's pony."

Follett was now out of earshot of the Kid's comments, but it did not stop the other men from blenching at the stupidity and danger of talking about the lost horse.

Only Tarrant put their feelings into words. "Thou shouldest keep thy mouth shut lest you get some of the same."

The Kid made a gesture with his thumb, shucking his front teeth, and no more words were spoken on the subject.

The pace inside the tunnel was sedate, matching the unworldly quality of the stillness and the depth of the group's ignorance about their predicament. They made four more torches with rags and the last of the oil, and the men prayed they would reach daylight and the exit before the torches died. But secretly, they knew they wouldn't.

UROOBSH

Friar Benedict's arm was in a sling fashioned of the finest black silk, a luxurious and extravagant fabric for the poor brethren to possess. Nobody had ever seen it before, so the monks assumed it was a remnant of the holy man's previous life and, therefore, better not mentioned. The smell of mothballs it emitted helped the brothers to focus strictly on the present.

Since his blasphemous and painful meeting with the pumpkin-like Woebegot, the staunch old man had changed his view on the nature of what he had considered exotic animals. He had put aside his rampant compiling of the community's consuetudinary and now collected stories and eyewitness accounts of these new and worrying creatures that were infesting his neighborhood. Benedict had even ventured outside the monastery to investigate reported sightings. On one such expedition, he had stopped at the humpbacked bridge on the other side of town. There he had heard chanting coming from the muddy waters. It had sounded like one nonsensical word repeated over and over again by a group of small voices. *Uroobsh* was a new word for his journal and the only word he had ever entered there that he did not understand.

Friar Benedict rarely shared an opinion with the peasants, but since his ordeal, he had started to listen to fragments of their gossip and folktales. Some of the occupants of the Lowlands believed that these new creatures must have come out of the mountain, that their origins were somewhere in its labyrinthine tunnels and fallen passages. This reasoning fit with certain legends passed down by the old families of the region for centuries.

The keepers of those memories told impossible tales of the building of the mountain that rose from sea level to the heavens. They told of its vast library of books in all known languages—a physical manifestation of the knowledge of the beings and the peoples of those distant times. Their wisdom and communications were housed in a ziggurat, a pyramid, a tower whose hubris had offended God so much that it was crushed and broken into a Cyclopean cone of silence. Collapsed into a mountain, the integrity of its thousands of careful tiers was destroyed. Superstitions about its interior whispered of endless corridors and fallen bookshelves, stairways and halls swallowed by rubble.

It was a perfect place for those abnormal creatures to grow, but exactly how their conception and evolution occurred had never been explained. Benedict wanted to tease out all the possibilities, so he asked for an audience with Abbot Clementine to share his concerns about the reality of these creatures. The Father Superior had already banned his research into the origin and history of the Gland of Mercy, making it very clear that he must conduct his studies in another subject. Benedict did not receive this edict well; however, he had taken a vow of obedience. Still, he could allow only so much academic control. He would obtain his "superior's" blessing on this investigation at any cost. He would seek the abbot's scholastic opinion on how new breeds of animals found their way into this world—a complex but honest inquiry. He would even pretend to find the abbot's words interesting and of value.

Five days after his request, Benedict was informed by Friar Cecil that the abbot was ready to see him and could spare this last quarter of the hour of three.

"He has much to prepare before Shrovetide; his time is sparse."

Idiot, thought Benedict.

So they made their way to the abbot's chambers, then waited. Twenty minutes later, Clementine arrived and offered the old monk a seat. While the abbot prowled around the room, Benedict presented his observations and questions about the genesis of natural and unnatural beings and how such beings might now dwell in their domain.

He was quoting Empedocles of Akragas about the variation of lost species when the abbot interrupted.

"But Empedocles also thought that the application of love had an effect on water. The most popular ideas about the origins of some exotic animals are centered on a version of spontaneous generation, which uses the evidence of fossils to prove its validity. According to this theory, some of God's creatures, presumably arriving after Genesis, were halted in the act of becoming. Locked in the core of the earth, they waited to be pushed gradually toward the surface and life. Once exposed to the sun and the outer living world, they broke away from the surrounding inanimate rock that had contained them and scurried off into their newly achieved vivification. Those that did not quite have the energy remained fixed and ended up as fully formed creatures, but atrophied in untransmuted stone: thus explaining fossils."

Benedict was stroking his bristling chin and murmuring approval, and then he added, "This is not unlike what some common people use today to explain all kinds of natural phenomena, like the generation of mice. Many know that if you wrap bits of cheese in old rags and hide them in a corner of the house, they will spark and give birth to mice in their stinking folds."

"The same miraculous conception also occurs in meat, with flies," said the abbot, smirking.

"Yes, and all these 'facts' might also describe the perverted use of a talented man's imagination. Pictures that slither out of the minds of men who conjure them in their own corruption," said Benedict.

Clementine looked confused, not realizing that the old man had suddenly changed subjects and was now hobbling down a completely different track of baffling contradiction.

During his studies, Benedict had unearthed reports of portraits, paintings, and pictorial inventions of unnatural creatures. These accounts had sparked a whole new set of ideas he was now trying to unravel. . . . But without seeing the paintings or meeting the artist, it was all conjecture, and that was dangerous ground on which to build a theory. This lack of evidence was the curse he had to solve.

"Are you talking about witchcraft and the raising of familiars?" asked the abbot.

Benedict looked horrified and crossed himself. "Certainly not; who would dare discuss such things these days? No, I was talking about artists, painters—a painter who, it is said, has chronicled all the variations of creatures that God never imagined. One man who quietly started the most enormous bestiary of blasphemy the world has ever known."

"But carvings of demons and church paintings of Hell exist everywhere," said the abbot.

"Not like that man in 's-Hertogenbosch made."

"Ah! That man. I, too, have heard tell of him. Do you believe it's true, what they say?"

"Impossible to know without seeing the paintings and meeting the man."

"You are thirty years too late. Jerome of 's-Hertogenbosch, or Jheronimus van Aken—or, as he is now more slovenly called, Hieronymus Bosch—is long since dead."

Benedict looked shocked and defeated.

The abbot continued, enjoying his little revelation, "It is difficult to imagine one man in a cramped attic, in an insignificant town not unlike the one outside our walls, inventing such an obscene zoo. Creating new beings in encyclopedic detail of variation and contrivance. Imagine the influence of such a gibbering plague and the momentum of its unnatural consequence."

"It might attract others to copy him?" offered Benedict.

"Yes, and in much more dangerous realms than fictional representation. This is why I must advise you to be restrained in your work and in what you say about it. You, too, might gather a controversial momentum with conjectures that I do not want inside this house of God."

Something about the abbot changed as he made this pronouncement, a sliver of anxiety peeking out from under his mantle of perfect superiority. Benedict flushed under the growing weight of the insults and was attempting to answer when Abbott Clementine began again.

"Have you heard of Friar Livin Wuursberg?"

"Of course, I have heard terrible things about Wuursberg's crimes, but I don't understand why he should be cited against me."

"Then I will explain. The lunatic crimes of that man and his heretical followers nearly destroyed the solidity of Tertius Ordo Regularis S. Francisci, and it all started with an empirical conjecture about the primacy of sight. Do I make myself clear?"

"Do you mean because I have actually seen one of these creatures myself?" Benedict asked. His blood began to boil as Clementine continued to preach and suggest similarities between his research and the heretical order of the Fraticelli Wuursberg.

The abbot, refusing to acknowledge the old man's distress, continued, "Wuursberg had a maniacal contempt for the debasing of 'God's natural children.' In ten years, he managed to convert the gentle sermons of our patron saint of birds into a furious rant against any invention or elaboration to the 'natural' forms of men and beasts. This tangent eventually led to a declaration of physical denial of all human visual representation. Wuursberg believed that the insemination and dispersal of all blasphemous acts and imagery were literally carried in the eyes of those who had seen them, and that one style of painting was more virulent than any other. He called for those artists and patrons—they who transmitted the contamination farther into Europe—to be severely chastised. More and more burghers and dignitaries wanted paintings made in the style of this Jerome of 's-Hertogenbosch of whom you speak, either for their mansions, their secret societies, or their churches; and more and more copies were made of his ungodly deceits."

"And then God struck Wuursberg blind," snarled Benedict.

"*No, God did not!* Wuursberg's dogma ultimately led to his own enucleation and the development of the Blind Brethren of the Ardennes. They all removed their own eyes to save their souls from visual contamination."

Benedict was much shaken by this disclosure and placed one hand over his heart as if to offer it some protection.

"Wuursberg and his stumbling brothers eventually made their way toward Ghent, after hearing that a congregation of artists were meeting there to erect yet another and, some said, far worse version of *The Temptation of St. Anthony*. Each monk carried a crucifix with a concealed dagger as they crept up the steps into the new gleaming church. The workmen who were constructing the altarpiece thought nothing of them and mistook their falling and stumbling as the normal inebriated condition of priests in the late afternoon. Some workmen even laughed out loud when the monks unsheathed their daggers. They took the workers' eyes. Chaos reigned; paint, plaster, blood, and stone flew through the sacred air. The monks, who quickly lost their 'real' targets, grabbed anyone they could to sanctify them from the evils of satanic sight. Their victims included a woman and a small altar boy . . . the act that paved the way to their own pyre."

Benedict adjusted the sling holding his aching arm and bit his lip in salty silence.

"After the cinders of the good brothers were brushed away, a rumor spread that their eyes, having been removed years earlier, still existed. For some of their now-clandestine followers, this was wondrous news. A few jars of the pickled relics could be used to seed a revised form of their master's doctrine, preferably in a country that showed more understanding of its wisdom. So a search was conducted by somewhat less-than-scholarly disciples; during the following months, no fewer than thirty-seven individual organs were collected. A fine harvest, considering that the brotherhood had only ever numbered ten, and two of those had not fully committed to its essential requirements. Around this time, a grave misunderstanding emerged in the ranks of the unwashed flock about the holy relics. There is one written testament from those times that might indicate how the problem arose.

"The fourteenth tractate of the thirty-second manifest of the Diocesan Annals of Puth, in the province of Limburg, claims that the eyes carried the very contagion that the monks so detested.

Their last offending sight was somehow locked and moldering in the sullen meat of the eyes. If thine eye offends thee . . . What must be seen here is a strong parallel to the life-forms contained in stone, which we discussed previously, and an echo of Isidore of Seville's bestiaries. Much quoted by Philippe de Thaon is the belief that certain stones found in the eyes of hyenas give oracular powers if placed under the tongue of the seeker. It is also worthy of note, considering the downfall of the great tower, that Isidore's most significant work, much praised by Braulio, the bishop of Saragossa, was entitled: *Etymologiae*."

The abbot finally stopped speaking and looked down at the old monk, offering a condescending kindness that made his suffering even worse. "Which I am sure you are familiar with?"

Actually, Benedict did know the volumes, having read them before Clementine had placed a restriction on them.

The abbot continued, "Needless to say, these revelations doubting the sanctity of the eyes only helped to divide Wuursberg's followers into factions. They spent the successive years eradicating each other's views—until all was erased or debased into squabbles over minor subjects, the origins of which were mostly forgotten. The precious organs themselves were lost, discarded, or stolen."

Finally, Benedict was allowed to speak.

"All that may be true, Revered Abbot, but these creatures I am researching are actual, and any debate about their origins is secondary to what their purpose and meaning are to us now *in this abbey*!"

Clementine straightened his back and looked away, so Benedict could not see the guilt and fear in his eyes. But Benedict had already read something of these emotions in the abbot's demeanor, and he quickly closed on Clementine. "Have you *seen* any of these beings?"

The abbot could not answer and, in that jagged pause, Benedict asked, "Have you seen one here?"

Both men turned inward in this frozen moment . . . and both emerged with entirely different versions of the truth and its application.

"I think you miss the point I have been trying to explain," said Clementine, drawing himself up to his full height.

"Your simplistic trust in empirical evidence will not allow the appropriate depth of philosophical speculation and may cause unnecessary controversial momentum, the kind that might alert investigations from Rome, or worse, from Toledo. It is important that you do not vainly trust in what you see to be a truth. All great philosophers warn against the simplicity and deceit of that manner of explanation. I suggest that you focus your studies on the wisdom of profound scholars, rather than becoming obsessed with the fictions of the ignorant."

Benedict was speechless. His irregular teeth gnawed at his lip furiously, while his arm ached and his hand clawed in its black-silk sling. He would not tolerate these grievous insults. The abbot's arguments were wrong, his philosophy was misguided, and he obviously had an agenda that excluded any wisdom Benedict might offer. He would not be bullied by such thuggish and insecure debate. Something was driving Clementine's blindness. Something relentless that needed to stop all speculation and to lock up all the books. Something impatient and hidden that was tangled up with the approaching Shrovetide.

HEXEN

The night visitation in her garden haunted Meg, mainly because she couldn't be sure if it had been part of her dreaming. Its reality was also aching inside her; returning to her marital bed had been a mistake. She had gone back to sleep next to the stinking Cluvmux, sandwiching her starlit conversation between nightmares. All the contradictions of significant movements in other worlds were now turning in her. But the strongest memory that insisted on staying was the sadness her explanation had caused in Yellow Hat. She hadn't meant to disillusion the poor creature so. The combination of uncanny knowledge and regret had produced a conundrum, a thing little known to her. Even though it was uncomfortable, it was somehow reassuringly matter-of-fact. She thought of a windmill that caught the wind to turn a stone to crush a seed into the flour that made the daily bread.

Meg was in Grietje van der Elzen's garden at the very edge of the town, sitting on a tree stump, watching a nearby windmill and listening to the grumble of its wooden gears. Grietje's house was boarded up, desolate; her precious plants overgrown and unwa-tered. This was where they had always talked, away from gossiping ears. All knew Grietje was a Wise Woman, and great care had to be taken on how that was perceived.

Women like her had to watch their actions and pretend to know their place. Women who were wise in the old ways but who had married into the world of men and the church. Her eyes had been kept low for so many years that they had taken on an unbalanced weight, swollen outside the squint that marked their servitude.

Meg had seen many women less wise than Grietje, humiliated in village ponds, half drowned in rivers, and turned to screaming cinders by pious louts. Opinion was a dangerous thing to possess; its slippery temper had a way of hissing out and marking the speaker as at the least a troublemaker, at the worst a demon suckler. Opinion was generally removed from all females of her rank between the ages of eleven and fifty, so they could concentrate on more important things like stoking their wombs into constant activity and pampering their husbands' ambitions into whatever profiles they consider right.

Most Wise Women lived outside such drudgery and imprisonment, seeking seclusion and anonymity beyond the boundaries of villages and towns. Their distance earned them reputations for strangeness and conflict. The wild woods and the looming mountains were no place for the fairer sex. All these pronouncements were bleated by men who had no wisdom at all. They also said that such women were known to converse with the animals and the spirits that dwelled in those places. Some grew bark and vines about their bodies. All developed warts and crooked spines to blend in with the gnarled, unkempt boscage in which they hid. Or so said those in town.

Over the years many Wise Women had been dragged from their hovels and accused of satanic practices. Their homes were ransacked for evidence, as their neighbors and other goodly folk found great offense in their unnatural uniqueness. What sane woman could live like this? Shut away behind closed doors? Everyone else kept their windows open, curtainless, to prove that the same nothingness occurred in exactly the same way in each of their identical spotless hutches. This had been their last conversation, and it was only now that Meg began to understand what her friend was trying to tell her. Remembering more and more disjointed fragments of their talk as she sat alone with the wind gusting between her and the windmill.

Grietje had been strikingly powerful, both in her independence and in her beauty. Those were dangerous qualities in a repressed community that hid in its grayness.

"Do you feel safe out here by yourself?" Meg had asked while her friend was examining the quality of a big bunch of leaves.

"Safe as any, and I am not always alone."

"I was thinking about someone to protect you."

Grietje stopped looking at her leaves and squinted at Meg. "What, a man, you mean?"

"It has benefits."

"Benefits? Having an oaf under my feet all the time, making demands that would turn me into a slave or a whore. Benefits!"

"There are a lot of strange animals showing up, and some of them look dangerous. A man could see them off for you."

"I'd rather have their company than a man's. They might have something more valuable than a prick and a bad temper."

Then, out of frustrated perplexity, Meg said, "Sounds like you been talking with them."

"I have and frequently do," said Grietje. " 'Tis part of what I am; it's always been like that. You should know, it's strong in you, too."

Meg made small sounds of denial that refused to solidify into words. So Grietje continued, "I use all my talents and powers and have grown sick of hiding them."

Suddenly finding her tongue, Meg insisted, "But that's what you could use a man for. His normality could shield you."

"Not from the Inquisition, it couldn't. I know what I am. There is nowhere left in our world to hide. It is coming to take me. The best I can do is to prepare my revenge."

"You could go farther away."

"Where?" Grietje laughed. "Most of the Wise Women I know have died. The patrols of the Caballistas del Camino scooped up anyone in the surrounding lands that had the faintest wisp of unorthodoxy or paganism. Or were just humble, shy, and scared. The Spanish invaders, their king, and all else did so under the great power of the Inquisition. Its fires had to be continually fed with the confessions of the blasphemous and the bodies of those who refused to kneel. Those who lived alone, outside the city walls, no longer exist, and soon the soldiers will be coming in this direction. My home, like my sisters', will crumble and give a dwelling to other beings, and become a sanctuary for the birds of the air and the beasts of the woodlands."

Meg could no longer hear the rumbling of the windmill. The only sound was the pumping of her heart. All Grietje's words had come to pass.

The caballistas did turn their attention to the less obvious, to those who concealed their witchcraft in the poorer alleys of the growing towns. Meg had known three women who died in the pyres, and she had heard of countless others who had been ducked or weighted and drowned. Almost all had been innocent of the charges brought against them, but the last one, Grietje van der Elzen, embraced her guilt and admitted to every shocking accusation. Then she had startled the courtroom by adding lurid details of her licentious communion with dark forces. Some of the clergy had to shield their ears, and others left the chamber in disgust. Toward the end of her list of transgressions, she had modestly announced that she had also sat as a model for the great master of 's-Hertogenbosch, the Brabantisch Lame-Vanger himself—and that the combination of her comeliness and the contortions she performed gave birth to at least seven Filthlings from the promiscuous tip of the artist's pencil.

Grietje knew she had nothing to lose as the last flame rose around her, so her descriptions became more and more lurid under the insistent questions of her tormentors. Scribes transcribed the details in thick ledgers that would eventually join countless others, giving a massive weight of proof to the Inquisition's holy purpose. As she burned, she spat out her name like a flag along with the names of every devil she could remember. As she fell away into ash, a vortex of what she had been erupted, focused, and inseminated a vengeance of change into the world.

TUNNEL

The riders plodded in single file inside the tube of featureless stone. Their flickering torches gave a knot of animation to the closeness of the wall and their isolation as they moved between pools of darkness. The Oracle's odd unpredictable sounds cast back into the darkness they had left behind and forward into the darkness they were heading into.

The men barely spoke. The abnormality of the place and the unknowing were becoming depressing. Then the first torch spluttered out.

"Jesus," said the Kid. And Follett commanded that they stop.

"We must feed the horses whilst we still have light," he said, and the simple statement made things much worse. Its normality undermined by a future dread. Only Follett and Tarrant got off their horses and found the nosebags. Attaching them to the animals' heads provided a distraction. The sound of the horses' eating was both disgusting and comforting, and it gave the men an opportunity to mutter, their machinations smothered by chewing noises.

When the horses finished, Follett and Tarrant crawled back into their saddles and gave the word to continue.

"How far have we come, Captain?" asked Alvarez.

"Impossible to know. It feels like three or four hours, but the tally of it is difficult."

This was the last understanding of and conversation about time. Both were silenced with the extinction of the last torch. The inevitable arrival of the endless blackness changed everything.

They stopped as if frozen . . . hopeless and blind. A horizontal vertigo reached into the lost memories of their traveled past and the unknown distance of their future, and the containment of standing still made it worse. The continual movement had given them hope. Without it, the dismal fear of eternal entrapment engulfed them all; the horror of the living grave overwhelmed every man in a black flood of realization. The horses sensed their riders' unease and became agitated.

Tarrant whispered into his mount's ear and urged it forward. Eventually, the animal accepted the command and moved on. The others followed.

Occasionally, the horses grazed the men against the rough walls; the animals were losing their coordination and their spatial awareness. The steady line faltered, men and horses nudging and stepping sideways. The only thing that had improved was the temperature. The limb-numbing cold of the cave had given way to a uniform chill that sat outside their bodies like a claustrophobic shroud.

From the back of the line, Pearlbinder said, "This tunnel is getting steeper, like it's climbing to Heaven, but it feels like a descent into Hell."

His voice seemed unattached and his words abstract. A single sob was heard among the men, who could see absolutely nothing. A single anonymous and automatic exclamation of despair.

When wicked men of wicked caliber lose part of their lives, they never come back entirely. Some part accepted death as a better option than the life they found themselves trapped in. One of these scarred and charcoaled souls had entered that state of mind, but he would never admit it.

The only other noise growing between the sounds of the horses' hooves was the growling of the men's stomachs, which gave a modest indication of how long they had been locked in this corridor.

The next hours or days were appalling. The plodding rhythm in the rising tube caused a nauseous drowsiness that swallowed the last remnants of their willpower. So the riders would plummet into thick, meaningless dreams and then startle awake into a reality that was far worse. They had no control left. Alvarez began to moan involuntarily, and the Kid's teeth were chattering. Starvation and the grave became their reality, and eyes that had shed tears were now parched, constipated, and locked open.

The men were barely conscious, staring blindly, when the Oracle began to whistle a soft, bright sound that filled the thick darkness like a memory of a spring day. The contrast was cruel and terrible in their despair. Then Tarrant's lead horse walked headfirst into the closed end of the tunnel. The Oracle whistled again and the wall before them fell asunder. The men and horses shrieked, reared, and fell.

A vast magnitude of whiteness hit them as the space in the wall opened into a brilliant morning of sun-dazzling snow. Their eyes, wide open in the tunnel's night, were now stunned and hurt by the intensity of the light. They rolled and stumbled in the snow's purity, hands covering their faces, screams turning into tears and laughter, drinking and eating the whiteness. The Kid rubbing it into his eyes.

The Oracle sat in its crate and observed everything quietly. Gradually the men calmed down and confronted their pitiful state and their desperate need for food and shelter.

"Where are we?" asked Alvarez.

They turned to examine the hole they had just passed through onto this plateau of virgin snow. The men spread out, finding themselves on the edge of what felt like a summit; each man walked to a different place, their bodies becoming markers describing a roughly circular space.

"There is a track down this way," called the Kid, "and there are rabbits down there."

No more needed to be said as the men tore open their packs to grab anything they could use to hunt. Pearlbinder moved up behind Follett.

"You know what this place is, don't you?"

The old man didn't turn round but answered quietly, "Das Kagel."

Pearlbinder looked around him. "How do you know? We could be anywhere. There is no land in sight, just clouds."

"Isn't it magnificent?" Tarrant called to them. "We are above the clouds, like birds."

"Not an albi-tross, I hopes?" said the Kid, with a foolish grin and a handful of wire traps.

Pearlbinder looked deeper into the clouds and forgot his question to Follett. For a moment, all the men took store of where they were in this world, because it was easier to believe that they had entered another. A vast dome of radiant blue sky crowned with the ragged mountaintop was the only solid feature in the middle of this impossible landscape. The black, negative space of the hole they had just exited was the darkest thing around. The blinding snow covered a softly undulating circle that led to a rim: the edge of the summit. The descending track was clearly defined, spiraling down into the top surface of the clouds, which extended to the horizon in all directions. Its myriad colors were iridescent and warped and whispered through with blues, silvers, and whites. Undertones of gray slid in temperatures of opacity, which were seeking the space to become transparent. A vast sleeping ocean whose undulations were too slow to see and too fast to ever be remembered. It was easier to believe that one could walk or sail across this seascape rather than travel down through it. Even in their desperate hunger, or perhaps because of it, the men were mesmerized by its beauty, lost in its endless potential. Even in the cinder hearts of the most callous, there is a cusp for rapture. Even in the souls of those who would joke or spill life and death, there is a pause just long enough to be surprised by the taste of air. So it was with these pilgrims on the brink of their night. Soon they would descend into blindness, cold, and terror, but they had been given this day, this vision, and the sweet taste of rabbit flesh before they devoured the inevitable.

UNYOKED

There was only so much "guidance" that could be tolerated with a monk's academic research, and Benedict would take no more censorship and patronization from the abbot. He would continue his investigation into the creatures and demons that were infesting the land and the abbey. Moreover, he would do it with greater relish now that he had seen the effect the subject had on his "Father Superior." Distaste, fear, or something stronger had disclosed a weakness in the abbot, and it smelled like a secret. Benedict would put all his might into exposing or exasperating it. So, with his typical ruthless obstinacy, he would accept the abbot's accidental "advice" and deepen his knowledge of the subject.

The old monk would use the insult as a command—a key to the long-locked inner sanctum of the library. He would quote the abbot's scorn in a slant that would allow him to be in the company of old, forgotten volumes, scrolls of demonology, and hierarchies of unnatural beings in the Kabbalah.

This task he undertook ferociously, sending novices scurrying in and out of the library's every nook and cranny, seeking every word or image on the anatomy and origin of these creatures that God had never created. He was, of course, now far too frail and injured to take on such strenuous physical labors. His vigor must be focused on scholastic endeavors, where he had already made impressive progress. He had already laboriously annotated Saint Augustine's *De divinatione daemonum*, one of the very sources that the artist Jerome, the Brabantisch Lame-Vanger, was rumored to have used when visualizing such monstrosities. Of course, he had never seen any of the works of this Jerome who, since his death, was now called Bosch; most hadn't. Benedict had suspected the rumors that abounded inside the holy orders, rumors of the horrors this obscure artist produced, were exaggerations invented by others who had never laid eyes on the actual pictures. The abbot's announcement that Bosch had died years ago, far from taking the wind out of Benedict's sail, had sharpened his resolve to find an answer, a conclusion. So much better for a scholar never to meet the subject of his investigations rather than ask him what things mean or how they came into being. That would be the ultimate act of empirical misdirection.

Benedict had recently heard that one of the noble families who supported the abbey had such a painting in their possession. Since that disgusting thing's attack in the kitchen, the old monk's curiosity had deepened into resolve. He was beginning to think it was his duty to witness one of these "masterpieces" in the flesh. Because the flesh had proved itself real, and he wanted to understand the relationship between the artist's imagination and the reality of the new life-forms that were infesting his home and his peace of mind. To his logical mind, there could be only two possible explanations, and they were both evil, heretical, and unthinkable. The first line of thought was that this Bosch had willfully created pictures of these atrocities without reference to anything at all; they were pure fiction. But surely this was impossible, how could one man create an entirely new unnatural history? And if so, how did these things become sentient and slide off their canvases into the real world?

The second possibility was even worse. Bosch had opened a portal into Hell or some other dimension, allowing this vile bestiary to enter a Christian domain, so that he could make portraits of them and secure his reputation forever. There was some evidence, albeit secondhand, of recent witch trials where some of those accused said that they had "modeled" with demons before the artist in his studio in 's-Hertogenbosch. Normally, Benedict would have ignored such fantasy as foolish tittle-tattle, but certain parallels were beginning to take shape. These were his main lines of explanation. All other notions about the generation of these beings placed his scholarship in direct opposition to his faith and life thus far.

Benedict had no intention of stumbling into the blind footsteps of the Wuursbergian brothers. He was far too canny to court martyrdom on such a troublesome road. His crusade was to become an expert on these creatures, to fuse his technical and esoteric knowledge, so that he might be called on to inflict injury or oblivion to every one of them. Especially those that he now believed had burrowed into the walls of his home.

In this new fervor, he needed help . . . someone younger, who had physical and moral strength. Benedict had become cautiously impressed by Friar Dominic, having kept an eye on him since Cecil's miserable description. Even the way Dominic conducted himself when his voice was stolen suggested sensitivity and stoicism.

Dominic was sitting on the edge of his bed, reading, when Benedict arrived. The young monk was surprised and a little intimidated.

"How are you feeling?"

Dominic nodded and stroked his throat, followed by a small hoarse whisper that did not gather into words.

"Don't try to speak, not in daylight."

Benedict pulled two candles from his pockets and held them out to Dominic. "Take them and cross them over your heart."

He waited until Dominic did as he was told.

"Do you know of the sacred works of Saint Blasius?"

Dominic shook his head.

"He was an Armenian doctor of great virtue and wisdom and a patron saint of illnesses of the throat and voice. And he, like our own good Francis, understood the beasts of the field and the birds of the air. Except Blasius understood wild creatures, wolves. Perhaps like the dog you tried to draw so poorly on that crumbling wall?"

Even at his most benevolent, it was impossible for Benedict not to be acerbic. But Dominic did not hear it; he was enraptured by the story of this unknown venerated man.

"I have found his prayer, which sadly was forgotten for far too many years. Its blessing will return your voice during the night to come. Speak to nobody during the day."

Benedict then retrieved the candles, still warm from the boy's grip, and lit them. Holding the candles high over his head and incanting in a deep, resonant language, Benedict then brought them down and crossed them, still alight and dripping, across Dominic's throat, under his chin. The old monk spoke three more words and then put one candle in Dominic's hand and kept the other for himself.

"Tonight, Saint Blasius will be with you in your dreams, where you may search together for your voice."

Two days later, Benedict recruited Friar Dominic, after persuading him that a nest of Woebegots had most likely infested the cloister wall. They, therefore, were the cause of his traumatic loss of voice, rather than the ghost of the Quiet Testiyont. Nothing like the Oracle's voice had been noticed, but whispers and yappings had been reported. And all had heard the ungodly screeching of the word *vanished* in the stairwell. Well, perhaps they had not vanished but simply had dug deeper into the fabric of the monastery itself?

With the younger monk's strength and energetic faith, Benedict would prove the sanctity of their home had been breached. He would accomplish this with or without the abbot's permission. Fortunately, Clementine had been called to an ecclesiastical gathering three days away. In his absence, the brothers were technically under the guidance of Friar Thomas, a dim and vacant man whom Benedict could sidestep any day of the week.

So with the year sliding near the great schism between Carnival and Lent, and the absence of the abbot, Benedict decided it was time to discover the source of the mystery and mishap. There was nothing and no one there to stop him. He stood before the ragged gash in the Oracle's dwelling with a small posse of monks, some armed with crowbars and axes. Benedict took his good working hand away from his twisted lip and raised it to bless the tools, the place, and the worthy brothers.

"It is God's will for us to cleanse this sanctum from any malign beings that might now be infesting it. This is the Cyst of the last Holy Oracle Testiyont, of all those Blessed Ones that came before, and of all those that will come in the future," he loudly declared, then stepped aside, pointing the trembling finger of attack that had so easily converted from the gentle curve of benediction.

Dominic, who had been released from his confinement in the infirmary, was anxious to join the venture and discover what had taken his voice. He stabbed his five-foot-long crowbar deep into the gash, skewering it violently and destroying the union of crumbling plaster, matted horsehair, and decayed brick. A great deal of material fell out of the wound. On the sixth or seventh thrust of the iron rod, something farther back gave way. The crowbar, so impetuously impelled, was sucked deep into the wall, a victim of its own momentum. Dominic looked startled, staring at his empty hands until two other young monks stepped forward and set at the wall with axes, adding cascades of loose dust and islands of surface plaster to the growing pile of debris. Soon a great quantity of the wall was gone, leaving only a gaping maw in its place.

Benedict raised his hand to stop the attack. One of the brothers pulled the last remnants away with a long-handled rake. They all drew closer, bending down to see what might declare itself in the nest's destruction. Dominic balanced his crowbar like a spear, and Benedict fisted a crucifix like a dagger.

For many moments, they stared at nothing because nothing was there. Gradually their postures changed, dissolving the tense muscles of attack and the lean sinews of flight. Some stepped back, others stepped closer; one touched the loose, saggy wound with his hand: nothing.

"I fear we are too late," said Benedict. "It must have escaped."

He returned his crucifix to the chain around his neck. This action allowed the other monks to begin their own gestures of disappointment and departure, when suddenly a small movement in the rubble attracted their attention. The dust and fragments were being stirred, as if by the wind. Particles were in motion, a loose spiral, not unlike the rotation of cats before they settle to sleep. Dominic started to make a terrible sound in his throat, which was seeking the profile of words. Friar Ludo came to his side and stared into his face. He made the same sound again and pointed in little stabs at the rubble.

"He says," said Ludo, "he says it's his voice."

"What is?" demanded Benedict.

"There, moving, there; it's his voice," answered Ludo, while Dominic nodded and pointed in frightful agreement.

The monks stared at the ripped wall and its little shelf of activity; no one moved because a great terror, a singular and vindictive root of unknowing, held them to the spot. A few loose stones, tufts of horsehair, and plaster fell to the ground. Then the movement bellowed in a language that no one knew, but that all understood: "Unyoked."

Benedict was the only one to shake himself free of the spell of icy bewilderment. He grabbed his crucifix and held it out before him, the chain yanking his head forward, turning his dramatic pose into a surprised comic stooping that belied his command.

"I bless thee in the name of Christ. Depart!"

His voice, which should have commanded authority, exposed a quaver of uncertainty. It did unlatch the other monks, who now fell away from the wall, moving sideways and backward without taking their eyes off the voice's invisibility. Soon only a tiny echo could be heard as if something were crying as it vanished.

A quick breeze entered the courtyard, chasing a few leaves and some of the debris around the cobbles. Its matter-of-factness broke the spell, and almost under his breath, Friar Benedict said, "It is done."

A few drops of rain followed the breeze and the clouds leaned toward twilight with a wideness of sky. The monastery bell began to toll as some of the company worked with their brooms and shovels.

"Leave it. We can clear it away tomorrow."

Nobody argued, and the call to evening prayer seemed a relief. The rain came in with a new bluster as the last monk closed the heavy gate behind him, allowing the locked garden and empty cloister to give themselves up to the growing dark.

Near the chapel, Benedict drew Friar Ludo aside and said, "Take the boy back to rest."

"Yes, I shall, but tell me, what do you think was in the wall?"

"A manifestation of something gone or of something that is to arrive."

"Not the ghost of the Testiyont?"

"No, not completely, that manifestation was confused. The Testiyont was never that. But there was a trace of it, I think, mixed with something else. But not evil, that is why I gave it a blessing, not an exorcism."

Ludo rubbed the back of his neck and shook his head. "But it did steal the boy's voice. Surely that is a malign act?"

"Did the voice, which shouted that last word, sound familiar to you?"

Ludo moved his hand to pull at his ear. "Er! Well . . ."

"Did it not sound like Abbot Clementine?"

Ludo's eyes popped, and he crossed himself quickly. "It did, it did sound like him."

"Then, perchance, what was in the wall doesn't steal voices, it just borrows them."

"For what purpose?"

"That I don't know, but my faith tells me that now the Testiyont is truly gone."

Ludo looked more closely at Benedict's face. "At rest?"

"Unyoked."

FE-FI-FO-FU

Follett and his men soaked up the bright sunlight from a blue, cloudless sky and the white, reflecting snow. There was no wind, and a great peace sat with them on the peak of Das Kagel. It was a bleak bounty, and each man used it to heal the memory of traveling blind through the freezing tunnel that had burrowed into their hearts like a decaying parasite.

The men had found game to eat and wood for fires, warming their bones and stomachs with a stew of rabbits and foraged roots. The Calcas had shown them how to make primitive rugs from the skins of their dinner so they could sit on the snow. Each man had made his own shelter using the remains of the hacked-apart tents. Although they resembled ancient, sheltering saints, they had thawed out enough to believe they were not dead. They even talked about their journey before the cave and the tunnel.

The giant was discussed with the most passion, rehearsing the tales they would one day tell in taverns. Each wonder of their meeting grew in radiance and in dimension. Only Pearlbinder saw no humor in the subject, having been deeply affected by the experience. He had changed his headgear, removing his beaten hat and replacing it with a turban wound from a yellow silk scarf. The color amplified his sternness.

"What will befall O'Reilly?" Alvarez whispered to Follett.

Follett had no idea, but he had been practicing an answer for over an hour, waiting for someone to ask him.

"When healed, he will return home," he finally said.

"Dost thou think him safe?"

"Safe from what ill?"

There was no conviction in the question.

"From being devoured by that beast."

"Thou cared not to call him a beast when he bore thee over the falls."

"I knew not that thou hadst traded O'Reilly with him as payment."

Far above, a flock of birds flew languidly over them. It was the first normal life they had seen in days.

"The giant told me he would heal his wound and become his companion," Follett said, avoiding Alvarez's eyes.

Alvarez did not answer but violently spat on the ground.

Some kind of optimism was trying to grow among the men. They guessed they had seen the worst of the journey, but that was because they could not imagine anything worse. They all prayed to different gods for sleep without thought and to awake alive and to return to the world of hot blood and loud days.

The next day half their gods granted half their prayers. The weather was fine but changing, and the horses sniffed keenly at the departure, even though the track that spiraled downward from the top of Das Kagel was very narrow. It forced the men to ride in single file, leaning toward the mountain's tapering snow-clad walls.

"What manner of pathway be this?" asked the Kid loudly, to those traveling before and after him.

" 'Tis the only way down," answered Follett.

"I have heard the path gets wider as the height declines," added Pearlbinder, whose confidence had returned with a vengeance.

He now rode tall and gleeful in the saddle, and seemed to be enjoying either this new difficulty in the journey or the other men's unease in it.

He continued, "It is said that it was built by a race of men who no longer exist, and they had no knowledge of horses."

"Then it is not but a goat track, a footpath down," commented the Kid.

"It wasn't made to descend!"

"What then?"

"The few who keep a memory of this place declare it was made for escape or sacrifice."

"How the fuck do you know that?" snarled the Kid.

Pearlbinder would not fall into the trap of proclaiming his ability to read or of any other research he had undertaken before setting on Follett's quest, and he was smugly savoring the youth's ignorant irritation. He was just about to rub the Kid's nose in his own stupidity when part of the outer track crumbled under the hooves of the last rider, and Tarrant and his mount slid toward the edge.

The rider quickly gathered the reins and pushed forward on the mare's neck to make the beast step up onto the scree. The sound of the rocks and snow sliding down the incline and falling off the edge locked into the breathing and muffled heartbeats of both men and horses. Tarrant had taken one hand off the reins and was reaching up to find the hard rock under the snow-covered wall, as if to stabilize both himself and his mount. The men, witnessing the insanity of this pitiful gesture, shivered and pressed themselves inward and away from the precipitous drop.

Follett, who had been riding just ahead of Tarrant, unsheathed his lance and thrust it backward. Tarrant let go of the rock and lunged at the spear as if to grab its blade. With great disdain, Follett twisted the shaft and flipped it away. Then he twisted it back, let it fall against the horse's bridle, and yanked. The stickleback rear of the blade hooked into the bit.

Follett dug his spurs hard into his horse, and it jolted forward, pulling the head of Tarrant's horse with such force that it had no choice but to clamber over the slippery, disintegrating track. Follett pulled on the shaft again, and the horse shuddered and found firm ground. Men and beasts remained motionless, holding their breath and listening to the sound of an avalanche somewhere below.

Follett took the lead, slowing their pace for the next four hours. The silence continued until they reached a wide, sunlit plateau. Smaller footpaths spidered out from the path in different directions, some freshly used. It was the first clear sign of recent occupation, and the men assumed an altered stance and a heightened awareness.

"We will camp and make a Scry here," said Follett. "Alvarez, prepare."

They dismounted, tethered, and unpacked their horses, and stretched out in the stillness of the place, lighting pipes of tobacco and other leaves. Only Pearlbinder stayed in his saddle, pushing his head upward into the sunlight as if trying to breathe above water. The Kid lit a small, knobby black cigar and sidled up to Tarrant. "You were near a goner back there."

Tarrant turned his slitted eyes toward the Kid.

" 'Twas a dangerous defect in that pathway."

"I thought you were a goner." The Kid grinned.

"Weren't my time, then and there."

"Could have been."

"No."

"Could have."

"No."

"You old men pretend to know everything."

Tarrant ignored the insult and focused hard on the Kid. "I do, because I am much older than you know. I have lived in many times and have a bounty and a credence within the years. I will not die on this steep place."

"How the hell do thee know that? You didn't die because Cap saved thy spooky life. You all treat me like I know nothing. Just old men saying they know it all."

As he spit out his words, the Kid looked from one man to another for a glimmer of recognition. Then his eyes stabbed toward Pearlbinder, still seated proudly on his horse in the sunlight.

"What about him? What's his game?"

"He glories in the warmth. It brings memories of his homeland," answered Tarrant.

The Kid grinned wide and said, " 'Tain't what I mean. He's been different, changed since the giant lifted him up in his hands like a cricket. Made him something else. Look at him wearing that bonnet."

Tarrant looked away, not wanting to be drawn into the young man's disrespect. " 'Tis a turban, not a bonnet" was all he said to close the story.

"Easter bonnet," chortled the youth.

"Hold thine tongue around the Pearl, child."

"I fear no pansy."

"Thou shouldst be afeard of him. Don't let his ways deceive thee. There be no smut of balm in that man."

"He was mighty soppy 'bout his horse in the cave."

"That's a different matter; they shared travails together."

"Or he just fucked it too much. P'raps he likes 'em big like she-horses, or big dog-headed he-monsters."

Tarrant turned away from the youth, saying, "I want none of your mockeries."

The Kid sniggered and looked around again toward the statuesque rider, then unzipped the dead cigar from his grin and pulled the brim of his wide hat over his face, cutting out the sun.

"What sustenance will the Oracle partake of in this wilderness?" asked Alvarez.

"We must seek more bones," said Follett, cringing at the memory of his feeble attempts to save the contents of the spilled box from the fast waters. He could still hear the giant's mocking laughter.

"Or thou couldst send the Calcas back to fetch what remains of O'Reilly."

Follett ignored the grim jest.

"But giants eat bones, do they not?"

"Tend to the Blessing. I will go ahead to forage. We need to find some bones with haste and steep them in confession, or we won't get the saturation needed for the next prophecy or direction."

"Thou wanteth human bones, then?"

"Verily. I don't want to go down this mountain blind."

"Are there people up here?"

"We are no longer in the wilderness. Common men dwell below. I have seen signs of occupation and husbandry already. Those woodpiles were made this year."

Alvarez grunted, and Follett turned his horse back toward the other men, stopping to have words with the Kid, who got up, dusted his clothes with his hat, and rode after his captain.

"Blessing?" Alvarez said to himself, and spat again.

Only he and Tarrant could face seeing or dealing with the Oracle more than once. And Tarrant's interest wasn't practical; his was some kind of morbid fascination that Alvarez had no time for. Something about his superstitious, injured soul was resigned to disgust and used it as a cleansing, preferring it to the black, ornate guilt demanded by the religion of his birth. Each time he had to confront the box, he looked deeper into it, trying to see the squirming thing inside, forcing himself to experience the repulsion on a deeper and deeper level.

The other men moved aside as he lifted the crate from its pannier and carried it over to an outcrop of jagged rock. In the shade, and before releasing the latches, he begun to hum his way into a song. The sun gleamed on the other side of the rock and the brilliant sky stretched itself beyond the rolling cloud. Even the breeze seemed coddled in warmth. The sound of the world floated up in the rising air, and the birds that had been so far above them before now began to wheel below. All was settling into a crippled belief of kindness until the Blessing sang back. Alvarez gritted his teeth and continued his song, letting the resonances meet and entwine. Some of the men covered their ears or walked away, hoping the wilderness might dilute or smother the duo in camp. Time passed slowly in the warmth, and the trees' branches waved aside the hours. Some slept in this moment of calm. Some reflected on future wealth, allowing the sun to glint on invisible coins and to dapple all the dark shadows of life into an unfocused haze.

Then came a far-off call that opened everybody's eyes.

"Cooee."

One of those well-used but meaningless words that has mysterious properties. Up close and said quietly to a child, *cooee* can instantly demand joy and affection, but cried loudly, and with the right emphasis, it can travel miles, defying all the laws of normal acoustic velocity. Now the word echoed up the mountain, announcing that Follett and the Kid had completed their task and would soon return to camp, and that they should not be mistaken for intruders.

"Captain found bones," said Tarrant.

Alvarez stopped for a moment, but he was prompted to continue by a different sound coming from the wobbling box.

Outside the small forester's hut, cleated into a large fissure of the mountain, Follett and the Kid were packing up their spoils. The old man had just given the first long-distance call.

"Will it do?" asked the Kid, wiping the blade of his broadsword with a stolen rag.

"Yes, if we pour enough into it. Gather the legs of the small one and the woman," said Follett. "And I want thee to steep tonight."

"Ah, boss! I made the obligation just before O'Reilly."

"I am aware of that, but they were old confessions. Tonight thou canst add these fresh ones."

"Dost thou think what I just did will make my confession more juicy?" the Kid asked bluntly. "Because if thou dost, then thou hast the wrong man."

Follett looked long and hard at the Kid and saw that it was true: there wasn't the slightest flicker of guilt, not a smidgen of regret. And for a moment it made his old blood run cold. The murder and dismemberment of the forester and her child would have driven most men insane, the constant reliving of its brutal details erasing all ease and composure from the soul. But for the Kid, it meant no more than chopping wood or gutting a fish. Follett's momentary shock was suddenly replaced by a sudden wonder, which was instantly supplanted by pride in his own acumen in selecting such a troop of heartless men.

"Thou should have taken Tarrant. He's a family man; he would have given thee buckets of shame."

The Kid was right, of course. Follett had missed a major opportunity.

"Sometimes thou talkst like a cunt priest." Follett spat.

"That's because I be fluent with the Scriptures; had every damned one of 'em read out to me. I even had to write some down."

"Writing will wither thee, child. Scriptures should only ever be spoken out loud, not hidden away in books. Thou art a man, not a squirrel or a termite."

The Kid braced himself. "I ain't no kid! Nor will I be compared to any rodent or vermin!"

"I compare thee not to vermin but to those creatures that would be all-knowing in the parasites of words. Scrawl down the heart's voice of what should be spoken from one man to another."

The Kid did not understand and it was boldly displayed on his face.

So Follett explained. "Writing is the shame of man. It dilutes the guts of meaning. If thou be not man enough to hold great learning and the saying of events in your memory, then thou should not attempt to keep them imprisoned. The world was turned by scrolls and books. The making of those bricks of paper even contaminated the tower of language itself, making it less than a woodpile or an old maid's collection of rags. Words are power, and writing is only a pissed shadow."

"And that is why you condemned Scriven?"

"Damned right, I did. I wrote a line of text in his guts with my lance for the stealing of words."

The Kid looked at his feet and considered his next words very carefully.

"But some of those words he wrote were his own."

"Makes no difference. If he be stupid enough to scribe what he already spoke, then serves him right. But stealing other men's words, worthy men's, and Steeping and scribing them after they been said are acts of blasphemous contempt."

"Enough to die for?"

This was to be the Kid's last question.

"So be it, surely enough to die for. Especially when those words be mine. He dared to gather and steal the words of my Steeping and set them on paper, and that condemned him and stopped any future such disgusting acts. Make no mistake on this: if I find a book of paper about thy person, I will dispatch you instantly. No thief of notions or speech rides with me. And I will do all in my might to wipe out such things, even if it means winding everything backward with sacrifice."

The Kid had no more words in any shape or form, so he left Follett's side and went to collect the bones. On the way back up to the other men, the Kid remembered the bloodstained pages of Scriven's hidden notebook as they were thrown into the wind. He remembered Follett's rage as his red hands tore the thing apart, fury in his eyes and spittle flying from his mouth in a bellow of curses.

They did not speak until they were in sight of the thin gray column of smoke rising from the campfire. Both men could already taste the reassuring warmth of hot coffee and feel the heat of the tin cups. The Kid would never again speak of books to this man, so he returned to the previous question about getting the best out of Tarrant.

"Naught is lost by using me to do the slaughter!" the Kid announced.

"What?"

"I mean thou canst still get a juicy one out of Tarrant if you give him the job of peeling and chopping the bones, and then giving a Steeping directly after."

Follett nodded and then made a funnel of his hands. "*Cooee.*"

It's difficult to explain a sound, especially one you will never forget or ever want to hear again. That was the kind of sound that issued from the box as its occupant heard the call from beyond the camp. Alvarez removed the slatted lid. When the air touched its wrinkled skin, the Oracle shivered and emitted an offensive odor that was mellow in its discord. As Alvarez stared into the box, his voice cracked and became dry, and the lullaby he had been singing vanished. The voice from the box also changed, turning spitefully human.

"No, Mumma, more, give more."

It was a demand, not a request, and every man heard it in a part of his body that he could never admit to having. Pearlbinder's hand instinctively moved toward his hunting knife, and the Calcas joined like twins. Some of the party were not convinced that the language came from the box at all, thinking it more likely that Alvarez was speaking ventriloquy under his tongue, either in mockery or, worse, in some kind of possession.

All went quiet, and then Follett and the Kid rode in, large hanging bundles slung behind their saddles. Follett stood in his stirrups and looked at the silent men.

"Tarrant," he called.

BLEAGH, GARRRGH, AND EUEUW

Meg found herself standing on the spot where Grietje had burned alive and knew that some traces of her friend must still be there under the scorched cobblestones, even though the snow, rain, and sunshine had worked hard to remove them. The square had no crowds in it today, just a flutter of people getting ready for Carnival. Meg knew a few by name, and they waved greetings at her as they hurried by. *Best not to be seen here, standing alone,* she thought. Why was she here, anyway? That was the question that let the names in, all those strange and difficult names that now echoed in her stomach.

"Not here," she or they said. "Not here."

She looked up above the squat houses and the rampant church spire. She looked past the mass of the monastery and up to Das Kagel. And the names seemed louder inside her. She left the square, the streets, and walked past the allotments and the gardens into the fields, where she could feel the mountain without anyone knowing. There was something in or on Das Kagel that needed to make itself known. She stopped and sat by a small brook. The sound of the water eased her anxiety. The names needed to come out. She looked around and could see only a distant figure, well out of earshot, ploughing the land. As she spat out each name, she tried not to hear them. Occasionally she would stand and look about her to be certain that she was alone before continuing. She did not realize that she was saying far more names than poor Grietje could have had time to say before the smoke and the pain stopped her.

Meg started dredging more names from somewhere deep inside her.

"Vinegar Joe," she called. "Elek. Gef."

"Here, Mistress."

She spun around to confront a weasel wearing a yellow hat. Was this the same thing that had spoken to her in the garden? The one she had so upset by explaining that it was not a member of her family? But this one was bigger and had a different air about it, a different kind of personality. Perhaps they had only one hat that they passed around.

"Were you in my garden? Did we speak before?" she asked, tentative.

"Might have."

There was no doubt in its voice, just a cocky playfulness.

"What do you want of me?" continued Meg.

"Nothing yet."

"Then why are you here?"

"Because you just called me."

Meg was horrified.

"I . . . I just said those names to get them out."

"And you did. We are all here."

"All?"

"All the names you called."

"No! No, I didn't mean to."

Gef lifted its tiny yellow humanlike hands palms upward in a shrug—the same gesture of baffled resignation that another Woebegot had made to her. The one she had sliced in half. A terrible cold guilt flooded over her. These things had intelligence and speech!

"Can you all talk?" she dribbled out.

"Nah, not many, but they are learning. None of 'em as good as me cos I've been here longer."

Meg's mouth was making small gulping movements like a fish, but her amazement was beginning to settle.

"They understand more than they can say. How many languages do you speak, Mistress? At the last count, my own tally was up to nine. There will be many more on the other side of this place."

Meg had no idea what this creature was talking about, but she thought she caught a glimmer of very human condescension in its expression as it finished speaking. Then there was a rustling in the tall grasses and reeds nearby that made her jump, and she remembered what it said about them *all* being nearby.

"Tell them to go away. Please!"

"Just talks to me then?"

"Yes, but please make them go away."

Gef let out a ricochet of agitated squeals.

"All done, Mistress, just us for now."

"For now?"

"You called; we came."

"But I don't want you."

"Thens you gonna have to tell 'em yourself, each one."

Meg could not believe what was happening to her.

"I can fix that in time."

"But I don't want to do this! Can't they just go away?"

"If you don't dismiss 'em proper-like, then they will never go away."

"What must I do?"

"Understand."

Meg hung drab and exhausted at the prospect.

"I think you need to meet some of the others in the Tower, the hill."

"In Das Kagel?"

"Mostly," replied Gef as it turned, beckoning Meg to follow.

———

Two hours later, they were inside the mountain in tunnels that were never made for Meg's proportions. It was pitch-black and smelled of the sea and of cellars. Gef led the way with a fish lantern. He had given Meg her own, which was more rotten and therefore brighter than his. Like all animals, Gef had a deep fear of fire, so phosphorescence was the only alternative for those that were not nocturnal. Many of the tunnels used by the Woebegots were impassable for Meg, but fortunately they had found ways into the taller, arched structures that had lost their true shape to decay and ruin over the centuries.

The last thing Meg ever suspected was that the mountain was hollow, but as they traveled deeper and deeper, her initial trepidation was overtaken by wonder at its gigantic strangeness. Gef stopped and signaled Meg to be quiet and watch. There was sound and movement ahead. Three shadows could be seen digging in the shadows and sifting through rubble.

"These three are blind and are looking for their names and other words," whispered Gef, so close to Meg's ear that she felt his whiskers tickle her face, which made her giggle and blush in the darkness.

The rotting-fish light showed that the weasel disapproved of such behavior, but he did not comment on it; instead he cupped some of the broken wall and earth in his yellow hand and gave it to her to inspect.

In this place, the stone and earth had been crushed with rotting paper and parchment, what was left of decomposing books and scrolls and their wooden shelves. The tremendous weight of the collapsed floors above had compressed them into a dense material. Although solid and impossibly thick, the substance was porous and resembled gritty frozen chocolate, or stale, atrophied cake. Word had spread among his kind, explained Gef, that the application and usage of this stuff induced states of knowing and development in the art of speech, especially in those creatures that possessed mouths.

Bleagh, Garrrgh, and Eueuw had found their names here by eating quantities of this material. Bleagh had the advantage of being faintly luminescent. A cold blue glow rose from the short feathers that covered most of his egg-shaped body and the small patch of his bald head just above his long, pointed beak. He pecked with care and diligence like a heron. Garrrgh was less delicate and shoveled the mudlike stone into his wide-open mouth, which looked like a baggy purse. Eueuw licked the nutrients of wisdom after snuffling the particles loose with her flat head and paddlelike hands and feet, much like the duck-billed platypus she almost resembled.

They were eating their understanding, which had nothing to do with learning through experience and the accumulative lessons of cause and effect. Those abstract properties did not abide with them. They thought they could learn their names by chewing on great mouthfuls of the stony paste until words and ideas began to be released, but its insufferable taste made it impossible to swallow. So, after a tolerable amount of mastication, they spit it out with great force, not unlike the later practice of chewing tobacco or betel nuts.

Gef explained these details to Meg so that she might learn how to communicate.

"If the juice obtained in this process gave them their names, why did they choose such ugly ones?" she asked.

"This is the great mistake I mentioned. Each one receives a proper title but cannot say it. Instead, the chewers hear one another spitting and misunderstand these loud expulsions to be the exclamations of their new names. Thus, Bleagh, Garrrgh, and Eueuw became the names by which each recognizes the other, even though their real names sound quite different. In fact, a certain Latin loftiness emerged from the mixture, so that Bleagh thought his name was Phlenaphonion Candidius and Garrrgh considered his to be Ugax Chrempsicholicus. Eueuw was still a little uncertain of the magnitude of his name. Needless to say, this process leads to much confusion, especially when some gather enough confidence to call out the name of another, which, when heard by the others, is then considered a declaration of the speaker's name.

"The only good thing is that when mobs of them spew up chunks of words and totally misunderstand one another, it is much like the behavior of your people in hostelries and public houses. In many ways, this pleases most of the Woebegots and further establishes their belief in their similitude to you, whom they call the Great Ones."

"This is all very difficult to understand. How will I be able to un-call them?" asked Meg.

"You won't have to, because these are not those ones."

"Then why did you bring me here?"

"To show you that it is not going to be easy, working together."

"But I don't want to work together." Meg was getting angry and tired.

"O but you will."

HARM

"When thou hast done here, it be thy turn for Steeping," said Follett to Tarrant, who was covered in blood.

His eyes were cones of vicious contempt swallowed in a ruff of disgust. His hands, feet, and clothing were covered with splinters of bone and smears of skin.

"Didst thou hear me?" commanded Follett.

Tarrant nodded without moving and eventually said, "With these very bones?"

"It's all we have."

"Where did you find them?"

"Down in trees. Their woodsmoke smelled different than ours."

"I thought this frozen hell was deserted?"

"'Tis mainly, but there is always one or two forest men in the deep woods. Me and the Kid found these."

Tarrant stood up and attempted to brush off the sticky waste that clung to his clothing. "Was it his idea that I make the cutting?" he asked.

"Someone must. We need might in the Blessing to give us a sign before we go on, and the feed will do that."

"But it was the Kid's idea?"

Follett said nothing but lifted the Pyx and opened its damaged lid.

"I shall pack them."

Follett worked quickly and frantically, arranging the chopped bones in the box, while the man with the stiffening red hands and lead eyes watched with morose concentration.

When it was time, Tarrant took the box to a place higher up, where he thought he could not be seen. The Kid followed him to make sure he actually went through with it. Sitting out of sight, the Kid glared up at the small figure on the cliff. He could not believe what he thought he saw next. Instead of keeping the box closed and mumbling over it like a tenderfoot, Tarrant opened the lid wide and forced his entire head inside, singing his confession.

"I will not disgorge the fury of now. Of the burning rim of what just occurred, the stiffness of which no longer dries on my hands. That all exists in a skin of the moment before. I suck in my breath and swallow to another time, away from these idiot, despicable men.

"None of whom know that, like O'Reilly, I come from a different place in a different time, and that my acts there were infinitely worse than any I've perpetrated here. That is how I know these men well. I will not say that I have always been like them, but I have done worse when I knew better. And now I know why I did those things: to show the side of me that was good and kind, to show that my will and the power of its perversity were greater, and to show that I would use it to purchase myself the viewing of wonders and mysteries in this gray world. And it worked; all the butchery and disgust that places me beyond the forgiveness of God and man buys me the right to stare into the mouth of Hell and witness every rare and abnormal sight in this twisted path of life. And this is what I share with you, what I gift unto you, Most Sacred and Unique One. What I spill into the bleeding bones that I have hacked apart this very day is not my guilt or horror, which my comrades think I have, but the savagery of the knowledge that it buys. Unlike all these other foolish men, I commit my crimes without passion. The promised wealth that Follett uses to lure these men means

nothing to me. I will be given nothing by him at the end of this journey.
You are my reward. The time and observations of you, and your kin,
and every other abnormality that will be exposed on this journey. I
will charge myself on your existence in the same way that you feed from
my suffering. When the light is shut, I will enter a lower ring of Hell
than any other man here. Lower than any has ever reached before. In
that place I will transform. Forged under the hammers of pain that I
create today and all those days back to when (as I have told you before)
I took my own little children's lives to seal the exchange of my soul for
the ability to transgress time. To obtain a vast knowledge. To challenge
Satan himself. In a poem like this:

"An Emperor
Of antiquity
Sought harm
& harm
& harm
& harm
& harm
& harm
& harm
& harm
& harm
& harm
& harm
& harm
& harm
& harm
& harm
& harm
& harm
& harm
& harm
& harm
& harm

& harm
& harm
& harm
& harm
& harm
& harm
& harm
& harm
& harm
& harm
& harm
Until he reached
Iniquity.

"Amen."

When Tarrant finally emerged, his face and his eyes were red and blotchy and his mouth could not stop moving. The Kid had not heard a single word, because the shouting had distorted the sounds. Tarrant had been more cunning than Scriven; only the Oracle would suck and gnaw on those sweetnesses.

After the Pyx had been saturated in Tarrant's Steeping, Follett collected it and put it in Alvarez's gnarled hands. Then Follett raised his eyes to point to a bold rock that could be used as a platform for the Oracle. Alvarez still seemed disconnected and fatigued, like a somnambulist or a user of holy toxins.

"That rock."

Follett did not care to give the same order twice. Together, they carried the Oracle crate up to the humped rock and peeled open the lid, trying not to breathe in any of the odor that came from inside.

Alvarez had no heart for the next feeding. It had all stacked up wrong. He felt that they had disturbed and hurt the Oracle in their last meeting. He had no way of knowing how it would behave. He also feared that the nutrition he was about to give it was seriously lacking and that Tarrant's Steeping may not even have taken. True, the man had a gloomy edge that would sicken its telling, but there was something about Tarrant that was unpredictable, almost moral. The combination of fresh marrow and only one Steeping of questionable quality might not be enough for the Oracle. Dismally, Alvarez sat with the Pyx on his knees, the long, thin spoon held like a tense silk in his big, nervous hand.

The first spoonful was difficult. The Oracle squirmed and lost purchase on the food. Alvarez held it closer to his chest so he could align the spoon with the reluctant mouth, but the Oracle's slithering wobble missed the spoon. Alvarez was like a patient mother, trying again and again to position the necessity. Suddenly, in a random instant, the Oracle found the marrow and gnawed the shaft of the spoon as it tried to swallow everything, a great ferocity overcoming its previous clumsiness. Alvarez struggled to hold the thing while he stabbed the spoon into the still-bleeding bones. He had never seen the creature respond like this. In his eagerness to finish the matter, Alvarez dropped the spoon and brought a shaft of bone to the Oracle's sucking mouth. The effect was instantaneous; its loose flap of a mouth wrapped around the bone and began to suck. The noise and the vibration of its thrashing made many of the party turn in surprise. Tarrant looked in the opposite direction and smiled.

"Watch thy paws, amigo! It will eat them and suck out thine very life," the Kid jested.

Nobody laughed and the joke turned sour in his mouth, but the Kid would not let go, sensing contempt on the track of humiliation. He spun his head and called across the gathering, "Hey, Tarrant, what hast thou fed them bones? Juicy stuff, I would hazard?"

Everybody present knew this was a great mistake and closed their eyes. Even the Oracle stopped eating.

The Kid was irritated by the lack of response and pushed further.

"Nuthin' like young bones to soak up a good man's words," he chortled.

No one looked at the Kid, so they did not see that his mouth was still when his voice next spoke.

"You got kids at home, ain't ya? I bet you've had a good taste of them."

The Kid, who before had been turning his head to look at the others, trying to catch a morsel of approval, stopped dead when he heard his own voice, his grin reversing. The air thickened, and Tarrant waded through it toward him.

"I never said that!" the Kid said to himself, in his horror and confusion almost expecting an answer.

Tarrant was there, swinging the ax with all his might, the wild, wide arc dividing the dense air. The Kid could not see the blur of it as it became embedded in his face. This was not a death blow; Tarrant had not designed it that way. He had not made the equation of angles for the cutting edge to carry all the force of a slicing blow and split the Kid's head in two. This blow was an eruption, unfocused, but brutal in its intention to silence the yapping gob with a measure of devastation. The strength of his rage and the weight of the steel made the velocity of the arc excessive. The blunt back of the ax lifted the Kid off his feet, crushing his nose, teeth, and gums into concavity. His cheekbone shattered, shearing up and into his eye. Tarrant enjoyed the jarring impact as it shuddered down the shaft of the ax and into his hands, his arms, and the rest of his body. He stepped forward and stood over the sobbing boy, the ax ready to strike again, just in case the Kid was stupid enough to fight back.

Follett was about to bark a halt when he realized it was already over. The amount of blood indicated that some grievous damage had occurred inside the Kid's head and that Follett was another man down. There was always wastage with such a band of men, bringing destruction on themselves and squabbling over nothing. But to lose three before the road even started to decline was not a good sign; well, at least the departed had been peripheral. Losing Tarrant, the Calca brothers, Alvarez, or Pearlbinder would have been a more serious matter.

The Kid was now standing between the Calcas, his buckling legs gauging the blood loss and shock. He was trying to speak to Tarrant. "Wassntme, wassnmt mi, Oracle say it, wassnt mi . . ."

But it was impossible to understand the numb splutter that came out of his wrecked face.

"Wilt thou finish it?" Follett called out, and the Kid's head lolled in the direction of the sounds, strings of red spittle swinging in the air.

Tarrant looked more closely at his handiwork.

"Ain't that grievous," he said.

"Wilt thou doctor him, look after him on the rest of this trail?" Follett snarled in choking fury.

The Kid's head was now hanging, exhausted from his effort to look around. The Calcas swiveled the Kid around so Tarrant had a better view. He stepped forward and lifted the Kid's face by his chin, turning it with quizzical indifference.

"The eye's gone, but you could patch up the rest," he said.

"He is fucking useless to me now," said Follett, and pointed behind the group. "Put him over the ridge."

The Kid suddenly started to struggle in the brothers' grip. Tarrant wiped his hand on the Kid's back as he walked away.

"I yum . . . um well, weel," the Kid said through a thick redness.

"Do it," barked Follett.

The men looked at each other and then at Tarrant, who nodded. They turned and pulled their burden through the trees toward the ridge and the cleft in the gorge. The Kid's knees buckled, and Tarrant stepped in to take some of the load at the edge. They stopped and lifted away their hands dramatically in a grand, operatic announcement of release, stepping backward, not wanting to be the last man in contact with the boy as he fell into the quiet granite ravine.

THE DIRTY BRIDE

The monks were preparing themselves for the austere privations of Lent while the town was deeply engaged in the debauched week of Carnival. Outside and against one of the walls, a ragged shadow hastily propelled itself home on long legs and flat feet. Meg had just left her drunken husband and his cronies pretending to joust. Cluvmux had once again slid off his barrel to lay giggling in the dirt.

She was coming to remind him that the most recent batch of sausages needed to be blooded again before he attempted to sell them. But first, she decided to watch the stupidity from afar. Entering the tight square from the south side, Meg was instantly framed by the town's tallest building, the dark, brooding high church. Engulfed by an overcrowded squabble, she pushed her way through the swells and splutters of shabby humanity, finally finding protection beside the vast wooden tuns of beer outside the inn.

Stopping to gain her breath, Meg gazed into the writhing throng of more than two hundred filthy, raging souls, each out-shouting, out-stinking, and out-jostling their oblivious neighbors.

Momentarily she lost her place in the real world as she looked into this mass of everyday life and beheld a thing unknown, trying to focus through all that spun, crawled, and ran in the square. Dashes and thrusts of color flared in the rampant air; mouth-stained voices furred and belched, coagulating in the upturned jigsaw spaces between every human shape. She breathed in the colors of woodsmoke and the smells of bread, herring, straw, and piss and the roasted bristles of hogs and swine, all mixed with the sugar of a waffle iron. Wet feathers were being lash-boiled to laughter and gutted to swearing. She heard the squeaking wheel of the town's well pulling up slopping pails of water and saw the dusty yellow ocher of the earth as it gulped down the spillage for cleansing, gasping a retreat from the littering rabble who would bruise it black over the next three days of the festival.

Bagpipes scrawled the air, smearing the stink of fish-gutters and griddle smoke into the cries and the lute of "The Dirty Bride," a farce being performed between the jostling tavern and a shabby canvas tent housing stained lepers: A bedraggled Nysa is pulled from a travesty of the nuptial bed. Mopsus, the groom, prances before her, indicating the physical joys of betrothal and occasionally forcibly inviting a passerby to visit the squalor of their domain. This little gem, which had been performed forever, was a debased transcription of Virgil's "Eighth Eclogue," the Roman poet's famous version of the Greek *Bucolics*. Meg grinned at the lewd caravansary and the warmth overflowing from it and from its audience bubbling in the tavern. Other plays could be glimpsed between the crowds, but only by the artificial difference of their movement.

But now, on her way to find her useless Cluvmux, she thought she had already seen the Devil and Death that day. The Devil was hooded and cheating at dice, while Death was present in the white and sea-swollen body of a man dragged before the public eye: a proven drowning. The naked corpse was positioned next to its poor widow, who held a begging bowl in her waving hands. Her swaddled child was propped against an upturned chair.

The dead did not worry Meg—their place in Carnival was

valedictory and portended toward life. The Fool was another constant in this seasonal ritual. And he had the strangest behavior of all. Meg spotted him in the same place, over and over again: at the center of the square, purposely plodding on squat, bowed legs. The small, intent man, whose face she never saw, would lead couples out of the crowd by the light of a torch, which burned stupidly against the bright midday sun. They were always sauntering forward, but never made any progress. The Fool was always impossibly constant, in exactly the way the Devil, still shaking dice in his scarlet leather hands, was not.

Meg shivered and turned her head away from the corner where she knew the Fool was watching her, and, as if in his good jest, shifted into the tide of rotting beggars. She gathered her clothes tight about her and began to move away. That's when she saw what was happening with her husband's company.

In the time Meg had taken to enjoy the mummery, the rolling barrel had been brought down. She recognized a man dressed in yellow and wearing badges as Ingisfort Pleumps the wickmaker, and behind him was Mewdriss van Keulen, who earlier had been carrying on her head a table laden with bread and waffles. In one hand she held a tumbler, and in the other a candle—symbols representing deceit. It was an appropriate role for the slut Mewdriss, who, as Meg watched, suddenly slid and fell among the spilled and the broken, including a wrecked pie that Cluvmux had been balancing on his own head—a pie Meg had made the day before. The slut now had her hands on Cluvmux's ample thigh, pretending to try and gain purchase on it and stand upright but instead falling back on top of him in more and more indecent postures. Both were laughing and falling, as were many around them.

Meg had had enough. She was not prudish, but she hated the time wasted and the amount of pleasure her husband was enjoying. He should have been carving pigs and blooding the sausages instead of feeling up the skirts of a better man's wife. Then she saw her husband's jousting lance: a long skewer, taken from her kitchen. It lay bent on the filthy earth. The pig's head, roast chicken, and sausages it once carried had broken away and lay ruined in the mire, now fit only for stray dogs, children, and lepers.

This was the final straw. She stalked out of the frame of watchful buildings and into the alleyway, her eyes gathering the closed perspective of normal days back into the sensible scullery of her head, while her lips spewed venomous words under her breath.

By the time she reached home, she was more like the name she had been cursed with: Dull Gret. She sat in her low kitchen. Her head filled the space of the frame, a huge, white, sweaty close-up that squashed the edges of everything else, bigger than the room in which she sat and the world she occupied. Her head was propped on the hard spidery fists of her long bony hands where they screwed into the sinewy pistons of her arms, which fled down to crimson elbows chiseling into the scrubbed oak tabletop.

Like this, she was all detail, red-rimmed, long-nosed, becoming chinless. The last bloom of health and hope had burned her chapped pallor ruddy. Her tears were so dry, they had etched straight lines that could be mistaken for vertical contours. Once, when she was small, the distortions of her features had possessed a moment of cuteness. She had been all elbows and knees, nose, ears, and gawky eyes that asked so many questions with unblinking, birdlike pecks at the world. Goofy teeth, many lost now to rot and a thin diet, had made her food smile before she ate it. Citrus and ash had shrunk her face to almost a pucker, a mad hen growing whiskers and staring into what should have been despair. But something else was happening in her old hen brain, which smelled of ammonia and chalk. Something not unlike revenge that wanted payback for the squalor and foolishness she had been harnessed to for so long. Something that stirred the long-wasted child in her into insolent wakefulness. It was resolve.

She had never understood the words that Lady Grietje bellowed at her when she was being cooked, as the yellow hat in her garden had put it, but now she did. The blinkers and the safety catches had been taken off. She sat stationary for another twenty minutes and then rose to authenticate what was occurring with an act that would seal it in a signature of water and grease. With great, exaggerated purpose, she stooped over the overflowing sink, wiped her nose on the back of her hand, and began to wash up.

All fantasy was earthed. With her arms deep in the filthy water like lightning conductors, she experienced the separation of worlds. The one she knew simply slid apart from the one she was going to know. Deep in her body, salt flowed down from her mind and sulfur pumped up from her cunt and womb, mixing with the mercury of her solar plexus—and Meg was reborn.

THE MASTER

Friar Benedict had become saturated in the ancient images of demons and creatures that shudder between fiction and the accounts of worthy travelers who had ventured to the far side of the world. He had sought out every picture in the monastery's library and read every scrap of text related to them, but it was not enough. Not enough to explain what he had witnessed firsthand in the kitchen. Surely this was proof of the heresy that he so feared: A new race of horrors had procreated from the paintings of one disgusting art-ist's imagination. His knowledge told him that such a thing was impossible, but his instinct gnawed at his curiosity, or was it the other way around? He was wise enough to listen to all the rumors about the recent paintings that had been made in the proximity of his home, and he decided that he had to see one for himself to confront and understand this work. It would take a pilgrimage of a week or more to reach the closest one. And he would need to take a sturdy companion to support his determination to lay eyes on one of the fabled "masterpieces."

The consuetudinary could wait. There might be a new level of scholarship knocking on the wooden door of his cell. So with great fortitude, he confronted the abbot and made his request to go on the journey and take Dominic with him.

The relationship between Benedict and Abbot Clementine was at an all-time low, although it had never been more than mildly amicable. The old monk's legendary scholarship and his accepted seniority in the monastery proved to be a vexing sore point. From the moment he first arrived as the new abbot, the younger Clementine had felt his authority being undermined by Benedict's questions and by his over-watchful eye. The abbot had done all he could to marginalize Benedict's influence and to keep his acrid curiosity as far as possible from his own esoteric research, but their meetings and confrontations were inevitable in the confines of the abbey and during the commitment to shared prayer. He also had the same disparity with time, always moving on to the next subject, the next of period of the day, which frayed and irritated him, making him impatient with the ponderous Benedict.

So a formal meeting was the last thing either man wanted. The abbot barely listened to the pedantic, slurred words of the old man, until he explained he was asking for a leave of absence.

Benedict had just begun his careful and detailed explanation of his journey to witness an actual painting when the abbot, who had closed his eyes, interrupted. "And when do you plan to leave?"

"Why, I, eh . . . was thinking . . ."

The abbot opened eyes that were brimming with heavy, piercing annoyance.

"Soon, so that I may be back for Lent," Benedict managed to conclude.

He then listed the duties to which he would be anxiously returning, but Clementine's mind was already elsewhere, and Clementine ignored Benedict until he asked another favor.

"Because of my years and recent tests of endurance, I would very much like to take Friar Dominic with me to assist with my studies and to extend his cultural knowledge of sacred images."

Benedict was unaware of the abbot's change of posture. He had shifted into a suppressed gleeful stiffness and was almost smiling.

Getting rid of this cantankerous nuisance at this time was a great gift. Clementine's clandestine planning had been meticulous. The arrival of a new Blessing had been designated for the beginning of Lent. He had to be first to speak with it, to become the prophesied one to whom the Oracle would cleave. He would need time alone with it before its internment as an anchorite. This would have to take place behind closed doors, locked protocols, and forbidden prayers, beyond the prying eyes of anyone in the monastery, especially Benedict and all who backed him.

The abbot shook himself out of his reverie and turned his full cunning and concentration, and his gaze, on Benedict, which silenced the monk instantly.

"A most beneficial and illuminating project. I will send you my consideration very soon. Thank you for your time." And with that the abbot was up and out of the room before the old man had risen from his knees.

"In days or weeks?" Benedict snarled under his breath, but his assumption was wrong—he had his answer within two hours, along with a further suggestion from the abbot that he must not feel the burden of his tasks at this busy time of the year. Others would be told to fulfill his duties so that these important studies abroad might be given more concentration. The old man scratched his head and wanted to feel a sense of honeyed triumph, but the cankerous alum of deceit prevailed.

The next morning they started to prepare for their journey, Benedict glowing in the reluctant sin of appreciation. The monks knew very little of the lands that existed beyond the circle of towns and villages huddled in an intimate cluster around the base of Das Kagel. But everybody knew there were only three roads out—the spiral road up over the mountain, the seaward track to the east, and the inland road to the northwest—and most shuddered at the thought of taking any of them. The eastern coastal road was easiest to follow, keeping to the shore for many miles before it found a valley and gently climbed north. The only problem was that all manner of foreigners and brigands were continually washing up on its beaches. Worst of all, it skirted the Eastern Gate and all that lay beyond it. The inland road, however, was tough, steep, and barely populated, although it was a more direct route to the north and its cities of treasure. Benedict, with the wisdom of his years, chose the ocean road.

He also had been reading more about the paintings of this Hieronymus Bosch, but he could find little information about the man himself. His rucksack was now heavy with notebooks. This was not Benedict's problem, however, because it was Dominic's job to carry the cumbersome pack. It was the price of the education he would receive on their journey.

The artwork was owned by Caspia Nassau, the third son of one of the abbey's greatest patrons. The families Van Bronckhorst and Van Bosschuysen were said to have originally owned the painting. It had been part of a commission to make three works of art that would dignify the wealth of their mercantile kingdom. Disagreements, conflicting canons of taste, and religious bias within the famous clan had caused the triptych to be broken up and the paintings separated. The left panel, known as *The Nassau Depiction*, was hanging in the chapel of the southernmost stronghold of the family's realm.

Benedict had been scrupulous in his studies and note-taking, copying the few maps describing the passage to the distant citadel. He had heard much about the richness and grandeur of that sin-drenched place, and he knew his companion would have never seen anything like it. Wealth and loftiness of this proportion could contaminate a young mind such as Dominic's. He would be subjecting the young monk to a world that most from under the mountain could never imagine, and to this purpose, the old monk made their journey longer and harder than necessary. He told the boy it was a holy duty, a mission.

It was his obligation to educate and temper Dominic, as well as to take advantage of his youth and strength, which he would do without a moment's consideration for the hardship of those duties. Benedict also wanted to use the boy's innocent eyes, to appropriate his perception in the translation of the painting. He would be the litmus paper that would classify and gauge the occulted power inside this mythical composition. Benedict was growing a holy determination to dissect the process and glamour of the picture, and therein find its means of influence over the imagination of all who witnessed it. He, too, would sharpen his resolve on the troublesome road toward the confrontation. Every hour of every day brought the two pilgrims closer, and the minor delays and necessary diversions that slowed their passage ripened the old monk's enthusiasm and irritated his anxious heart.

Their passage to the painting had its own volume and momentum, and Dominic in his old age would often tell a lurid tale of all manner of demonic and queer folk that he and his sainted master met on their pilgrimage. Even though the incidents in the abbey were far worse, Dominic had taken an oath of secrecy about them. The most vivid and unlikely encounter was on a lonely crossroads with Veronica the Gibbōsus, a three-quarter werewolf of blurred origin and gender. Rolling up his sleeves and baring his chest to show the wounds received during the alleged encounter, Dominic would often insist on telling and retelling the tale until he found somebody who would believe him. Such stories would have been wasted on Presbyter Cornelius, a high-ranking academic of the fine arts. It was he who had given them grudging permission to view the painting, and under his decree, all the clergy, merchants, scholars, and noblemen who were given access to the great painting were expected to show decorum, restraint, and cleanliness. When Friar Benedict and his novice showed up at the fortified gate ragged as tramps, they were instantly shooed away.

MURMUR

As the mercenaries descended the mountain, its shape became clearer, the rock outcroppings more uniform, and the angle above and the drop below more regular. Their spiral track scratched into the steep massive sides of Das Kagel was becoming constant, its downward curve dizzyingly inevitable. The snow on all the surfaces had become smoother and animal tracks were more frequent; there were even a few the Calca brothers could not identify.

Occasionally, bits of field and distant landscape appeared as the men circumnavigated the great mass. On the sixth day, Follett guessed that they had been around it once. As they wound down, the days of passage would get longer, even though they passed through the same vertical quadrants over and over again. He looked up, realizing the place they now stood was not more than four chains below the exact spot where the Kid had been thrown over.

Pearlbinder saw Follett looking into the wide branches of the trees and thought he was hunting for wild bird nests and eggs to supplement their waning food supplies. In fact, Follett was searching for signs of the Kid, splayed in the branches like a scarecrow or decorating the canopies in torn fragments. But there was nothing.

They had almost cleared the stone chasm without incident when a shrill cry sounded below them, and a white shadow sped above the snow-filled trees. They were near the sea again and the drifting gull had confirmed it. The riders stopped and leaned sideways in their saddles.

" 'Tis an albi-tross," said Tarrant.

Pearlbinder dismounted and walked closer to the edge, straining to glimpse the sea and a horizon he had almost forgotten.

"Canst thou see it?" asked Follett.

"I care not to. Some animals have omens written into them," said the big man in the turban, closing his eyes and rolling his head in a circle.

Pearlbinder's carefully chosen words hit their mark, igniting an instant anger in Follett.

"I wasn't asking about the damn bird," he spat back.

"Damned, indeed."

"The sea. I was asking about the sea."

Pearlbinder turned into the old man's glare and said slowly, "I see naught, but I canst smell it."

No one spoke, knowing this was a dubious claim. Pearlbinder mounted his horse in the manner of a dignitary who had just been given the keys to a city, or that of a commoner dubbed knight. He moved ahead without so much as a glance at Follett, and they all followed the slightly declining track.

Three days later they were facing northeast again and their speed on the icy path had increased. Directly below them was the Gland of Mercy, invisible and outside hearing but casting its terrible influence upward. The horses turned their long heads inward, and the men were silent, taking interest in the clouds or in the snow's intimate patterns. No one looked over the road's edge.

Alvarez suspected that on the next rotation it would be much worse and marked this place on their descent with a curse, an oath, a prayer, and a gob.

Only Tarrant knew the legend of this great secret and its meaning for humanity. It had been a large part of his reason for joining

Follett's expedition. He kept his knowledge to himself, sharing nothing with this company of animals. It was not a difficult choice, and it also gave him a modicum of pleasure.

Follett had been told a bit about what to expect from his commissioners, but he had closed his ears to such things; it was better not to know. Ideas and stories like that can get inside a man, like worms, and eat at his brain. It was better, cleaner, and safer to trust his instincts.

They were now more than halfway down the mountain and the snow was thinning, patches of foliage and clumps of trees becoming more frequent. The view from the edge of the path was clearer; the low clouds and unidentified mist were now above them, as if belonging to another realm. Different sounds were climbing the mountain to join them now. Tarrant said he could hear a faint bell tolling, but nobody else could. They continued in silence; the only sounds were the shod horses walking on thawing ground, their breathing, and the creaking of the leather saddles.

Follett noticed that boreholes had started to appear in the face of the mountain. At first he thought they were failed attempts to chip away the frost, loosen the snow, and dig into the earth and rock. But as the group descended, the holes seemed more frequent and more successful. He couldn't figure out what nature of animal could make such cavities: they were too large for rodents, badgers, or foxes and too small and irregular for men. Then, as they approached the deepest excavation, he realized they were not incursions, but exit holes. He looked back along the line of men and saw he was not alone in his observations. The distance between riders had been growing as the track widened; the confidence of the horses and the relaxation of their men had increased. Their long, slow line embraced the subtle curve of the mountain.

Bringing up the rear, Abna Calca bent sideways on his mount to look into the largest hole he had yet seen. Something glinted there, so he stopped and dismounted. His brother, riding before him, did not notice Abna stopping, or if he did, he assumed it to be a call of nature and continued the slow ride. Abna saw Owen round the bend, but he did not think to call out and tell him he was stopping to investigate the breach in the mountain. He tied the reins to a low, spiny bush and approached the hole with dagger in hand. It was big enough to walk-crawl into. The daylight haloed him for about three minutes; then a sharp bend cut it off.

Abna stopped, straining his eyes to see through the murk.

A soft feminine voice spoke to him from the darkness. "Young master, don't hurt me, I shelter here."

The words were ill-formed, but the quality of the voice was mesmerizing, a hum of total innocence that vibrated up his spine.

Abna's words came to his mouth without being shaped, and he sounded different, clearer than ever before:

"I mean thee no harm."

After a while, with almost a sob in its voice, the reply came, "I think I am lost here, or I forgot my way."

Without hesitation, Abna said, "Come forth, so that I may see and help thee."

Had something happened to his ears?

"I fear, for I am naked. Please speak to me further in the dark."

Something like arousal and protection ignited both sides of his masculinity, and he became confused and hopelessly engaged. "How didst thou get here?" he said, forgetting he had never spoken so eloquently.

"Das Kagel is made of knowing," it spoke again.

"Dost thou mean thou hast found the way into it?"

"Verily. Everything is here. Come and see—there is a wealth."

"I have heard of hoards in these mountains," the young man said.

"This is not a mountain; it is a fallen tower. It was made by the other sons of Adam in another time."

The tingling was growing stronger with the cadence of the voice, but the cold wind on his back still attached itself to the outside world, his brother, and the other men, who were steadily moving away from him.

"I will bring others to help thee," he said.

"But there is barely room for you here. Come closer and see."

Abna looked back and could still see the faint light of the

entrance, so he shuffled a little deeper inside. The smell changed
as he moved, as if he had rubbed up against a different substance;
it was less earthen and had a tinge of the smolder of fired bricks.
Suddenly the space opened upward and he was able to stand. A dim
glow came from farther on, a luminescence that had nothing to do
with the sunlight outside.

"Wait a moment, I must not lose my brethren."

His words were taken up by an unexpected volume. Resonance
held them and savored their length and texture. It was like speaking in one of the great churches of Iberia, and he was appalled,
proud, and heightened.

"Do not be afeard. They will return for you shortly," said the
naked voice. "Come hither. I seek the Murmur Stone."

The voice moved toward the inner glow, and cautiously Abna
followed. As they did, luminous forms rose on the wall and began
to pulse. Slowly, the contour of the creature took form. He stopped,
his heart in his mouth.

The voice belonged to a beautiful woman. She turned and
exposed her small elfin face. It was pointed, with a very wide mouth
and eyes of abhorrent innocence. Her slender arms had been folded
across her belly, and now they rose to modestly cover her delicate
pointed breasts. Her legs did not seem to exist; instead long, quill-
like tendrils flowed from where they should have been and hung
over the lip of a large, pale shell. This conch-like strangeness made
up, or contained, the rest of her body, and its pearlescent sheen was
absorbing much of the dim light.

"Do you see the arch?" she asked, and as she spoke, she moved
her arm to point above them. Her hair had been tightly pulled
back and fastened with what looked like a fish made of metal with
a sliver of precious ivory.

"You cannot lose words here, Child of Paradise. Here, you must
gain them."

Her tongue was long and had the same nature as her quills.

"Are you in fear?" she asked.

Abna did not know, because his shock had been poached by
glamour. All other emotions, ideas, and memories became sub-
servient to it.

She glided closer to observe what had happened to her silent companion. Something new entered her eyes, and she brought up her hand to cover her mouth. Her gaze stopped him.

"You do not have knowing of my kind?" she asked.

There were only three fingers on her hand.

"No," he whispered, but somehow his deep voice boomed around them, and he sheathed his dagger.

Outside, Owen Calca had been riding half-asleep. The careful monotony of his mare stepping slowly down the safe spiral track had conjured inevitable drowsiness. The growing warmth of the Lowlands and the increasing scent of pine and oak soothed away any strangeness. He nodded with the movement of the horse, its rhythm passing through his body; he and the beast became one. As they passed through an alpine spinney of young trees growing down the side of the mountain in an unexpected scree of life, a tide of procreation began to rise inside his rocking sleep. Even some of the old scarred souls in the company marveled at this gentle surprise, lifting their arms to touch the shy new leaves and unbinding some of the smaller branches that remained furled against the winter. One of these now swung across the track and brushed against Owen's face. His blinking eyes opened and closed on two entirely different worlds. The smell of the rising land turned inside out, and the filtered light reversed into a luminous gloom born of total darkness. It was not a leaf that touched his face, but a hand—a transparent hand composed of tenderness.

Owen tightened the reins to stop his horse, sitting up in the saddle to smell the air and the sunlight, his spine becoming a tauter aerial. He turned and looked back up the track and saw Abna was no longer with them. He remained stationary awaiting Abna, but the other place that had reared up in his daydream had left a rind of disquiet in his heart.

In the cave, Abna and the female in the shell held hands in a magnetism of proximity, but none of their other physical parts fitted together. Even their faces, which shared some basic similarities in function and symmetry, could not join. In that touch, though, the sexual exchange was absolute and overpowering. No previous congress with a woman had prepared him for this, and every practice that he tried, from his limited carnal knowledge, came to less than naught. When he pushed his hand down inside her shell to find more of her inclinations, she elevated on her tendrils.

"Sir!" she cried, thrusting harder. "O, Sirrah, tear not my proximities with thy devotions."

And he, at this bidding, grew savage; his eyes shook with tears until he fainted.

A great sense of foreboding made Owen Calca turn his horse around and go back up the track to find his brother. The pathway reverted into its treacherous self as his mount slid and stumbled, trying to gain purchase. So he stopped, tethered the horse, and continued on foot, still with great difficulty, gravity seeming to have a will of its own in this place.

He fell to his knees, landing badly. From this low position he could see more clearly, and spied the back of Abna's horse beyond him. He quickly climbed up, toward it, sometimes scrabbling on all fours. The horse was tethered close to one of the holes in the mountain, and Owen knew his brother was inside. "Abna," he called out, the name swallowed without the faintest echo. Owen unsheathed his sword and pounded the pommel against the ice and stone, still calling, "Abna, Abna, Abna . . ."

Time had no attachment for Abna, who neither forgot nor remembered he had passed out; he awoke a silent man. He held her fingers the best he could, weeping for solace because he could not grasp the breadth of the world he thought he had known. The luminescence had changed hue, shifting into a pale amber and making her shell gleam with pink radiance. In the core of the mountain, which had once been the greatest library on Earth, the ghosts of books drank deeply on the sounds of their union, counting the sighs in their pages, amid discarded oaken shelves that lay on the damp ground. The vaulted arches above dripped punctuation to the translations of the joined species through endless hours of midnight echoes. And each rotting brick, between purple and brown, considered itself as pale as the white stones that sleep untouched on the unlit side of the moon. In truth, that pumice is only turquoise in the reflected light of Earth's blue seas.

Far off, Abna thought he heard someone yelling, then banging and yelling. Someone he knew, someone on the outside. But it was too distant, and slowly the arches closed around them. The light and the consequence of everything beyond this moment dimmed.

DEPICTION

They sat outside in saddened defeat, Dominic disappointed in the mist and rain of their alienation and Benedict furious enough to turn it all to steam, so that he never really got wet.

A day and a half later, Presbyter Cornelius was told of their existence and they were allowed inside to dry out and be recognized.

Cornelius looked as if he had never been outside stately homes, rich cloistered walls, and sanctified libraries. His fingers curled and uncurled constantly, like two separate creatures trying to escape an invisible web of unparalleled stickiness. He walked around the two outcasts, stroking his chin, deaf to Benedict's rambling explanations.

Suddenly he commanded a nearby servant, "Give them food and warm water, clean clothing, and find them a bed. Tomorrow, bring them to the chapel."

Benedict thanked him.

"I would not allow anything as filthy as you within ten feet of our masterworks, and that would include the Sacred Baptist himself."

The fresh water, new soap, and soft towels were unlike anything Dominic had experienced. The youth was delighted, even when they rubbed and stung against the bites and scratches on his pale skin. Gradually, a glow of redemption hummed about their clean bodies as they warmed themselves around the narrow fire in the closed stable where they would sleep. The wind outside rattled the slatted door, but brought no nightmares to their modest security.

In the morning, they were ushered into the lofty chapel to set eyes on the fabled icon. The servant who had brought them to the door disappeared the moment they were inside. The scent of an incense unfamiliar to them gave another kind of depth to the darkness sporadically illuminated by flocks of candles in elegant gold holders. They knew they were not alone because they could hear Presbyter Cornelius giving instructions and orders in a tone that had nothing to do with prayer.

They quietly homed in on its squeaking, insistent whine. Cornelius was in a side chapel, which looked more like a stable than a place of worship. He and three other monks were standing around a wooden box and a heap of straw packing. Behind them glowed a painting resting on a large black easel. The dark silhouettes moved back and forth, crossing its illumination without paying it any heed.

The painting made Benedict walk on his toes, as if he did not want to disturb the scene: a sunlit landscape of yellow fields and lush green woodland. The foreground was occupied by an old man in prayer or meditation beneath a dried hollow of a tree. A pig slept next to his tranquil form. The painting made Benedict stop moving. He knew instantly that the old man was Saint Anthony of Thebes, Saint Anthony the Great, the anchorite father of all monks. A marvelous warmth flooded into the old monk; he was overwhelmed, as though he had come face-to-face with the saint himself.

Dominic, who was at Benedict's side, felt the change in his master but knew not to question him at this time. As Benedict stared at the painting, his analytical mind joined with his compassion; he began to understand why this work was so powerful. The secret was in its contradictions. A survivor of starvation, sun, and temptation, the hermetic father was always depicted in a harsh wilderness or in a cave where devils taunted him ceaselessly. But here he sat on soft green turf beside a gentle brook, like an old peasant fishing and dozing. Benedict walked closer, impervious to the nonstop chatter of the nearby presbyter and still unseen by those working there. His concentration and the unworldliness of the painting had combined to render his revelation invisible.

In the farthest distance stretched a celestial blue sky, and beneath it rose steeples and a cliff-like structure. Below them, and running into the middle ground, yellow fields were dominated by a white church with a blue gathered roof like a maid's hat and a stable beside it. The realism of the artist's vision was astonishing. Benedict imagined himself crossing the little bridge and entering the larch gate that bore a tau, the symbol identical to the one on the Great Saint's cassock. Then Benedict noticed the other folk in the picture, casually going about their daily business, carrying ladders and shields. But they were not normal villagers; they were identical to the things that had been materializing in the streets and fields around his home, his monastery. Some appeared to be minor demons, but ones that were not found in any bestiaries or grimoires he had consulted, although they were hinted at in the Voynich manuscript and, indeed, in the descriptions of the savage excesses of this artist's other paintings. Benedict stepped forward again and this time nearly touched the box the others were working on. Presbyter Cornelius stopped jabbering, and the whole chapel listened to the resounding silence.

Then Benedict saw that they were indeed demons, but they were unlike the savage clawed horrors he had seen elsewhere. These were almost comical. Their monstrous intentions were subdued while they grinned and picked at the saint's composure. The most violent action was the threatening of his dozing pig or the pouring of water or oil near the tree, behind his back. What was happening? Had the saint found tranquility in this gentle landscape after all his perils?

Dominic wandered into his view and blocked the painting, peering intently at its center. Benedict, irritated by this rude interruption, was just about to say something when the boy asked, "What's that? It looks like a fire at the back of the church."

"I can't see anything if you stand in front of me."

"Sorry, Master, it's just that it is the eye of the painting."

"Eye?"

"Like the eye of a storm."

Benedict looked closer at the scene and realized that it was exactly that—poised. He examined what the boy had seen behind the church. Then he saw the alarm bell in the tree. This moment of revelation was broken by the barking Presbyter Cornelius.

"This is *not* what you are here to see," he snapped. "We have important business here and cannot be bothered or disturbed by visitors. What you have come to see is over there," he said, fluttering his hand toward the other side of chapel.

Benedict tore his eyes from the painting and stared long and hard into the presbyter's twitching face.

"Very well, but what is this?" he asked in cautious, rigid words.

The presbyter took a deep, irritated breath, which he would release only once.

"It is, of course, also by Jheronimus van Aken, or so they say! We are sending it back to the Inquisition for safekeeping. It is merely resting here during its passage."

"Is there any doubt about its authorship?" asked Benedict. The question seemed to enrage its temporary keeper even further.

"Not really. Some even say it is the artist's last work, that he died finishing it. I find that questionable. It seems far too quiet, too gentle compared to the epic artistry of his other work. Especially the *one* you have come here to see."

Cornelius gathered himself, becoming taller, and held out his arm in a matador posture that signaled their moving away. Dominic understood this gesture and led the way. Just before he left, Benedict turned back to scrutinize the detail Dominic had seen in this "gentle" painting, and there it was. Squeezed into a tiny gap between the hollow tree and the bottom right-hand corner of the church—a tiny bright light, a glow of fire. Compositionally, it flickered between the blind side of the church and the woodland behind it. But in the flattened perspective of the painting, the fire also sat just beneath the dry sheaf of straw, which was threaded through the desiccated tree to give shade to the saint below. This one brushstroke undid the apparent peace of the picture and made it a tinderbox of tension. It was the moment before the total conflagration that would devour the entire landscape and turn its gentleness into ash.

Benedict understood enough about painting to know that such a bright detail would have been added last. If this really was the artist's final work, then he was now staring at the essence of a vision, a signing in time. One tiny stroke, a lick of paint. A sable flame.

To suggest a localized Armageddon in the near future. To show such a possibility in a tiny detail that most would never notice . . . and in the artist's last breath. This was the end of the world set in miniature. It was not a graphic depiction of total destruction but a seed, a whisper, a waiting. A suggestion. What kind of artist was this?

Dominic had been led to the large painting on the other side of the chapel. He stood gnawing on his index finger, his eyes wide as he tried to see all that was within the radiant rectangle. Benedict now joined him but seemed lost in thought. Cornelius stood several paces behind them, alert to any potential indignity, arms folded, hands still working in their cuffs. His bitter eyes caught glints from a series of perfectly trimmed candles that illuminated the painting without a flicker. This was just as well, because any more spluttering agitation in the picture would have sent its viewers stampeding for the door.

The painting dominated the farthest wall of the dark chapel. The movement that seethed inside the contours of the frame seemed twice the size of the actual picture. Its density, detail, and power spilled out of its dimensions. Benedict's eyes had finally settled, and now the painting was looking at him. Dominic remained the same, incapable of understanding. The young monk had only ever seen a few pictures before, and they had been mainly the tiny near-abstract embellishments in illuminated manuscripts or the occasional inn sign, rough in depiction and execution. The church artworks that dwelled in his monastery were indistinct renditions of the crucifixion, encrusted with smoke and disinterest. After these dull facsimiles, any kind of pictorial version of the world would have nailed his attention. But the *Nassau* panel opened his eyes and tormented any understanding he had held about reality and artifice. His visual cortex was swelling dangerously; it strained and tangled the confining membranes of normality around it. In colors brighter and clearer than he had ever seen, an impossible world delineated itself in searing truth. A swarm of comic, bloodcurdling creatures was setting about a clutter of undressed people. He had never seen such nakedness. The white, strewn bodies were calm in their defeat; an exalted indifference, far beyond passivity, amplified their vulnerability, as they limply awaited the arousal of their torture. Nothing like this had ever pierced his eyes.

But the worst feature was the background of the painting. The nightmare orgy of unimagined clarity was occurring in a landscape he recognized. The muddy earth and the brown crumbling wall, the stunted trees were all signatures of his homeland. He even thought he could identify a turnstile or gate if he dared look that closely. The things that scurried in the foreground cast their shadows on the contours of everything he had ever known. The languid naked figures were hanging in trees identical to those he had climbed as a boy. Their skewering and debauchery were snuggling into the folds and furrows of the gardens and turnip fields that had belonged to his parents, and to their parents before them.

Amid this fearful revelation was another looming possibility. Was the world really like this? And was he in some way deficient in not seeing it as it was? Because this painting was true, so conspicuously observed from nature, no artist could invent nightmares that cast such genuine shadows. Had his church blinded him to what really roamed the wide world and the confines of his own pastures?

Benedict was unaware of his comrade's anguish. His real consideration was still locked with Saint Anthony. And he knew it would not be dispersed, much like the nameless residue clinging to vessels that once contained pure substance, as the alembic process distilled the obvious to its essence and then to something else. All he could do was gently nod and reply very quietly to any question with a simple "Um. Yes!"

"It is, of course, a masterwork of perspectival composition."

The words came from another universe and meant nothing.

"And the rendition of the phantasmagorical far exceeds all the artist's previous works, a positive ascent into stylistic maturity. Pay attention to the brushmanship: a sharper, terser touch, with much more command than before. A mastery of fine brush-point calligraphy, permitting subtle nuances of contour and movement, is it not evident?"

Presbyter Cornelius had closed his eyes to concentrate on his own erudition, and his quill-like fingers helped expel the still-blind words with the impatience of a damp, ruffled cuckoo. He was in mid-crescendo when Dominic took one step closer and pointed with a shaking hand.

"It's the one; it's the one you met."

Nobody paid much attention until he actually touched the canvas.

"There, that one."

"Get away from the picture," Cornelius hissed, his hands now like moth and flame.

The old monk leaned closer, at the young monk's insistence, and saw, perched high up near an overturned dog kennel, a creature, which in the fine brushwork shadow, did indeed look like the pumpkin monstrosity that had hurt him so.

"It's the one; it's the one," sang Dominic, turning his attention away from the transfixed old man and explaining to the furious, looming keeper. "We know this one. It came to our monastery and took hold of my master."

Cornelius ignored this nonsense. He wanted these foolish peasants to acknowledge his distress and cringe under his reprimand.

Benedict spoke without his eyes leaving the painting and the pumpkin-like figure skulking there. "There is fear amongst some of our community that the fevered imaginations of this artist, and some others, have escaped to spawn a calamity of actuals in our lands," he explained, and in a different tone concluded, "and that veracity has been born underhand."

"Actuals?" fluted Cornelius.

"Like this one."

Dominic pointed again, his twitching finger within inches of the flat canvas and Benedict's face. "This is the one that escaped in our kitchen."

Cornelius's scholastic sphincter tightened. He would waste no more of his precious knowledge trying to educate these lunatic bumpkins.

"I don't understand what you are saying. This work of art has nothing to do with freaks of nature, or any other kind of farmyard mutations you might have seen."

"But it is identical—"

"Not quite, there are different blemishes of the skin, and the arms are more masculine," interrupted Benedict.

The young monk could not believe that the old man's pedantic observations were about to lose the argument, so again he pushed his point.

"But it is the same animal in a way that a cow is a cow and a dog is a dog."

Benedict quietly agreed and turned his head as if trying to see around the painted body of the leaping figure.

"Preposterous, preposterous," inflicted Cornelius, his hands taking on the ruffling of starlings, which squabbled and stabbed their now-carrion nature toward the contours of rooks and crows.

Dominic ignored the insults and pressed his case. "Where was this picture made?"

"What do you mean?"

"In what part of the Lowlands did the artist find these things?"

"'Find'?"

"I ask because I think I know this wall." Again, his finger touched the pigment.

"Don't touch it, ever!"

"But I think I did, I think I climbed it."

And as if to give physical emphasis, the young monk's finger rubbed up and down over the painted bricks. This was too much for the presbyter: talons suddenly sharpened, dived, and impaled Dominic's shoulders, but instead of lifting him out and away from the painting, the presbyter's momentum made Dominic lurch forward, the innocent finger bludgeoned against the canvas. Its nail furrowed a perfect curl of paint from the gentle, recognized wall.

Cornelius screeched in horror, falling to his knees, his hawks turning into doves as they moved to soothe and bless the abused picture. The old monk took his confused comrade by the elbow and guided him out of the room. The stern candles remained aloof and unblinking at such poor, human behavior.

On their way out, Benedict and Dominic passed the place where the empty easel stood. The wooden box with its precious cargo of Saint Anthony, and the conceptual firestorm, was packed in straw and heading south, and would never be seen in these lands again.

Something had happened within the old monk; he was quiet in a different way. Dominic had seen him in deep study before when he was not to be disturbed. He had also witnessed Benedict in a stern and terrifying silence, when the old man was fighting his own rage over the stupidity of others. And, of course, Dominic had seen him in the concentrated stillness of prayer.

But now there was a softness in Benedict's quietude. As if he were using a different part of his mind, a part that had never been witnessed inside the monastery walls. Whatever this was, the young monk knew better than to disturb him in his contemplations. So the air between them remained crisp but warm until Benedict said, "Tell me, do you think the artist who made those works was possessed by a vision of evil?"

This was an astonishing question, and the entrustment it

bestowed on Dominic was overwhelming. So much so that it took a good while for him to answer.

Benedict smiled, as if in approval of Dominic's pondering. This was indeed a great change.

"No, Master," Dominic eventually stuttered. "Although the creatures painted in these works are disturbing, I do not believe their purpose and invention is to taunt the faithful into sin. And the given talent of the artist cannot be a property of Satan, because it is too fine in its execution and too wondrous in its surprise."

"Excellent," announced the stunned monk.

"You have the wisdom of innocence in your fresh mind. But might not that very quality of brushmanship be a ruse, a trick of the devil, to ensnare the viewer in its glamour?"

"No, Master, because all such gifts come directly from God, and any other version of them would be base and counterfeit; obvious in its usury."

"My son, you give an old man hope in a weary world."

Dominic was delighted at such praise and was just about to continue the debate when Benedict suddenly announced, "We will leave this wretched place at dawn."

"After morning prayers?"

"No, before them—we will pray on the road. Nobody prays here."

The annoyed soldiers let them out before the first light had touched the throats of the birds. The cold folded their bodies inward, their arms enclosed across their chests, their heads down as they headed out from the shadow of the citadel. The curl of paint in Dominic's clenched fist had remained hidden, safe from the presbyter's anger, and was now tucked deep in a pocket, the only thing about the two men that stayed almost warm. Dominic hoped it would be a talisman to secure a safe passage home. A good-luck charm to their comradeship and solid proof of their witness of an impossible and wonderful thing.

As soon as they cleared the outskirts of the citadel's domain, they looked for shelter and waited for the rising sun to warm the new day. Four hours later, their prayers were answered and most of the cold was subdued by a brightening sky. The road home now seemed urgent, and they took to it with surprising fortitude. It took another hour before they felt able to talk again.

"Master, will we be back in time to see the arrival of the Oracle?"

"It is hoped so. That would be an important thing to witness, but it also depends on the length and quality of its journey to us." After a pause and some facial adjustment, Benedict continued, "And the will and purpose of Abbot Clementine."

"Surely the abbot will be pleased with our expedition after we report our findings?"

"That remains to be seen. He might decide that we have discovered too much."

Their damp cloaks were steaming in the sunlight and their rough path had a gentle decline, which seemed to make walking easier.

"Why would he think about new knowledge that way?"

"Because he has done so before. When he discovered that I had accidentally found a cryptic document and successfully translated it, he was furious and made unpleasant allegations before confiscating both the document and my rendition."

"The abbot cannot blame you for something that you found by mistake. He cannot punish you for stumbling over obscure facts."

" 'Stumbling'!"

Benedict stopped walking in a shudder of rage, and his hand leaped up to help his face.

"I mean discovered by accident."

"There is nothigf accidentalf or loutishf about the discofery of new wisdom or the purposeful excavation of ancient knowledge. A true scholar is led to these understandings by divine grace and a trained methodology, not by blind luck. It's only the malign application for self-gain that is so despicable."

"Apologies, Master, I was only responding to your assertion that you were not seeking problematic doctrines."

The old man was about to spit fireballs again; then he swallowed and considered. He lowered his hands and breathed the new words fiercely, but without flames, slowly so even a dunce might understand.

"Inspiration often comes unexpectedly. A true scholar must train himself in the recognition of it and how he might coax results from its surprise."

He gulped again and reshaped his mouth.

"There are nuances between words and dates, histories and statements that nudge in unexpected directions. Tiny ungainly shrugs and whispers suggesting opposites to what is formally preached in the sentences of the document. These glimpses and tracks have a way of explaining what may not be openly said. Sometimes they have been inserted by cunning scribes to catch the attention of similar minds. Sometimes they escape from the writer's concentration. The new scholar must open himself to shifts of language at the very center of the composition.

"Exactly like the paintings we have just seen. The artists, taking the talents that God gave them, paint new images and let their creative skills be not fettled by limp-minded bureaucrats who know nothing of the gift of intelligent imagination. They must hold their talents in a loose and flexible way so the work may evolve around the idea that generated it."

The old monk was again pleased with his erudite mitigation to the dull boy. His patience had been worthwhile, and he had also accidentally illuminated his own purpose. He must act on what he knew to be true. Something about the confrontation of this painting had strengthened his resolve and his own need to confront.

He was about to permit himself a smile when Dominic said, "But, Master, that's what the presbyter said about the painting and the artist's skills!"

The sound of small stones being turned to powder under the old monk's sandals was the only thing that filled the time before he spoke, or rather spat, again.

"*That* moronic paiderastïs knows nothing of artf. He only burbled about craft. *Brushmanship* is nothing to do with fvision, talent, or purposfe. *Brusfmafship* is the obsferfation of a weak-brained elitist that God pafsed by when the talentfs were being gifen to the worfy. He should not be allowed anywhere near a painfing or a bookf, he should be afsigned to swilling out the pigfs after hafing his ridiculous manicured fingerf crushfed in a wfine presf."

Spittle had gathered in the corners of the good master's mouth, and he savagely wiped at it with the back of his shaking hand. Then he lurched forward, leaving the stunned Dominic still standing in his dust and with the sound of "*Bruffmanfhif!*" still being spat onto the path beyond.

BRETHREN

A great exhaustion had overcome Owen Calca from his hammering against the implacable mountain and his calling for Abna. Instinct told him that his brother was inside, but hope suggested that Abna might have taken another path, even though there was none. He also knew his brother was not alone. Distorted glimpses of somebody, or something, came to Owen every time he bellowed his name. Did his sibling want this? Had Abna found a genie or a demon? Was he in rapture or in imprisonment? If Abna needed him, he would find a way out or leave a sign, a message, for Owen. But there was nothing, excepting the disturbing flashes of his brother's phantom liaison inside the mountain.

Defeated, with a sick feeling in the pit of his soul, he reluctantly limped back to retrieve his horse and turned down the track to find Follett and the rest of the party. Dread and hollowness filled the time of his descent.

"Calca! What be it? What ails thee?" Follett asked as the weary and sick-looking rider joined the men, who'd stopped to await him.

Owen could barely speak, but he coughed out words made of saliva and fear. "It's Abna. He's been taken."

"Taken?"

"Taken by whom?"

An echo of enormous capacity and loneliness lived in the space below where the men stood. The words caught there, no matter in what volume they were said, and were called back, making fun of them, turning the word *taken* into a flock of derisive, distant crows. Owen opened his eyes wider and blinked hard until his eyes became his brother's. He felt as if he were staring into a dark tunnel, into the very core of a shadow where he saw a creature in the dim light. An impossible beauty, a female not of this world: A thousand careful words could never describe this enchanted being. The awe of the vision forced him back into the company of men, with one wrong word stapling his tongue to his limited powers of description.

"A demon," he said, with unexpected force. "A demon has taken Abna inside the mountain."

The echo snatched up the words in a mocking song.

"Demon, demon, demon, taken, taken, taken, Abna, Abna, Abna . . ."

Follett unsheathed his spear and spoke sharply to his horse while turning it tightly around, a sign to the other riders that they were going back. The men rearranged themselves in their saddles; some standing in their stirrups to look around. Only Pearlbinder remained stationary, blocking Follett's path back up the mountain.

"We'll lose valuable time here," he said.

"Can't be helped. We will make it up later."

"Thou knowest we couldst miss the tryst if we tarry here."

"What tryst?" snarled Follett.

"Lent."

The men glared at each other vacantly. Follett's horse skidded, hooves clattering on scree as it tried to remain stationary on the steep incline.

Pearlbinder remained rock-solid, barring the way. Then he turned on the shivering brother. "Hast thee seen this demon, Calca?"

Owen blinked at the harshness of the question. "It came to me as I was riding. It's in the form of a woman."

"Have you seen it with thine waken eyes?"

"It has beguiled Abna with its—"

"*Have you seen it in the flesh?*" bellowed Pearlbinder.

"N-no," spluttered Owen.

The echo was in exaltation at all this shouting.

Pearlbinder turned his back on the defeated man and cleared the path for Follett, whom he now addressed with determination and respect.

"I believe thou means to give up the creature to the abbey below at the beginning of Lent. When all fleshy matters are quenched, and prayer becomes the only language of strength."

"Damn thee, Pearlbinder."

"I estimate we have two days before Shrovetide. Send Calca to chase phantoms and to find his brother alone, and we might just make it. If we all go back, we shall lose the day. The church needeth this treasure on time, and I wager the top sum of our reward depends on it."

All the other men were now paying great attention to this conversation.

"Am I not right, Captain?"

Follett swore, spat, and said, "Thou are always right, Samuel, but this is not the place to discuss that matter."

"I think it might be," added Tarrant, who had turned his horse to face Follett.

"I will not tolerate insubordination."

"'Tain't that," said Pearlbinder. "Just best that we all knoweth the price and the time of our delivery of this Blessing."

"I hath told thee, individually, the price you will be paid when we make our delivery. Your percentage of our bounty has increased since the loss of some of our party."

"And the timing?" asked Alvarez.

"The Pearl was right. Lent, at the beginning of Lent," Follett answered, turning his spear and horse around, speaking loudly as he descended.

"Owen, do you want to go search for Abna or stay with us and pray that he joins us below?"

There was so much stone, gradient, time, and fear between Owen Calca and his lost brother that failure seemed the only outcome. So he announced, "I will stay with thee."

It sounded almost gracious, but everyone heard the husk in his throat, and Follett immediately elected him for the next Steeping. The raw edge of his anxiety would add much to his confession. Slowly the men continued down the path toward the tangle of towns below and the tryst that they now knew awaited there.

No one looked at Calca, but they all watched Follett more closely than ever.

Three hours later, the vertiginous track wallowed out onto a slope. Gradually, it became a narrow, flat bumpy road with the mountain on one side, and a screen of tall trees guarding the next drop on the other. They were on the southwest face, and the day was in full force beyond the fringe of trees. Tarrant steered his horse close to the branches and looked through onto an uninterrupted view of the landscape. Pearlbinder joined him at the edge, sliding open a long brass telescope he had retrieved from his pocket. He put it to his eye and reached out through the branches toward the blur of houses that nestled in the valley below.

"Civilization," he groaned, handing the instrument to Tarrant, who eagerly took it.

The world bobbed and floated disconnectedly as he pointed the lens down and saw the villages and fields below free from snow. The world down there was normal in the flattened space. Silhouettes of different kinds of trees broke the continuity of the sprawling horizontal lines of smoke rising from the chimneys, like spiderwebs in the clear, breezeless air; then there was another movement on the green blur at the center of the community—a pond or some kind of lake. It took him a while to make it out while his hands shook in the cold. The sight connected to a long-exorcised memory of a different time, and a despised emotion crept into the self-tempered hollow where his soul once lived. For a second or two, he saw his wife and their children alive, and he hated it.

The horses were becoming restless, their hooves stamping impatiently on the frosted ground. They smelled pastures and warmth and wanted to move out of the high, tight cold.

"What hast thou seen?" demanded Follett. Tarrant was lost between the lens and what it captured, unable to answer. Suddenly, and more important, a huge black blur filled his view: a moving mass that seemed to float above the distant village like a solid cloud. He stopped looking and wiped his eye. Nobody paid him any attention and he returned to the view. The blur was another group of men, far below them, making their way down through the steep snow, dogs following behind, their misty breath panting into the air. The men carried spears. Warriors, or stray caballistas, Tarrant thought for a moment, until he saw the single thin rabbit carried on one of their backs. Hunters returning after a dismal day's event, the one animal all they carried home. The chill of poverty inside the warmth of home and the faint sounds, perhaps imagined, of a smithy and church bells, sent a wave of longing that gilded the air above the village and plucked at their purpose.

Pearlbinder looked at Tarrant and saw something he did not like. He reached out to take his telescope back. The removal of the metal tube unlatched Tarrant's mouth.

"People, just people," he said, in response to Follett's question.

DELIVERANCE

Benedict and Dominic had just entered a spinney of wiry juniper when they noticed the air was tinged with its rich scent. The land around them was unkempt and ragged, giving no encouragement to cultivation. Patches of dry woodland sprouted out of hard earth, old irregular stones, and jagged outcrops of slate. At least the knotted trees gave some shelter from the swathes of rain and the parching sun. The way back, so far, was without incident. They had not stopped to sleep properly, only dozing in the sun and napping under the shelter of trees.

They were nearing the far edge of the wood when they saw the rude shelter in the trees. Benedict approached cautiously, his staff held out before him. The hut was a simple but sturdy thing, probably erected by foresters or shepherds. Long slabs of bark were lain up against a frame of roped branches, some still with leaves and galls. It was more a wooden tent than a house. The old man poked his staff into its entrance and rattled it back and forth. Nothing ran out. Only the echo and the falling leaves, dead twigs, and fungus responded to the movement. Dominic questioned him with a sideways look.

"Foxes, vermin," Benedict said, his first words since his fury on the road.

"We will stay the night here." His words were ruffled by tiredness, his maimed lip over-sipping the cold air.

They allowed themselves a small fire near the hut. As they departed the great home of the painting, Benedict had poached some food from the overstocked kitchen. He unwrapped his spoils in silence as the night grew thick in the trees and the brightness of the stars burned away any remnants of lingering clouds. After a poor meal, they crawled into the tight space and curled up like children. The woods were all eyes and ears around them. In these sparsely populated lands, the reality of the monsters in the paintings seemed more possible.

Both monks unsheathed their knives and crucifixes before falling asleep.

In the darkest hour before dawn, a noise hooked Dominic out of his sleep. He lay rigid, listening, trying to identify it. It sounded like chattering, like chattering human teeth, and it was growing louder. His heart froze, and he shivered under his blanket. He did not want to see what was making such a ghastly noise, but knew he must. He stretched out a hand in the dark to raise Benedict, but the man's body felt cold and stiff. A sliver of moonlight illuminated the monk's snarling lip and transformed it into the death grin of risus sardonicus. Dominic threw himself outside and fell to the ground, where he lay panting madly until the chattering dragged his attention to the trees.

High in the branches, strewn and woven throughout the leaves, were the people from *The Nassau Depiction*. The painted naked men and woman who awaited or adored torture. Their obscene paleness gloated inside their thin, elegant bodies. Their hollow eyes watching him; their jaws chattering. Their faces were all alike, as though they belonged to one family without age or gender— except the one who was climbing down the tree, headfirst. The one Dominic knew. It was the naked man he had seen on his visit to the Gland of Mercy. Dominic had not recognized the man then, but he did now, even though his features had been smeared into the likeness of all the others. He had reached the base of the tree and was now walking like a dog on all fours straight toward the young monk.

Dominic's screaming sounded like that of a burning skylark. Friar Benedict shot straight up in a moment of alertness, banging his head against the side of the hut and bringing a shower of beetles and tree crust onto his blinking face. He gathered himself and crawled out of the shelter.

"What's a matter with you, boy! Control yourself!"

Dominic's eyes were like saucers gleaming in the moonlight. "You're dead!" he croaked.

"Not yet," Benedict said, confronting his companion. "Pull yourself together, you have been dreaming."

The words seem to slap the young man back to wakefulness. They both sat on the stony ground and stared at the reality of the hovel. Dominic was reassured by the old man's bad temper.

"Oh God! But it was so real."

"You have been sleepwalking."

Benedict pushed past the boy and looked up into the trees where the boy had been pointing. Nobody was draped in them, and the soft sounds of the night were without the faintest curse of chatter. Nothing moved, not even the wind.

"It was exactly like the painting. The victims in the painting were here."

"*No, they weren't!*" said Benedict emphatically, while rubbing his eyes, stretching his taut mouth, and rearranging his disobedient lip. "It was a dream, only a dream."

"I never dreamed such things before; now they're here with me. How will I get them out?"

The old man returned to his blanket and sat down in the impression that he had formed in the earth. He took a long breath, one that reached down into his compassion.

"Dominic, my son, you have seen a great work of another man's imagination. A vivid, overpowering picture that has imprinted itself on you. There is no place inside you for such a thing to live. So it hides during the day and escapes in your dreams."

The quietness of the night sat between them for a while.

"Will I always carry the stain of what I saw?"

"It will fade. Work and prayer will wash it away."

"How do you know, Master?"

Dawn began to envelop the stars, and the moon was low.

"I know because I have had the same dream every night of my life. But time and study have dimmed it until now it is weaker than that light out there."

"What was it, Master? Was it a picture?"

"No, my son, it was a scent. Overpowering and detached from any reason or common sense, it was a scent of honey and ammonia, fused in an almost-noxious haze. There was never a trace of it during the day, only at night. After I had slept an hour or more, it came to me. It has haunted me for years; that terrible perfume seemed to fluctuate between salvation and oblivion."

"Did it ever escape from you, enter the world, and become actual?"

"Never."

"So I will not bring those naked terrors back into our world? They will not escape like the painted creatures, and occupy, haunt, the monastery?"

"No, they will remain bound inside you until they or you fade."

"But what about the abbot?"

"We don't have to tell the abbot about any of this."

"He already knows."

Benedict was confused and annoyed.

"He was there, Master. He was here with the other naked people."

"What are you talking about?"

"He was in the trees, like he was with the dead in the Gland. Naked by himself, but in there with them all."

Benedict's eyes had changed. His displeasure was a blunt tool to use now.

"Are you saying you saw the Gland here, just now in your dream?"

"No, Master, I have only ever seen it the once. All those years ago, when I first came to the abbey and Brother Cecil took me there."

There was a curdling of silence while Benedict slowly explained to himself what he thought he had just heard.

"You are telling me in all truth that you saw Clementine naked and alone in that terrible place?" Benedict was shaking his head.

"Cecil saw him, too, and told me to take no notice and come away."

"Did he now?"

"Why was he there and in my dream tonight?"

Very quietly the old monk replied, "I think it best to save any further speculations until tomorrow"—he looked at the sky and heard the birds—"or, rather, later today."

"But, Master, I have so many questions."

"They will never be answered, especially by me. Our pilgrimage is over, and we return with more questions than we had before. That painting was a confusion of truths. We must now forget all about it and return to our life of prayer and obedience. I will not speak of this matter again."

"How will I ever understand?"

"Through learning, study, and the day-to-day running of our community. But now we must rest; there will be plenty of time to talk on our way home."

The "confusion of truths" had already begun to open a deep channel of thought in Benedict, but he was unable to share it until it had processed into a nonvolatile distillation. His companion was not ready for this kind of thinking. And now he had a deeper, more disturbing conundrum to add to his contemplations. Benedict did not want to run this abhorrent new image on the same track as the enlightenment he had just received from the Saint Anthony painting. At their best, they would be antithetical. At their worst? At their worst, they might join and threaten in all manner of unthinkable heresies. He had not brought Dominic all this way to be confronted by horror and confusion.

The old man had serious doubts about the youth's capacity, both in his faith and in his ability to comprehend. The power of the painting had rooted fear and misgivings in his young heart, and they might grow stronger if he were subjected to more visitations of the abnormal. The only thing that balanced this terror was Dominic's good health and his trust in his elders.

"Master," Dominic said, taking the advice to change the subject. "Master, I keep thinking that perhaps I should make a journal of our mission. Write down the things we have seen, and the people and oddities that we have met."

The old monk's twisted lip began to snarl its way up over his teeth, preparing for a restrained bark.

"Such a manuscript might be of value," Dominic continued, "to other novices who never had the advantage of a journey like this, nor the wisdom and scholarship of a master with such devotion."

The snarl melted back to a quiet clearing of the old monk's throat. The conversation was over, and the morning was growing bright enough to seal it forever. They dozed, exhausted, a thin warmth radiating through the trees. An hour or two later, they gathered their meager possessions and set foot again into a slightly altered world. Dominic found something reassuring about the old man's moans and groans, his complaints about his bones and his age, and an hour later he found a subject to think about without pain.

"It will be Lent before we reach home," the boy commented.

"Aye, and they will be making a greater dog's dinner of it than normal," said Benedict.

"Why so, Master?"

"Because I am not there to oversee it and get the novices to pull their weight."

Unable to think of an appropriate response, and still wanting to ask questions that had been banned, Dominic blurted out something that he belatedly realized could be grossly misunderstood by the tetchy old monk.

"Is it not surprising that Abbot Clementine let you leave the monastery at all at this time?"

To his relief, Benedict seized the right end of the question with apparent appetite.

"That's precisely what I have been thinking," he said and, without a moment's reflection, continued. "In fact, he seemed enthusiastic about my departure, and yours. I have been considering this for the last few days and now begin to suspect something untoward might be occurring."

Their footsteps had been slowing, and now they came to a halt.

"What do you suspect, Master? Surely no matter what we know about the good abbot, he will always work with consideration for all his flock?"

"That's possibly true, but Abbot Clementine also must obey commands from the Papal See, which contain edicts and instructions that we lowly brothers will never know."

The abbot's name had a new, sour resonance in the old friar's mouth.

"But surely such a venerated brother as yourself would be consulted on all matters?"

"Venerated! You mean *venerable*! Old but not respected."

And here Benedict shifted his jaw and teeth into their more customary alignment for an attack.

"Do not confuse the two, child! Clementine has continually blocked and ridiculed many of my academic pursuits and achievements. His interference has held back my research for countless numbers of years."

Dominic was shocked to hear the vehemence of the old man's outburst. They were near an outcrop of rounded boulders, and Benedict waved at them, indicating that he and Dominic should pause for a rest. After fidgeting from one stone to another, and brushing dust and leaves off his chosen seat, the old man settled and began talking again.

"I always thought his motivation for curtailing my studies was academic jealousy powered by his ambition to become a prince of the church. I now think it was sometimes completely different."

He looked up at Dominic and gazed into his eyes, seeking a space of understanding that might not exist.

"Did you know that both of us were reading the same books and manuscripts in the library, and that when he found out I had a more in-depth understanding of the old languages, he began his censorship of my knowledge? I was banned from reading anything about the history of the Glandula Misericordia and its association with the Oracles who had lived in our abbey. I had to accept his authority in this matter, so I looked past those questions and sought their foundation in abstract reflections that lie deeper in the past. I studied the references that spoke of the suspension of physical death and the continuation of life. It was then I discovered that certain key books and scrolls were missing—and some were from the chained reference section of the library where books must never be taken away."

"Who has the key?" asked Dominic, puzzled.

Benedict groaned and bit his lip at the shallowness of the boy's prosaic response. "The abbot, I suppose, but nobody has tried to open them for centuries. Some of the locks are encrusted with rust."

"How do you know that, Master?"

The old man examined his tied feet in their broken sandals.

"Because I was trying to open one myself, and the abbot caught me." His voice dropped. "That's when he banned me from reading anything in that section of the library."

They stopped talking for long enough to let the voice of the wind pass between them and to cast their eyes on the distant patterns of fields and hillside. They could just make out the odd symmetry of Das Kagel, sheltering among the smudges of purple and gray that changed with the density and movement of the clouds. Flocks of shadows scurried in the foreground to keep up with the leisurely magnitude of their propagators above. While in the deep sky, longer, ghostlike tendrils moved under a higher and far more ethereal wind.

Dominic wanted to learn more about the secrets of the abbey, but he knew he had to approach the old monk with great stealth. A mistaken question could shut down Benedict for the rest of their journey.

"Master, I have been thinking that maybe we should go to the places where the artist of those pictures found those creatures. Go there on our way home . . . to the farmland where those fields and walls are. There might be traces of them and a possible new scent for us to follow."

"Maybe find and sniff at the upturned kennel?" asked the old man sarcastically.

Dominic smiled, thinking he had seen approval.

"You are more confused than the truths in those paintings, because you see only the component parts of some fantastic story or parable. Perhaps those pictures are not about the stories that they say they tell. Not about monsters and men, the living and the dead. Perhaps they are about perception itself?"

Benedict guffawed when he turned to look at the boy and saw a face that was the embodiment of incomprehension.

"If you draw the everyday things of the life we know next to creatures and situations that are grotesquely different, the contrast will make a joke. But if you make that picture with great skill and care, giving each part of it the same authority, so that the sun that warms the tree also casts its shadow over the Woebegots and across, onto the wall you know and the pumpkin your father grew . . . then, *then*, you have created a conviction by the keenness of your eye and the talent and practice of your hand. If the whole picture works with the same brilliant audacity, then the conviction becomes an enigma. And that mystery ferments in our minds—not as a mummery or a puppet show—as a demand to test our perception of reality. Both in this world and after it, and maybe in others of which we have never dreamed."

RELUCTANT
GEESE

Meg was making breakfast like a sleepwalker, disjointed between her home and the astonishing things she had seen and been told about. Two days must have waddled by without being noticed. The black core of the mountain and her brilliantly illuminated comic dreams of Hell's gate, merged and collided with housework and cooking for her husband. She had seen her friends eating demon shit and had had impossible conversations in her own backyard with things that could not exist, while the sounds of owls stitched all the opposites into a semblance of calm normality.

Cluvmux groaned his way to the table, the sweet smell of bacon fat shepherding his hangover to the plate. He scratched his unshaven face and spoke through his food.

"Another long day's rehearsal!"

Meg grunted, thinking about what her big day would be. She gazed out the window and saw ten women loitering outside. A conversation about the women being gathered came back to her, and she sidled quietly to the door, behind Cluvmux's hunched back. The women turned toward her, Willeke Dijkstra in front with her hand on the gate. Meg put her finger to her lips, shooing the women away, in the manner of herding reluctant geese.

"Wait until he is gone and then come into the yard," she hissed.

Twenty minutes later, Cluvmux left for another serious day's practice. Meg waited a few minutes and then waved at Willeke to herd the women in. Their reluctance seemed embedded, and they stood in a tight group, without focus or sound. No one spoke of how she knew to come here this day or who had told them to do so, but Meg understood it must have been the work of Gef, Yellow Hat, and the other Filthlings that had been Grietje van der Elzen's familiars.

It had never occurred to Meg that the accusations of witchcraft brought against Grietje were actually true. Slandered by the Inquisition, so many innocents had died horrible deaths. Yes, Grietje had strange and sometime unfathomable ways, and on her pyre, she did recite the names of demons, but surely that was the last tortured gush of her indomitable spirit? Meg started to allow this new, devastating notion to seep into her resolve.

Gef and his kin really had visited all these women last night, whispering through the down and straw of their pillows, keeping their voices pitched under and between all the husbands' snores. They had recruited the women to Meg's unveiled purpose. She looked at them again. They were dressed mostly the same, in long work dresses covered by near-white aprons, thick white material tied into caps about their heads.

All stood in lumpen anticipation of what would happen next. There was something in their drab tableau that was so opposite to her dream that it became a reflection, and she began to form words around it like building bricks, like the Gates of Hell in her vision. Or like what the Wise Women had always said about Das Kagel: that it had been a tower of words where the bricks were damp and smelled like books. There were no books inside the mountain that she had witnessed, but their ghosts and their corpses were everywhere.

She had once touched a book, never daring to open it; instead she had instinctively sniffed it to smell its meaning and nature. But the words growing about her now were her words, and they were climbing into her voice and sounding out to all those who stood dumbfounded, their mouths hanging open like fish. While Meg spoke, she held her arms out like a statue or a saint. The birds in the trees were silent and even the indifferent wind seemed to quiet.

When she finished her sermon, there was the kind of silence that sings in the ears. All the women looked at each other and then burst into a tide of enthusiasm that rang with a great hurrah, their red hands applauding. They mobbed her, putting their hands on her arms and shoulders to give proof of their solidarity, and to make sure of the reality of hers. They left her yard with eyes gleaming, happier and more powerful than they had been in years. The geese had flocked into gulls, homing toward hawks.

Meg stood silent, watching them leave, and then realized she was holding something; a small, scrunched-up yellow hat had found its way into her hand. She brought it up to her face to consult its odor, without the faintest idea of what she had just said.

POLDERS

Abna was no longer alone with his Bride of the Shell, moving in wonder through the crumbling miles of the mountain's interior. The Woebegot Eueuw, who had finally dredged up his true name and believed it to be Euglenens Paratrampsacus, had been burrowing in a ventricle deep within Das Kagel's great white mass. He had not used the same cleft of ingress as the bewitched Abna. Eueuw had tunneled in from farther down the track and dug upward like a mole. Indeed, he resembled one as his head pushed up into the great echoing open space. He blinked extravagantly and shook earth and dust from his whiskery pointed snout. When his large sloping eyes cleared, he saw he had entered the vaulted emptiness of one of the arches looming over the pathway. A place Abna and his disquieted lover would eventually take.

Eueuw crawled out of his deep hole and shook the debris off two of the panniers he wore about his shoulders. Into these he started greedily cramming the word-rich crumbling stone. He then feasted on a large quantity of two folios and three octavos. Then he attempted to lift the ponderous weight of the leather bags back onto his sloping shoulders, But they were heavier than he was. So he sat next to his hole, incapable of movement and unable to understand what had happened. The bags that were hanging around his neck and scraping the broken ground looked like two sagging ears or, worse, like two pendulous dugs, swollen out of proportion to the meager frame of their dame. Such were the travails of many of the Woebegots, the miracle of intention withered by actuality.

Their mimicry of humanity was more firmly attached to the foibles and failures of the species than to their splendors and achievements. Many said this was because the Woebegots must have come from the sea or the endless waste of worthless mud that created the vast shore around the Lowlands. Their marine origins made them inferior to humans, being more of the haddock than of Adam. This explanation also fit their growing velocity of generation. As time went by, more were seen; shoals of their kind were climbing onto and populating the Firm-Lands. Some historians suggested that the polders themselves were created to contain the Filthlings, rather than to reclaim land from the encroaching sea, and that the most significant development was merely a by-product of their original function. However, this bewilderment was never a proven part of history.

Eueuw had remained stationary for more than two hours. Unable to cope with his predicament and longing to return to the comfort of his hole, eventually he did the only thing he could. . . . He fell asleep.

Abna and his new lover had been moving through the broken arches all the time they made love, their passion losing compass but providing shifts of momentum. Their grip on each other sealed them from the world and kept all difference and misunderstanding at bay.

Eueuw sensed the lovers' approach through his whiskers, which twitched out of sleep at the first vibration of their entrance. He became anxious about their nature, finding the tangled mixture of scents confusing; he pulled himself around in scruffy circles, the weight of his treasures making him pant and struggle.

The lovers saw him far off. At seeing the mole creature, Abna freed one hand from the humidity of his love's shell and reached automatically for the dagger that was sheathed to his thigh. At the loss of contact, she also stretched out of the shell, away from their intimacy, opening and closing the long fingers of her other hand in a gesture of greeting. Eueuw did not know what to do: he had no speed because of the bags, he had no weapons, and he had no real language. So he just waited and shivered in advance of the oncoming meeting.

When they came within touching distance, Abna tried to hold his companion back, but she slipped her long fingers from his grasp. He was about to warn her or take command when he heard the word *demon* whispered over and over again in the translucent amber dusk of the arches. The condition of this strangeness overwhelmed him. The severing of touch had undone the spell; his blood ran back, pale and tepid, and sheltered under lymph. Abna shriveled into a reality that could not be, suddenly standing amid the crumbling arches in a light that had nothing to do with the world he knew and understood. He was with two beings that were more separate from him than any other beast or fowl that he had met or eaten. The temperature seemed to be dropping with the growing shock of his alienation. He looked at his hand, still tingling from her touch, but the sensation was wearing off as she glided away, toward the collapsed creature in their path. Abna's knife hand knew what to do; it had been tutored in speed and contempt, cutting questions to shreds before they had time to attack or ask questions of him.

But his intention was weirdly suspended between his opposing hands. Then she made a mewing sound at the other thing crawling in the rubble and touched its paddle-shaped claws. It rubbed its bristling snout against her fingers and made a harsh purring sound that sounded like coal being shredded on a kitchen grater. Abna felt disgust, and that emotion opened a channel to a deeper, sullen reaction of jealousy and rejection. He had been forsaken in favor of a repulsive joke. He had been separated from his brother; he had been betrayed. He stared at the thing, which she now fondled, in growing rage.

The beauty of her face was hidden from him, and he saw only the volume of her shell: she was a travesty, a slithering mistake that no God would ever have created. She felt his transformation, his withdrawal into his homeland of bloodshed and fear. She tried to speak as she turned, holding out her other tentacled hand toward him. But he saw no kindness in the gesture; rather, it looked like a lewd invitation to join these sudden abnormalities in a dance of depravity, to become one with them in some unknown coupling.

His recent experiences of love and warmth drained away, sullied into a mangled memory of physical slipperiness and unnatural contortion—and for that moment, it seemed true: they looked like dancers frozen in a collapsed dyad of grotesque sexuality. Then one of the leaking arches screamed and gave way, startling the fragile tableau into action: Eueuw let go of the beauty's wonderful touch and covered his head. Abna's knife hand took control, and he lunged at the threatening monsters. The lady slid sideways and around to block the progress of the meaningless attack.

The chamber shifted shape, its confines changing as earth and air shook with the collapse of tons of stone and words. After the sound settled and the larger stones agreed to stillness, lighter noises could be heard in the rubble: snapped and mangled words, some still twitching in uncontrollable incomprehension. Eueuw was making the most noise. Miraculously untouched by the falling masses, he had witnessed the blow that cracked the beauty's shell, and he was horrified by her injuries. Some of her delicate inner portion must have been squashed and then sheared by the sharp edges of her wrecked shell. A rope of white substance had bled and swollen away from her body; it was pungent but still alive, and it seemed to be seeking a place of its own to hide across the rough floor. The featured parts of her had gone, shrinking back into the interior of her shell for protection. Nothing of the gentle face or tendriled hair could be seen. Abna, who had been tripped by the beauty in the full force of his onslaught, had fallen headfirst into

Eueuw's hole, so that only his hips and legs remained in sight, waving in the gritty air. Clouds of stone, dust, and scribble spluttered around his frantic movements, giving his legs a wild and disturbing appearance and making their disembodied agitation the most peculiar occupants of this crumbling domain.

BELFRY

Abbot Clementine had escaped the books and the frustration of their enigma. He had gone to the bell tower, the highest point in the monastery, and looked out from there in all directions. First, north onto the symmetry of Das Kagel. He was restless and wanted the new Oracle to come now, so that he could fulfill the prophecy, take it in his arms, and bleed half its power. He had been preparing for this all his adult life.

From his tower, he hoped to be able to see something of the spiral track on the mountain. But low clouds had masked the entire top of the cone.

Clementine had removed five more books from the chained library and was attempting to translate them, seeking descriptions and formulas that matched what the remnants of the Quiet Testiyont had told him. He knew nothing would fit mechanically. There would be no hand-in-glove moments of absolute confirmation. These were esoteric matters, and the signatures and signs in them had to be perceived by resonance and reflection.

The abbot walked to the next set of slit archways, looking more westward, to where the forest at the base of the mountain would eventually meet the road to the town and its gates. He knew that if he had the three keys to the balance of ceremonies, then the power of the new Oracle would be his, and it would not affect the Gland or anything else. He was so close he could taste it, but he could not yet see it. He needed a deeper reading of the discovered texts. He was bluntly confronting his own ignorance and lack of imagination.

Out of the southwestern arch, he could see and smell the sea and its long, meandering coastal road, like an uncertain suture drawn between the horizon and the rising hills. Somewhere along that scar, the wretched Benedict and his dim novice would soon be trudging back to contaminate his life.

The books also contained a feeling of trespass and observation, as though somebody had been there before him, unlocking the sequence without any intention of using them. It could only have been Benedict who had saturated himself in this knowledge, but he was far too old and cowardly to take the next step of activation. Clementine was also beginning to believe that he could actually feel the presence of that old gargoyle in these books. As if his prying mind had stained the pages in some way as it absorbed their secrets. Perhaps even sealing their wisdom after he had tasted it.

Clementine turned his back on the sea and walked around the bells to face south and look out over the town and its sprawl of crowded houses. The buffeting wind was snatching up the sounds of music and of hammering, a chopped murmur of pointless life. He used the noise to drive away the notion of the old monk's haunting the books. Of course, Benedict did not curse or bless the pages. Such things were possible—Clementine had practiced spells like this—but deep down, he knew it was worse than that. His real belief was that Benedict had no such need or desire. His genius in these matters was purely academic, no more than a scholar's selfish fascination. An elaborate waste seeking a terminal seclusion.

This is what he so hated about the church. Its abundance was stifled by its myopic dogma. He turned eastward in the belfry and faced directly into the growing wind, looking down across the body of the abbey. Unlike most of those who dwelled there, Clementine was a practical man who learned things in order to use them. There was no difference between the shaping of stone that he had mastered in his youth and the gaining of magical wisdom that would give him perpetual radiance. The church held many keys to many kingdoms, and all of them were imprisoned by cowards who were too weak to even contemplate what the locks were and where they might be hidden.

His path through those hierarchies had been cunning and insistent, and what he now almost possessed was far too important to be lost to a dithering weakling. Clementine gripped the stonework to steady himself against the wind. He looked down onto the enclosure of the Triumph of Death and saw the morbid glow and smoke rising from its core.

He had been tempering his spirit in the harsh fire of that place, looking into the eyes of the damned, smelling their fetid decay, and standing his ground. He had trained himself to tolerate it for an hour every month, naked and resolute in the certainty of his ability to obtain celestial permanence. The wind moaned around him and the great cold bells moved slightly as if they were dreaming of a hollow mountain. It was time to go back to the books.

SKELLINGTONS

The road now seemed flat and broader. Follett and his men skirted the base of the mountain. The distance at this thickest circumference was almost as long as the mountain was tall and seemed to go on forever. Follett tried to explain that the distortion meant it was impossible to gauge distance by time, but only Pearlbinder understood him and Tarrant just chuckled to himself.

A day and half later, they passed into the eastern quadrant, and the horses shivered and strained against their riders' directions. The wind stank of smoke. A polyphony of lures and suggestions would rise and then fall into dumb quiet. The only persistent noise was the dull, faint beat of a drum, mournfully regular in its slow, steady rhythm—a pulse of servitude without the faintest taste of music.

Alvarez went to the edge, dismounted, and firmly tied the horse he had adopted after the Kid's death so it wouldn't bolt. He squeezed through the stiff trees to catch a glimpse of the fields below.

"It fades in and out of sight down there," he said when he returned, pale from shock. "Soot is running on the wind, but I think there is a multitude locked in combat. They glisten wrongly, and the surge is indistinct."

"Is it a war?" asked Tarrant. "I see naught!"

"It must be! What else would sound or stink like that?"

All the men tied their horses hard to the trees, pushed through the brush, and peered down. At times, it was possible to catch a glimpse before the view was obscured again, but this was not caused by the sun moving in and out of the clouds. It was as if the physical sight of the land and the incidents below could not be looked at for too long. Each time the vision retreated from view, it seemed to take with it a fistful of gravity, making the men feel a vertiginous suction beneath them.

"They are not all men," said Alvarez. "Some look like skellingtons or ravaged ghosts. Look at yonder flank where the drum plays. See how it moves like a great tide of bony heads locked together, all pushing forward into the fray."

"It may be a trick of the light," said Calca. "It's just helmets of a marching army, that's all."

Tarrant looked from one man to another, then to the distant valley, squinting. "But I see nothing down there. Where are these sights?"

Pearlbinder already had his telescope in hand. Follett kept quiet.

After a long while, Pearlbinder said, "It is not they who move. They only quake, marching on the spot and waiting. The movement comes from the fighting before them. A multitude of men and women are being herded into a great box or silo by . . ."

"*By what?*" shouted Alvarez.

"It's difficult to see. . . . By . . . thin men."

"Thin men?" pleaded Tarrant.

"Skellingtons," said Alvarez.

"Envious bones," whispered Follett.

"Something like that."

"What else?"

"The whole landscape is wasted, a field of ruin and despair where nothing grows. And the horses . . . No animal should be treated thus. The dead ride their innocent bones into horror, a great cruelty. It looks like Armageddon," said Pearlbinder as he began to withdraw from the others.

Follett had explained to each man as much as he could comprehend that the peril in this assignment did not come from other fighting men or rampant priests but from something much older, something they had all heard of before, either in myth or in actual explanation. He could barely speak its name, so instead Follett used parables and biblical quotations.

"It is said there are beasts that never encountered the ark still living in those lands. But far worse is the location of the Vale of the Shadow. It is the gully of death, where the endless battle between life and death is enacted under the same sun and moon we see every day of our short lives. But that place is not to be witnessed. It is not part of our lives or our mission; it simply exists nearby and its influence is terrible in the extreme."

He then counterbalanced this horror by telling each man about the wealth they would receive when the mission was completed.

"Why art thou surprised? Thou knew of this place and why it must be," said Follett.

"Yea, but not like this, not with horses."

"How else, then? How else can it be?"

Follett was becoming irritated.

"It is the Gland of Mercy," he said, "and thou knew it was there. It has always been there."

The other men looked at one another. Tarrant was the most perplexed because he could not see a single trace of what so grieved his comrades. Then they all turned their attention to Follett, who was given no choice other than to explain.

"Yonder is a cleft in the reality of the everyday world, there to relieve the monstrous enormity of death. It is a breaking in the crust of the normal where the Triumph of Death bubbles out and is exposed. The sight of the endless culling of men, women, and children all over the world would be impossible to behold, so it is concealed beneath the surface of life. Only here in this Gland may the full horror be seen, exposed, to burn off the pressure from within."

Owen Calca had lost all color from his face; a cold, sweaty whiteness seemed to envelop him.

"Can I use your spyglass?" he asked.

"It is not for thine eyes," said Follett, while Pearlbinder slowed and waved the tapering brass tube toward the anxious man.

"Take it, but turn it on itself instead. It is chaos and impossibility down there, and such things cannot be. Turn the glass and keep them at bay," he said as he moved away.

All the other men followed him except Calca, who pushed deeper into the resistant foliage, getting closer to the vision that seethed below.

Follett was furious at Pearlbinder's intervention. Both men knew what was being enacted in the Gland, but they saw it from different ends of the telescope, from opposite magnetic poles.

"Why did you give him the spyglass?"

"Because he asked," answered Pearlbinder, who had overcome his horror of tortured horses and was beginning to savor a curiosity about the torture of living men.

"If he sees his brother down there in that unearthly carnage, he will try to save him. And we can't afford to lose another man."

Ignoring the challenge, Pearlbinder deepened his inquiry. "Why? So far our way hath been without conflict; only the misunderstanding with the dog-headed giant shed blood."

"Thou knoweth I need a store of confessions to steep the Oracle's food. Only these men have a depth of sin and crime to draw from, and I need every ounce of it to get us to the end of this mission."

"But we are almost there. How many more times do you need to see that thing perform?"

Follett was offended by Pearlbinder's disrespect and hated being questioned like this. He tried to close the conversation by changing the subject.

"Anyway, things could get difficult on our way toward the monastery. I need the might of all of us."

"But surely we are working for the church in this mission and hath their right-of-way?"

Follett could see that Pearlbinder was not going to let go.

"The spoken pass is from the authority on the other side of the Inquisition, and they are disconnected from the caballistas, who rule below. They know nothing of our quest."

"And, of course, you carry no written authority," chortled Pearlbinder.

Follett bared his teeth and spat back, "Cease this now."

THE ORACLE

"I know little of the Quiet, Master," said Dominic.

"That may be just as well under the circumstances."

"I was too young in my novice days to have anything to do with the Cyst and the Blessing."

"Just as well."

"But wasn't Quiet Testiyont a holy man of great wisdom?"

"Whatever Testiyont was at his beginnings, he was not a man at his ends. He became one of those enigmas that the church can never resolve."

"Forgive me, but I thought anchorites held a profound and respected position in th—"

"Testiyont was not an anchorite," interrupted the old monk. "The Quiet was an Oracle."

In the far distance, layers of clouds parted, allowing beams of moving light to paint the sea and giving the whole landscape a framed sense of well-being, which was in stark opposition to the darkening tone of the conversation. The monks were walking more slowly now, caught between the momentum of departure and the velocity of arrival. The inertia rode where bones become heavier and distance seems interminable.

"Foreseeing future events is but a small part of an Oracle's talents," Benedict continued. "Those that the mother church finds for us, and installs within our walls, have a much greater duty. And I believe we are in peril all this time without one."

Dominic was frowning deeply and looking hard at the stony ground as he tried to digest what he was being told.

"But you were there when we were told of his instant demise."

"A great sadness," said Benedict before continuing. "But there was also something very wrong about the Testiyont's end. It was all far too sudden. I have found many testimonies in my research that tell how long it takes for such a blessed being to die, and there is a pattern in their departure, a layering in their passage from this world into the next—and that was not so here. The abbot suddenly announced the Blessing's death, rather than its disincorporation, and then quickly took the remains away to be buried elsewhere."

The old monk looked out from his words, deep into the perspective of the land. Dominic followed his gaze.

"Then was it his ghost I heard in the courtyard? Did his ghost want to steal my voice?"

"Others have heard things near that spot. Something is trying to communicate with us. That is the reason I insisted on having the writing material installed near the Cyst, even after he had apparently gone. And that is why my inquiries into the meaning and purpose of his kind were defiled by the abbot."

Dominic's face reflected a blank amazement that might easily swallow either incongruity or laughter as possible poles of respite. His master saw his struggle, and Benedict continued before any such churlish choice could be made.

"I believe the abbot wants knowledge for himself alone, even at the price of subverting an Oracle's purpose with us."

"With us?"

"Under our care and protection. There has been an Oracle in our abbey for hundreds of years. The Quiet was one of a long chain, and the absence of one is beginning to affect the world outside.

My studies have shown that there has never been so long a gap in the presence of a Blessed One. I think this void has weakened our resolve and the holy continuity of the world."

"Is that why the Woebegots have arrived?" asked Dominic, with a quiver of excitement at his own wisdom.

"Yes, I believe so. They are a symptom of the collapse of balance and of what will occur beyond the Eastern Gate if the matter is not rectified."

"But isn't the Oracle's purpose to foresee the future and warn us of any change in the Gland of Mercy?"

"That is the stated function, but I believe it goes much deeper. My studies leaned toward a suggestion of control. The books were trying to tell me that the Oracles in the abbey's eastern wall had direct communication with the Gland. And that they controlled, steered, or adjusted its function in a way I do not yet understand."

"Then it is a serious matter to find a replacement?"

"Yes, indeed! You are beginning to understand! There should have never been a gap between the demise of one and the arrival of its replacement. At the very first symptom of the Oracle's wearing out, a message should have been sent to find and prepare its successor. But I don't think that happened until it was too late. And this disaster is happening because the last days and powers of the Testiyont were being used and abused for another purpose, after it was supposedly dead."

"And you think the abbot did that?"

"It does not matter what I think. No one will listen to me."

Dominic looked into the eyes of the accuser in despair. And then he asked feebly, "But there will be another Oracle coming to take up its sacred post?"

"When they find it, and if they have been told of the demise of the last."

The old monk saw the horror growing in his companion's eyes and changed his tack. "No doubt the church beyond the Inquisition has been scouring the land."

"But what will happen if they can't find one?" There was a noticeable tremor in Dominic's question.

"There have been Oracles since the beginning of civilized time, and the church has always found them. Every known language tells of them, and some still exist today. But do not imagine a sacred man in a cave or a grove of trees, who recites the whispering of the angels in order to guide man in his capricious future. Rather, see a caged travesty of humanity warped into mania by drugs and potions, or twisted by the fumes of the earth into rages of meaningless screaming.

"The ancient and revered scholars tell us of such creatures, and the priests who maintained and translated their ravings generally did it for their own advancement. But they also indicate that some Oracles may not have been of human origin at all."

"Monsters, demons!" exclaimed Dominic, no longer seeming confused.

"Possibly yes, or something else we do not recognize or have a name for."

"Like that thing that grabbed your hand?"

"No, not like that," snarled the old man, which for once did not deter the young monk's enthusiasm.

"Then the church must cast them out, not encourage their voices."

"The church is clear in this matter: such things will not be tolerated. But it must understand them first, draw intelligence about their meaning before destroying them. The Testiyont was not the only such manifestation to be taken into the Holy See; it's been happening elsewhere since Byzantium."

Dominic was silent again and allowed his focus outside their exchange. More clouds had been shredded by the winds, and vivid sunlight flooded the plains, illuminating Das Kagel in a purity it had never possessed. The light gave them momentum. Dominic tapped the stones of the path ahead with his staff as if sounding for snakes, but really he was killing time while the old man straightened his bones and groaned encouragement into his aching joints. A mile passed before they spoke again.

"Have you heard of the *Sortes Astrampsychi*?"

Dominic looked hard into Benedict's face.

"I thought not," the old man said wearily. "It's an ancient document that gives a key to the understanding and practice of Oracles. It even developed the sacrilegious idea that any man may possess the powers of divination. It is one of the long-suppressed truths I discovered in my studies. What do you think the church would do about such inflammatory doctrines?"

After a moment during which all the heavens waited, Dominic said, "Burn it!"

The clouds shriveled from the old man's vehemence and allowed the sun to wince at his scorn.

"Idiot boy! You should join the Inquisition. *No*, they did not burn it. They made it their own—their recognition of it became the *Sortes Sangallenses*, and then the *Sortes Sanctorum*. Thus a dubious pagan superstition became sacred texts."

Dominic could see the fierceness in the old man's discovery, but he could not grasp the contours of its meaning. He also noticed that Benedict's deformed lip had caught, snagged on his long teeth and strange-shaped gums. This sometimes happened when he shouted or became enraged. The poor old monk had to pull his lip back into place with his fingers before he could continue speaking. This he now did, maiming some of the anxious words in the process.

"Thef churf absorbed oracular beings and the mongers who translated their dribble as a means of control. By making their power its own, the church is able to digest the bones of its dogma until there is nothing left of the original menace. But not all princes of the church think this way. Some would prefer the sanctity of the church to be influenced by such ideas. I found this in the pages of books in our own library while seeking a very different enlightenment. It came out of the pages without my will guiding it. That is why Abbot Clementine now wants to keep me away from further reading and concealed knowledge. He despises me for an erudition that he will never have."

At the thought of this, the old man looked around as if to make sure that they were still alone.

"Then the abbot must have his own purpose with those books," offered Dominic.

"Out of the mouths of babes and sucklings! More than you know or could guess, child. If we take the lesson learned from seeing those paintings and your own witnessing him naked in the Glandula Misericordia, then we have two lenses to examine his purpose with those specific books and my belief that he interrogated the Quiet before its death. It makes me fear for the safe sanctity and installation of the new Oracle."

"What did the painting tell you about the abbot's presence in the Gland?"

"The painting of Saint Anthony showed me that the inner core of its meaning was not its subject. The saint is in a calm meditation, and all the elements of the world around him are at peace or are becoming peaceful. Even the minor demons seem casual and indifferent. If you see only that, then you see only the surface depiction. Once you see that sable flame, you understand that its purpose, its driving force, is about annihilation held in abeyance."

Benedict was becoming excited. His hand was to his mouth, holding his lip aside, so he could speak more clearly.

"What do you think a mortal could learn or would see in the Glandula Misericordia?"

"Death, the triumph over death."

"Yes, of course, but that is only its subject. What is its force, its authority?"

Before Dominic could even gather up Benedict's casting of his revelation, the old man answered his own question.

"Its continuum, the perpetual that is its core—that is what Clementine has been seeking. Satan's greatest lure: immortality. Abbot Clementine wants to be immortal—and I fear that he will use the new Oracle for his own wicked longing."

"Are you saying Abbot Clementine is committing a grievous sin?" asked Dominic, a sad incongruity in his voice.

"It's not for me to make such an accusation. These are dark, deep, fast-flowing waters. Think what the Inquisition would make of such indictments. Their wrath would not only focus on Clementine, but also on me. The entire monastery would fall under their pitiless investigation and judgment."

Dominic cringed from the old man's revelation. All this deep thinking and worldly threat scared him more than phantoms in the woods, or in those paintings, because he had seen the actual spilling of blood in its name. He also realized that he had unwittingly become part of a darkening turmoil from which there might be no escape. He turned to confront Benedict, but he was gone, scrabbling in his rucksack. He came out with a notebook, and with great excitement he ruffled through the pages and stared at the one he was seeking. He clapped his hand hard against his forehead, exclaiming, "You fool! You fool!"

He waved the book before the boy's eyes. "*Cano, cano!* It's not a dog—not *canis*. Do you remember what you wrote on that wall? What the voice said to you at the Cyst?"

Again the old man did not wait for a slow-witted answer.

"It's not a dog. It's a song and a command!"

Dominic had no idea what he was talking about. His master was becoming intoxicated, his previous mood of despair transformed into elation.

"See here, it's '*Advenio, cano, obsecro te, salva me*'—not what I thought I read before. It's a command from the new Oracle, not the old one. It is asking you to help, to save it!"

"But, Master, I never wrote that. I do not have the language. I don't know what it means."

"It is asking you . . . *No!*

"It is asking *me* to save it. The message was for me!

"We must get back now, before it is too late."

CHATTERING

Owen Calca spoke to no one, not even when he dropped the telescope back into Pearlbinder's saddlebag. The warm brass of the telescope, still fully extended, had turned a sickly green. The men had all dismounted and now rested on the rounded boulders before setting up camp. After they ate, Follett told Alvarez to get the Pyx and Calca ready for the next Steeping. The lone brother was still deathly white and morose. He walked like a broken man, or one who had exhausted his view of the world. Owen was in prime condition for a deep and significant confession.

"It's got to be a good Steeping, this one. We might need its steering or forewarning to get us down and off this mountain and into the civil realm."

Calca barely lifted his head to acknowledge what he was being told.

Alvarez thrust the box into his hands and said, "Do it. Do it now."

Owen Calca's voice had always been strange. He and Abna shared the same split octave—a quiet rasp that shredded the softness of words—but now it had almost vanished, shrunk to the sound of a pin scratching slate.

"Pearlbinder was right. It was all too much, impossible, so I did what he said and looked through the telescope turned backward, to change the burning in mine eye and set such things in a distance, in a past. But the sound came in louder and with it the hollow of where One should be."

His voice faded. Its swallowing seemed to fill his legs with a jellied motion that propelled him toward a dim shadow behind an ancient boulder that had not moved since the arrival of upright men. He folded himself and opened the box and emptied the husk of his voice into it.

"All I be is shrunken. All I have done is nothing, and any word I had hath been eaten from below by the noise of teeth, all those teeth chattering, bone on bone, chattering jaws on head bone. Chattering more than pebbles in a tide.

"Chattering, forever chattering. Any word I had hath been eaten from below by the noise of teeth, all those teeth chattering, bone on bone, chattering jaws on head bone. Chattering more than pebbles in a tide. Chattering, forever chattering. Any word I had hath been eaten from below by the noise of teeth, all those teeth chattering, bone on bone, chattering jaws on head bone. Chattering more than pebbles in a tide. Chattering, forever chattering, chattering more than pebbles in a tide.

"Chattering, forever chattering. Any word I had hath been eaten from below by the noise of teeth, all those teeth chattering, bone on bone, chattering jaws on head bone. Chattering more than pebbles in a tide. Chattering, forever chattering, chattering more than pebbles in a tide. Chattering, forever chattering, chattering more than pebbles in a tide. Chattering, forever chattering, chattering more than pebbles in a tide. Chattering chattering

chattering chat-

tering chattering . . ."

And then he spoke no more but rose as if through thick water and walked to his horse, mounted, and turned back in the direction whence they had come. The three other men wondered where he was going, but the question needed no answer, so it never passed their mouths to reach the air outside. Only Follett shouted, "Where goeth thee?"

Calca did not turn but quietly said, "To find my brother's horse."

Alvarez groaned and made his way toward the box of bones, which lay on its side. He seriously doubted the nature of what Calca had said and did not relish feeding the bad, swollen marrow to their precious cargo.

Follett wisely decided that their final night on the mountain would not be in the eastern quadrant, so they moved farther down the spiral, farther away from the atmosphere of that terrible place. A night breeze of a different color rustled the trees as the last sunlight of the day vanished. A small stream crossed the path, and they stopped to partake of its benefaction. While Alvarez was preparing the Oracle, the others collected wood and thought about the Calca brothers meeting high above them and tried to gain some hope from the image. Follett cleaned his spear and thought about the reward that was growing larger as the number of men diminished.

"It won't eat!" shouted Alvarez from his seclusion. "It took but one spoonful."

"Try the bones at the bottom of the Pyx," called Follett.

Shuffling curses and mumbled squeaks came from behind Alvarez's rock. After another forty minutes, they heard the wooden lid close and knew the job was done.

"It's barely taken a cupful," Alvarez whispered as they prepared to Choir, the shivering bundle held between them.

Then it spoke: "Cloy of the earth bites hard, all those bone lips un-kissing the promise." The men looked at one another. "Thank thee for my new oncoming burial. Thank thee for thine own."

"Sounds pissed off to me," said Pearlbinder.

"Cos that weren't enough, it needs more. Let me go now," said Alvarez.

"It's got plenty to get us there and finished," answered Follett, preparing to leave.

"*It needs more!*" Alvarez growled back. "And I can give it."

"Fuck thee, Alvarez, do what you are damned well told and stop jabbering like some old wet nurse."

GIFT

Flowers had been placed on Meg's doorstep. Small, bent, and uneven. She could not remember the last time she received a gift. She picked them up and saw a scrap of paper was attached. Instinctively she looked around to see if she was being watched. Nobody was there, so she unfolded the paper: a tiny scratched *D* with a line running through it. She knew that mark as well as she knew her own—an *M* with a line running the opposite way. Dircx, it was Dircx's mark. She pressed the flowers to her lips and burst into tears. A sign that her son was alive and thinking of her. She held them to her heart and went inside the house. Doubt followed her—surely this was a trick, a cruel prank to give her hope. Who would do such a thing? She needed Grietje at a time like this; her insight and wisdom would have set this incident right, or wrong.

During the last few days, it had become clear that the other women were looking to Meg to unite them and to give them a voice against the authorities and against their husbands. How was this possible? What had she said to give such a startling impression? Fear was rising in her. This was not her life. She had nothing to say. What had she said against all those men? She needed Grietje's guidance and resolve, but wasn't that what she had been given?

Suddenly Meg recalled a memory, from before they had become real friends, when Grietje had given her a present. At the time, she did not understand it. It was a picture, a small drawing on wrinkled paper. What did Grietje say about it? She had seemed like a difficult person then; many of Meg's friends eschewed the Wise Woman, saying she was dangerous and would get people in trouble, always talking in riddles so. When Grietje gave Meg the gift, Meg hadn't absorbed the woman's words or the drawing itself—she had never planned on talking to Grietje again. But now she was certain: the picture was indeed the last present she had been given before today's flowers. But the memory of it was smudged and unpleasant, wrong in a way she did not understand. All its detail had been erased, along with so many other things, after Dircx's abduction.

Now she wanted to find the drawing, to recall what she had done with it. Even though she had little recollection of what it actually was. The truth was that she must have spent more time hiding it than looking at it. She certainly had not shown it to anyone else; of that she was sure. She had hidden it in her forgetfulness, but where? It must be in a place that Cluvmux and Dircx would not go, nor have any interest in.

The kitchen. Apart from eating there, they knew nothing of it, having never prepared a meal for themselves in their lazy lives. Meg held the flowers closer to her bosom and looked at the array of pots and pans, jars and bins, dried leaves, beans, smoked meats and vegetables. The butts and barrels of her domain, shelved and standing in her kitchen and her pantry.

She wove her distant, younger self through all these things, seeking that moment, years ago, when she had tucked the picture safely away from sight. She tried to layer the reality and weight of all these goods against the cobweb of memory to see if anything fit. But nothing adhered, agreed, or revealed itself. Automatically, she gave up on her sight, closed her eyes, and started touching objects, hoping she might feel a trace of the gift attached to that long-ago day. She was midway through this scanning when her instinctive sense of smell engaged in the search. A scent came back to her: earth . . . earth and musk . . . beans, broad beans . . . dried broad beans. The kind her family disliked but that were a favorite of hers. She had not used them for a long time. She opened her eyes and looked through all the containers until she found the one she wanted on a high shelf.

Meg climbed up onto a kitchen chair to reach the wooden box. Opening it, she cast her hand deep inside, blindly feeling amid the very old beans and the dust and the weevils. Her fingers touched paper, and she brought out the drawing; it was rolled into a loose scroll, fragile and uncertain. Carefully she climbed down and carried the gift to the kitchen table. Meg dusted off the paper before attempting to unroll it, but her eager efforts tore the frail tube before she could get it flat. She blew away all the legume and weevil dust and stared at the drawing. Finally, she placed a precious glass plate that her husband had stolen from a grand house over the paper, and then she looked at it. There were about thirty tiny drawings scattered and crowded within its confines. Detailed drawings of beggars and people with missing or disjointed limbs—some of which were craftily faked to gain sympathy—hopping, crawling, and limping in all directions. Under the glass, they looked so clear.

"Horrible," she said to herself.

Still, Meg could not take her eyes away from the accuracy of the depictions. Unknown to herself, she was smiling. Each figure's twisted portrait seethed and shouted in knotted character. They were alive and captured in the drawing. Their arrangement in the small paper rectangle also gave them a vivacious presence, as they tried not to fall over one another while staying aware of the outside viewer. Two even looked as if they were waving to her.

Then she saw one that looked like Cluvmux. It was not entirely him, but the bulbous, dumb, grinning expression could have been a sudden glimpse of her husband. The artist had made his particular deformity a comic swelling of a belly that needed its own crutches for support. Meg was now laughing out loud. Why had she not remembered this paper? Her quaking hand accidentally shifted the heavy glass plate, and all the figures changed. A very slight distortion occurred beneath the handmade glass; all the human debris of the street transformed. Minute adjustments had been made to each tiny drawing, so she was now staring at a page of Woebegots and Filthlings. The bent limbs, crutches, and wooden feet had become living extensions, absorbing the biological anatomies and peculiarities of other species. A sideways evolution had occurred.

Meg dragged her eyes to the Cluvmux beggar and saw the truth of her husband in another world, and in some way, its revelation excavated part of what Grietje had said about the drawing: " 'Twas given me by him in Den Bosch. Says it was an answer to be passed on. Now it was mine, and one day I would know when and who to pass it on to."

Meg had not understood back then and said so.

"Neither does I," Grietje had replied.

"But what is it?"

"That's what I asked, and he said, 'It's a mirror in which, like vampires, the ignorant cannot be seen.' And he just laughed at me and said I should go back and hold the beam that was sticking out from the wall, because the light was going."

Meg remembered the funny way Grietje had looked at her when she said those things, continuing, "I was slender and comely in those days, and undressed, pretending to be naked and hanging in a tree. That's the way he painted me, looking like somebody else."

That was the last memory Meg could drain from the gift. She took the drawing out from under the glass and stared at the page of beggars. Puzzled, mystified, and curiously elated, she rolled up the scroll and reinterred it back with the beans. But the evolution and meaning of all those creatures stayed with her and began to replace the questions that had so worried her just before. Every time some apprehension or doubt tried to gain her attention, the creatures would troop out from her memory and block the path of such miserable wraths. They were doing it now as she picked up the wilting flowers and brushed off some of the bean dust with her careful fingers. Looking again at her son's signature and knowing that it was true.

TETHER

They were almost there, making good time. Follett was beginning to glow inside his implacable clinker shell. It was all only a few miles away, and this was the best road they had been on in months.

Tarrant rode forward until he was abreast of Follett, and he said, "It maketh funny noises."

"So what is unusual there?"

"Alvarez could be right, it might be hungry or starving. I didn't trust Calca back there to give it his best. He was too webbed up in his brother's disappearance."

"Umph!"

"Nothin' to lose, Captain."

Follett, in irritated slow motion, pulled on the reins of his horse and brought it to a halt, waiting for the others to catch up. When they were alongside him, he spoke to Alvarez. "What's wrong with it?"

"It's leaking and talking in many voices."

"Saying what?"

"Difficult to hear, but stuff about not getting there alive."

"Jesus!" exclaimed Follett.

"Let me be its next Steeping. I have what it needs," begged Alvarez.

"Thou art very keen to do this. Why?"

"This will be my last time, and I saved the best for now."

"Wants to cleanse thy shitty soul before we get back into the world, is it?"

"And make sure this Blessing here is full to the brim before we get paid."

Follett squinted at the man to whom he had given trust over the Oracle and nodded.

"This is the last bit of wilderness. Do your worst, but do it quickly."

Alvarez looked deep into the box of bones. He decided to dredge up and expose the one thing he had buried deeper than anything else in his disgraceful life. To drag it out into the light so that he could see each detail and squeeze it until it gave up its hidden vapor of memory.

"I say it clear, I say it only this once, then I will be free, and you will be fed. But it might choke you:

"'Twas in a box like this, a room, a cell.

"Twenty years ago I ate an angel.

"I had arrived on the island of Chergui off the coast of Ifrīqiyyah, in a deep and stupid state of intoxication. I had been bewildered by alcohol and sanctified by opium. The island was no more than a hump of sand in the warm sea, only a few feet above the water, which was mostly calm. I say all this only to summon the place into my heart. To find the exact hurt, wanting to taste it again.

"It was a desolate place. A simple place. Hot and dry as a bone, with just enough water to drink, and chickens and octopuses to eat. Nothing much grew there except palms and saltbushes. A perfect place to hide, nobody ever went there. Of course, there was a church hole—a convent, tiny and run by a species of women without moisture, grace, or *hope. There is a level below all humanity where those cursed with being human always find themselves. I was there with them. Barefoot. Stepping off the painted boat into the warm sea and onto the warm sand.*

"The convent was the only place to stay, and surprisingly, I was allowed in for just one night. But that was enough to damn my soul forever.

"They used clay pots, rough terra-cotta vases, to catch octopuses on that island. Passive fishing, it was. They sank the vases in the sea, offering the creatures a home . . . sometimes with bait. Octopuses like enclosed spaces, away from the tides of the worlds.

"But on that fateful night, a great gibleh was coming out of the desert, heated into the speed that sucks out the madness of men. There were two unused cells in the convent. One was given to me; the other I was not allowed to see. While I was sleeping and the wind was at its highest, the nuns removed the straw roof of the other room and lit tapers of exquisite perfume: agarbatti of the Atharva Veda. I was near naked and unwashed, and it was in my dreams that I realized I was the bait. I awoke when the nuns started singing. I have never said these words before, and I will never say or hear them again:

"Forever will I tether thee, forever.
Tides tides o' moon
scythe thy ocean wide
hither to this clay chest
thy feast shall abide.

"Forever will I tether thee, forever.
Taste taste o' sun
with this song divide
thy heart's breath
in my mouth abide.
Forever will I tether thee, forever.

"Thus the angel was called, battered and damaged, into the clay-lined room. I broke open the door to the sounds of thrashing wings and the guttural cries of the violent nuns. What I saw in that room, I will

never forget: *The creature was gushing ink, blue-black ink, against the dry walls. The three nuns were soaked in it. The entire room was splattered and blurred with ink and smoke, and then blood as I ripped the wicked women away from their crime. At the center of the wings and ink was a white mist, squid-soft and helpless. I stopped the nuns' defilement of the unknown creature. I broke one over my knee and strangled another. The third one died when I beat her ugly head to mush against the ocher walls.*

"When I awoke from my fatigue, I took stock of what was around me. The limp white body of the angel had been ripped from the wings, which had become shadows, ink splatters and nuns' garments slashed and torn about the red-clay room. I carried the bodily remnant of the angel out of that squalor and laid it on a table. It was beyond repair . . . and so I ate it, raw, to relieve it and my hunger. The sweetness of that puttylike flesh I will never forget. I have never found anything like it. I have tried many women, but they are bland. I would give everything to obtain it again. Everything else is numb on my tongue."

TERRA FIRMA

The way down from the mountain passed through a well-maintained, working forest. The air was laden with the smell of sap and wood, and the sounds of saws and voices told the party that they were nearing their destination. They followed the track that turned into a logging road and could see the city wall below them. The men made their way toward the second city gate where fewer caballistas were assembled or loitering. There was no love lost between the military police and parties of traveling armed men. Follett, Pearlbinder, and Alvarez had had conflicts with the caballistas in the past; if they were recognized, it would be perilous to their mission. Their departure from the wilderness into civilization had not been authorized. Follett had been told in advance that this undertaking had nothing to do with the powers that ruled this land. It was none of the Caballista's business. The cargo was beyond explanation. So they hid their arms out of sight but kept them within easy reach. Follett's spear was camouflaged as a staff with a dead rabbit tied to its shaft.

The morning was bright; only a few patches of snow remained

at the corners of the buildings and the roads. As the mercenaries approached the two-story gatehouse, they could hear the hubbub of the festivities deeper in the town. The celebrations increased in pitch and volume, climaxing with a mock joust between the two teams of Carnival and Lent. The gatehouse was almost empty. All the populace were crowded into the city square, waiting for the ritual to begin.

Follett led the horsemen as they slowly approached the gate. In single file they rode: Tarrant behind their captain, Alvarez with the prize, and Pearlbinder guarding the rear. They lowered their eyes and slumped in their saddles as they passed through. Even Pearlbinder managed to shrink an inch or so, but he had refused to change his turban for the ratty headwear that the others sported.

Two guards were talking inside the gate, three more lingered around the apron of the town, while another pissed against a wall. Follett had cleared the gate unnoticed, and Tarrant was just behind him. Alvarez was midway through when the Oracle let out a long, loud *"Cooee,"* as if to announce its arrival. The sound bellowed in the archway, and all the guards turned toward its strangeness, one with his cock still in his hand. None of them looked ready to fight, blinking through their sickening hangovers.

But they did cease talking and started to be interested or annoyed. The Oracle's voice had stopped, but the unearthly pitch of the call continued to resound in the arch and in the guard's memories, where it tried to find a dovetail or recess of understanding— somewhere to fit. Since the sound was strange and unknown, it roamed about uncomfortably, generating disquiet, irritation, and fear. Pearlbinder quickly brought his mount up alongside Alvarez. A guard stepped in front of Follett, holding up his hand to stop his entrance. Two guards behind him drew their swords.

A ten-minute walk from the gate, through the maze of compacted homes and shops, in the main square, the ritual was about to begin. Meg's husband, Cluvmux, in the role of Carnival, was perched and slithering on his great hogshead barrel, which was being pushed on a heavy sledge of ancient wood. He was coming adrift before the first joust sounded. Cluvmux balanced a pie on his head and rested a lance—actually the iron spit taken from the rotary roasting frame, its cooked meats still attached and dripping—across his prodigious stomach. A tightly corseted shabby green jerkin tried to constrain the bulge of his belly, but it was held together more by stains than by the thin, breaking laces. Carnival's squire, the Dutch Ovenor, halted his topple by pushing his knight upright on the barrel without ever losing the rhythm of his fart-wanking instrument, which he worked furiously with the grave solemnity of a dedicated virtuoso. Wisely, Ovenor had tied a string through his device, so that it hung about his neck, allowing him to play one-handed, if necessary.

The opposing team, Lent, was on the other side of the square. Their squat red wagon, ready to grumble forward on its crude hand-carved green wooden wheels, was pulled by a grim-faced couple, one dressed as a monk and the other as a grotesque woman. The bitter-faced Lent jouster sat on a high-backed chair, wearing the tattered costume of a threadbare nun. He barked ragged orders to his crew between biting his lip in concentration and balancing two stinking fish on the palm of a long wooden paddle that he used as a spear. His miter, worn to announce his dignity, was a hive of spluttering bees that had tuned themselves to match the ringing in his ears. He pointed his spear at his adversary and yelled, *"Charge!"*

High in his saddle at the rear, Pearlbinder saw what was going to happen next, so he put the reins between his teeth and his hands on the hilts of the two scimitars scabbarded close to his horse's flanks.

"What have you got there, stranger, that makes such an ungodly call?" asked the closest guard.

He had been making his way toward Alvarez while asking the question, but he suddenly confronted Pearlbinder, who had moved forward and blocked his path.

"You all together here?" the guard asked, looking around to mark the other's position in the potential fray.

"Hey, shit-bonnet, stand aside, let me see what your dark-skinned sister is hiding there," the guard barked. A mail-clad hand grabbed Tarrant's saddlebag, causing his horse to flinch and neigh. The Oracle joined in the cry, and the soldiers shrank and twisted sideways, but they didn't let go.

The distraction gave Follett enough time to unleash his lance, dig his spurs deep into his horse, and shout, "*Take them!*"

Pearlbinder needed no further encouragement after being called "shit-bonnet." The scimitars cleared their scabbards as he turned his horse, spinning heavily to increase the ferocity of the curved blades' slashing sideways and outward.

Follett lowered his lance, shook off its disguise, and charged into the tight group of three men. Tarrant leaned down, thrusting his tomahawk into the guard who still held his saddlebag but who had turned his head away, toward Follett's screamed command.

The first vibration of the cart's wheels on the cobblestones sent one of the fish sliding off the paddle end of Lent's spear. The gormless youth, who was supposed to wave the flag marking the beginning of the battle, woke up and brandished his banner with great vigor. Both the cart and the barrel were suddenly pushed and pulled into action, their sluggish momentum charging headlong into each other's attack. They bumped and creaked forward with the urgency of a crippled tortoise. The yellow-clad candlemaker, Ingisfort Pleumps, provided most of the movement on Carnival's side; the tin cups he held clattered like dull bells with every shove from his strong, dim body. On the Lent side, the pull was taken up by Mewdriss van Keulen's idiot brother, his nun's costume sweatily chaffing and his breath huffing as he tugged the complaining wagon into the fray.

The nun's paddle slapped into the pig's head and the dangling sausage that decorated Cluvmux's spit. The impact sent the remaining balanced fish flying through the air into a pusher's grinning face, where it burst, splattering its yellow and gray guts everywhere. The first applause erupted from the crowd and found its way back to the gatehouse just as—

———

Pearlbinder's blade sliced horizontally through the face and head of the guard who had called him a shit-bonnet, just as he would have cut off the top of a soft-boiled egg. The reversed bowls of the guard's eyes, forehead, and hair flew backward, exposing a perfect cross section in stunningly clear anatomical detail, before it seethed into a pulsing, open wound. The man fell to his knees, already dead. In their panic to get out of the way of Follett's charging mare, two caballistas collided, muddling themselves. One lifted his sword above his head as if to fend off any harm, which gave Follett the target of a lifetime. He kicked the horse harder and brought the tip of his lance down into the guard's armpit and ribs. It plunged through his screaming body and continued to nuzzle deep into the bowels of the second man. He had skewered both on one lance with one joust, a legendary achievement for a cavalryman, akin to an archer splitting the first bull's-eye arrow with his second shot. The fierce charge continued, pushing its victims like skipping, spilling puppets.

The Lent nun bellowed a curse louder than all the onlookers in the square, making his unshaven, emaciated face even more grotesque, and shaking his beehive miter sideways, spilling a vanguard of irritated bees into the crowd. His pushers had fallen out of the way the moment the lip of the wagon dug into their raw heels, but seeing their master's anxiety, they picked themselves up, waving their arms to shoo off the enraged insects. The sledge, beer barrel, and wagon finally collided.

Cluvmux and his adversary looked surprised, and vaguely sober, just before they started to poke at each other with their long, unwieldy weapons. The most dangerous sequences they performed were verbal. Almost face-to-face, they swore blue and purple while trying to unseat each other, sending the disgruntled bees far away to escape the offensive language.

———

The Oracle was buzzing inside the protection of his box while all around were covered in blood, even Alvarez, who had never drawn a weapon while taking care of the Blessing, was soaked from the spouting artery in the guard's neck. The wound had been inflicted by Tarrant's lightning-fast tomahawk, just before he hacked the man's hand away from its fingers that still stupidly gripped his saddlebag. Alvarez guided his horse between Pearlbinder's slashing blows and the devastating pecks of Tarrant's ax.

Follett had finished the third guard by stabbing him through the eye as he gawped at his dancing comrades. The caballistas now lay dead or dying, one still with his cock in his hand, as the riders cleared the arched portal and were inside the city's walls.

The mock battle had finished in the square and a great applause arose, close enough for Follett and his men to share. Follett stopped and turned to face his men, sitting proud on his charger, grinning, his lance upright and scarlet, pointing at the blue sky. The two punctured men were sitting on the steaming red grass; holding each other, rocking gently like children praying for sleep to come soon.

Follett's men were enraptured with blood and success; they had almost completed their mission, and this last little skirmish had heightened their purpose after all the time spent in the wilderness of snow. They steadied themselves as the bells of the great monastery sounded above the boisterous rabble, telling them which way to go to triumphantly receive their reward.

Cluvmux lay giggling in a waste of food. He did not know if he had won or lost. Neither did anybody else. They had performed the ritual, and now they were running out of time for drinking and sucking on all the pleasures of Carnival before the austerity of Lent closed its strict gates. He got up, forgetting to look for Meg before he found his fellow revelers.

GHOST

They were skirting around the road that led directly from the gate into the bustling town when Tarrant fell off his horse. Follett had been talking about how to divide the bounty they would receive when they delivered the Oracle, and how it would be best done quickly, although they might have to stay for a week or so inside the monastery. The men had been riding single file, keeping their attention individually locked, while allowing their voices to travel along the plodding line. Tarrant had been speaking the most, wondering about the monks' possession of their prize.

"What will be their purpose?" he continually asked.

Follett was becoming annoyed. The sudden joy of a perfect conflict was being tarnished by this conversation. There was no point to it. They were completing their task, coming to its conclusion, and now that they had lost half their party, the spoils had doubled. The calculation of the exact amount he would pay each man kept changing as he tasted the possibility of keeping it all. He had already decided that even if the Calcas came back, they would get nothing. He was rehearsing telling them that they had broken the contract by going about their own business rather than following orders. Pearlbinder, Tarrant, and Alvarez would back him. He could deal with them later.

Tarrant's words were having the greatest effect on Alvarez. He had spent the most time with the Oracle, and, even though it still made his flesh creep, a bond had grown between them. He was beginning to agree with Tarrant's doubt and to think that maybe they should wait and discuss the matter before handing over the prize.

"Maybe we should make camp now and have one last Scry before meeting these wretched monks?"

Pearlbinder turned in his saddle to look into Alvarez's face, while Follett took a deep, enraged breath.

"We are not making camp, and we cannot make another Scry. We have just slaughtered a clutch of caballistas, which will stir up a hornet's nest. It will soon be Lent. We need to be inside the monastery now."

His word was law. No one spoke until Tarrant hit the ground.

Pearlbinder was off his horse first, crouching beneath it, using its thick body like a shield, looking in all directions for archers or crossbowmen or anyone who might be responsible for unseating a fellow rider. When no arrows flew, he came out and joined Follett, who was standing over Tarrant's body.

"He's dead," he said in total disbelief.

Pearlbinder knelt to watch Follett touch the fallen man's face and lift his stiff arm. He froze for a moment, and then pulled his hands away, wiping them with disgusted confusion on his tunic sleeves.

"He's stone-cold, like he's been dead for days."

The others shivered.

"How is this possible?" asked Follett.

Pearlbinder answered cautiously, "Because all of him was never really here. There was a distance in this man, as if he lived elsewhere while riding with us."

"You mean he was a ghost?" asked Follett.

"He had a likeness to Scriven," said Alvarez.

Then Tarrant's voice said, "Verily, he was the wisest of us all."

Pearlbinder swung around, dagger in hand, to find the origin of the voice, which was not coming from the corpse at his feet. He looked up at Alvarez.

"Alas," said Tarrant's voice again.

Pearlbinder and Follett lowered their eyes from the terrified Alvarez to the crate slung on his mount's side. A great terror overcame the party, each man frozen to the spot, waiting for the hideous voice to speak again. With a shuddering moan, Alvarez pushed himself from the horse, slithering backward so as not to touch the "prize."

"It has stolen Tarrant's soul," he warbled as he scurried away from his horse.

"No, I think it's just copying him," said Follett, who wanted nothing to do with any unforeseen manifestations so close to the completion of his quest.

Alvarez shook his head. He was having none of it.

"It's just another of its voices," placated Follett.

Meanwhile Pearlbinder was examining the dead man, turning him this way and that, roughly undoing his tunic and breeches. He finally exhaled, taking his hands away in a theatrical gesture of disgust.

"There's not a mark on him, not a single wound."

Follett looked at what was left of the crew and gathered the remnant under command.

"Leave him by the roadside, we have work to finish here. The conclusion is in sight and our reward awaiteth. Alvarez, make haste with thine horse. *Now!*"

Then the Oracle spoke again in the unmistakable voice of Alvarez: "Forever will I tether thee, forever I, will I tether thee, forever I, forever will I tether thee."

The sound in the box changed into a small crackling noise, like dry leaves under an empty wardrobe; it was the sound of human laughter, but physical, nonverbal, without emotion. Alvarez had regained his feet and was walking away backward, his eyes locked on the box.

"Alvarez, I said *now*!" shouted Follett. "You have come all this way, don't give up now."

Alvarez just shook his head.

"It's an order."

"I cannot, Captain. This is wrong."

Realizing that his command over this man had vanished, Follett tried another tack. "But your share is now a third."

"This is wrong; there is a taint of evil here. I don't want the money; it stinks of witchcraft. I was never here."

The now-insensible nature of their conversation was interrupted by Pearlbinder, who mounted and then grabbed the reins of Alvarez's horse, leading it out of the discussion. Alvarez strode quickly away without looking back, leaving everything he owned behind him.

THE LAST STORY

Dominic and his master were exhausted, out of breath and foot-weary, but they had made good time and were keen to be inside the confines of their home. They had taken side streets to avoid the great flock of masked revelers who were booming in the central square. The narrow alleyway they were in led into the smaller square that housed the monastery's eastern gates, but they were going against the flow of excited and drunk people. It was not easy to push through because three horses and two riders were plodding ahead of them, slowing the pace and dividing the irascible crowd. People were swearing at the riders until they noticed how heavily armed they were. With a great sense of relief, the crowd opened into the square. On its far side, Dominic, who was two heads taller than his master, could see that the gates of the monastery were open, giving entrance to a cartload of supplies.

"We made it, Master!"

"Yes, but I hope it's not too late."

Their view of the gate was suddenly blocked by two men on horseback and a riderless horse who stopped in the middle of the square. Benedict hobbled faster now that his task was almost complete. He was within ten paces of the riders when Dominic's voice yelled at him from the box attached to the vacant horse. He stopped dead, and his young companion collided with him, eyes wide and hair standing on end.

"I have occurred. Save me," it sang.

At the same moment, another voice echoed the words deep in the monastery's interior. Screaming them into the circular stone stairwell that rose up to the abbot's door.

"This will be our last Scry," said a commanding voice from inside the Oracle's crate. Its force made the crate splinter across the body of the horse that carried it.

Pearlbinder turned to see the wood warp and the chamois leather and silk peel apart, exposing its occupant's gray, naked flesh. Then it twisted and slid down the horse's side to flop and groan on the hard cobbles below. Bits of silk stuck to its irregular body. The spooked animal shat as it pranced sideways, leaving its naked passenger in the steaming, rich odor of digested hay.

Follett barked at Pearlbinder, who still held the reins of the startled beast, "For God's sake, don't let it trample the thing."

Abbot Clementine was running down the stone spiral, a bag of gold coins clutched tight to his chest.

"Come hither, ye cunts, and read the outcome of thy days."

"That is Scriven's voice," shouted Pearlbinder, his own horse now trying to make harsh backward turns against the pulling of the other animal.

The Oracle had never spoken so clearly. It was as if the stolen voices had given it a sense of the world in which they lived, had nailed it down into the awareness of the now and to whom it spoke.

Benedict was making the sign of the cross as he neared it, not caring about the panicked animals and their owners' obvious savagery. Dominic remained bolted to where he had stopped, his hand over his mouth for fear his voice would be stolen again.

The angry riders were becoming more agitated, unhinged. There was a great shift in their understanding, as if in direct proportion to the clarity of the rantings from the shit-covered flesh beneath them.

One word stuck in Follett's craw like a kernel of ironstone.

"Read," it said.

The Oracle smelled the distemper the word raised in the captain's confusion and said it again, louder.

"Read thy story, the workings of thy minds, the twisted journey, the crimes, and the demise. Read it all forever. That is my gift to thee. A picture of your cunt lives, read by all. And every word you ever spoke, *for all to read.*"

Follett's lance was in his hand and spinning over his mount, the scabbard thrown aside. His mouth worked in silent rage and the color drained from his face, except for his red eyes, which were locked on the Oracle.

"*No, Captain, not now,* we are here, *it is done,*" said Pearlbinder, letting go of the reins of Tarrant's horse and urging his mount forward to block the attack and shield the Oracle. He reached out to stop the lancer's practiced gesture, while his other hand automatically retrieved his scimitar. The sun reflecting on its polished steel cast a glare into Follett's charging wrath.

The Oracle pumped itself up into the conflict, a perfect target, chirping, singing like a demented mynah bird in the shrill alternating voices of Scriven and Follett.

"*It will all be.*

"*Read read read read read read!*"

MAGNITUDE

Alvarez was numb and relieved as he followed the trail of noise that splattered into the center of the drunken town. He stopped at the first inn and drank a flagon of ale without pausing to look at the raucous mob around him. He considered the great loss of recompense for only a moment, before the next flagon rinsed his concern away. Two inns later, the taste of the Oracle's voice had washed away and he was ready for anything.

Follett was a good man and they had traveled together much over the years. Maybe he would keep part of the bounty for him. Maybe they would share it in taverns and on the road again. The thought made Alvarez grin and raise the mug in a concealed salute to himself.

As he lowered the mug, he saw a man laughing at him from the corner of the shabby room. It was another stinking caballista. This one was older than those he had witnessed being dispatched earlier. For some reason, the man was staring at him and then he began imitating Alvarez's quiet salute, complete with whispered toasts and muttered oaths. This drunk was taking the piss out of *his* drunkenness, and that triggered a rage in Alvarez that was totally out of proportion to the guard's oafish jesting. It was a great spite for the Oracle and what it knew about him. An unspent violence seething. It was also the wrath he had swallowed to give that disgusting, evil thing safe passage. Halted adrenaline sheathed and now infused with his lifetime contempt for all police and for the caballistas. The fury he had not shared with his comrades at the gatehouse curdled his expression and vibrated the air around him. The caballista mimicked this last face, then donned his helmet, emblazoned with a wreath of metal laurel leaves, and swaggered out the door. He stepped out into the bright sunlight and took a deep breath of the warm, fragrant air, sucking the glory of the world into the glory of his pride.

Alvarez was out of his seat with a speed that was surprising for one so awash with ale. He knew no one was near enough to stop him or take this cunt's side. He rushed outside and, with all the force he possessed, drove his dagger hard into the guard's lower back at an angle that ripped through his liver and worried the point up toward the bottom of his lungs.

Alvarez walked around to the face the guard and stood, sword and dagger in hand, making a comic impersonation of the man's agonized face as his victim fell to his knees. Still wearing the mimicry, he raised his sword in a decapitating curve, but the sun caught the metal leaves of the helmet, and it seemed far too pure and desirable to be splattered in gore. Alvarez stepped sideways and raised the sword vertically, bringing it down parallel to the guard's neck and through the gap in his collarbones, into the open top of his rib cage and straight down into his unprotected heart. The wound obediently closed, and the man bled to death without a drop marring the trophy, which Alvarez quickly retrieved. He knew he would look magnificent in the helmet, and any fortunate female who happened to see him would be overwhelmed by his grandeur.

The volume of the stink of Carnival aroused every Filthling within three leagues of Das Kagel. Even some creatures from the eastern side lifted their orifices out of smoke and torment to savor the distant breeze. The meeker Woebegots, which hid in the villages and farmlands, cautiously made their way along the riverbanks toward the city square. Some crawled in the hedgerows and woods, being careful to avoid both vindictive foxes and intolerant hermits. Some came up from the cellars and silos to discover why the Great Ones had become so loud in their odor. The long-winded plays and the short-breathed drinkers competed in their praise for and denigration of the street musicians who cursed the air with brass and strings. In so much confusion and noise, another band of mismatched grotesques marched unseen with their weapons and ragged skirts through the throngs of revelers.

Meg had pushed a tight metal bowl onto her oddly shaped skull, and its dull pewter glint reflected in the metal breastplate that was three sizes too big but which gave hollow space and protection to her ponderous, sagging paps. Her army of outraged wives was more traditionally dressed in long skirts and aprons. They had obtained all manner of weapons in their passage, having fleeced and knuckled the weaker men they crossed; their passion and their purpose engulfed them.

The bleary, shuttered metal visor that Alvarez was now wearing softened and compromised his focus, his desire, and reality itself. Drunk and adrenalized, he saw these women as active and wholesome. He saw only their curves and force, so he lurched toward them, waving his long black sword. He met Meg at the foot of the bridge. She was one of the tallest women he had ever seen. From her large flat feet to the beak of her raw, red nose, she was pure Lowlander, and an exotic urge filled Alvarez's senses. He had never had such a long woman as this towering vision. Now was the moment for a bit of the strange: a lick of the abnormal, a different sweetness.

"How now, longshanks, wither thou goest in search of a man?"

Meg stopped midstride in total disbelief.

"Thou looks like a mare who might match my magnitude."

She was just about to spit out her answer when she saw the

green metal laurel on his helmet and instantly remembered the loudmouth who had taken her son and refused any mercy to either of them.

Alvarez swaggered forward and looked up at the swaying giant. He rested the point of his sword in the ground and placed his other hand on her thigh. Such a length of bone! She smiled without opening her mouth and leaned down toward him. He took his hand off her leg and started to undo the strap of the helmet; he wanted it off, ready to receive her stooping kiss. In his rapid fumbling, he did not see her hand dive to the top of her boot and retrieve her prized gutting knife. The helmet came off to a great shout of applause from the women, who were gathering around to watch, or maybe to join in.

A great warmth overwhelmed him, and all the colors of the world swam, splashed, and paddled before his bulging eyes.

BLE//ING

Abbot Clementine was at the gate with Friar Cecil, whom he had demanded go fetch a blanket. The abbot had been horrified by what was occurring on their doorstep and by the dreadful jeopardy the Blessing had been put in, but he was even more horrified by the apparition now walking toward him. The new Oracle, the one alleged to have the greatest powers, was being carried in the arms of the last person in the world he ever wanted it to meet.

Brother Benedict had snatched the Blessing from under the hooves of the maddened horses and the pumping blood of the madmen. He approached the monastery with the Oracle clasped tight to his bosom, like a child, and both were singing in a quiet unified hum that had no words. Clementine stood speechless in the gateway, with no idea of what had just occurred. All his arrangements had worked perfectly until this last moment, when, for no apparent reason, the mercenaries who had brought the Oracle so far turned and butchered one another within a few feet of the journey's conclusion and the abbey's doors. The sack holding their money hung limp in Clementine's hand. Dominic followed his master and the prize, striding into the Monastery of the Eastern Gate. Neither of them looked at, or acknowledged, the man who had been its abbot.

Some of the brothers even applauded, and Benedict held back a smile, conscious of the sin of pride and the sin of triumphant wrath, which followed in his wake and nearly drowned the Father Superior. But mainly he didn't smile because his mouth couldn't do it.

Benedict took the Blessing to the warm kitchen, the place farthest from the abbot's dwellings. There he, Dominic, and Friar Ludo washed the filth of the horse and the cobbles and the blood of the savage horsemen off its peculiar body. Then they wrapped it in soft linen and placed it in a basket in a quiet cell; Benedict alone held the cell's key. Then both travelers bathed and slept, leaving strict instructions to be awakened immediately if there were any "difficulties."

The next morning they prepared the hole in the wall and lined it with straw. A quantity of stone, plaster, and lime stood nearby. Dominic, sleeves rolled up, was ready to help the mason. Benedict pulled him away and told him to inform the abbot, who had been conspicuously absent, that in an hour's time they would be ready for the ceremony of internment.

Dominic returned looking puzzled.

"The abbot said to do nothing until he arrives."

Benedict shook his head and snarled. It was raining outside, so they placed the Oracle into a comfortably lined and lidded wicker basket. Dominic was given the honor of carrying it out to the hole in the cloister wall, which he did with great solemnity. Five monks were already there, chanting softly.

The basket shuddered in Dominic's firm grip as the Oracle started to speak, repeating the same two words over and over again: "Sing *cano* sing *cano* sing *cano* sing . . ."

Dominic looked at his master.

"It's what you said: *cano*, sing. It is asking us to sing," he said.

And so they did, joining the incantation. The rain was falling gently through the bright sunlight, and far off to the south, a rainbow was forming over the sea. Everything had a clear and optimistic atmosphere until Abbot Clementine arrived with Friar Cecil. The abbot went straight to Dominic, seizing the basket from him with all his might. Benedict stepped forward and was quickly blocked by Friar Cecil.

The abbot turned away from the congregation and the Cyst and walked swiftly back the way he had come.

Benedict hobbled after him, shouting, "Where are you taking the Blessing? All is prepared for its entombment in the wall."

The abbot faltered and shouted back, "I must examine it and perform certain rituals before it enters the Cyst."

"What rituals?" demanded Benedict.

"None of your business; you would not understand," snarled the Abbot.

"The Orphic Separation?"

The old monk's quietly spoken words made the abbot falter and seethe. "You know nothing of such things. I command you to stay away and to keep your tongue."

Abbot Clementine gripped the basket tighter and spun around to go through the door. Instantly a shrill, warbling cry corkscrewed out and was answered by another somewhere inside the monastery; the pitch made Clementine shudder. The Oracle then nudged hard at the wickerwork lid, pushing it up into the abbot's face, where it scratched the underside of his nose and drew blood.

The basket started to fall away and the creature squirmed as if in anticipation of escape, but Clementine's strong hands grabbed it ferociously, without any sign of care or compassion. He held the Oracle at arm's length and refused to look into its squawking, spitting eyes. He kicked the fallen basket aside and walked stiffly into the building. The Oracle tried to squirm out of the abbot's large, powerful hands, but it did not have the strength. It suddenly went limp in the painful vicelike hold, shrinking into inertia as its captor charged through the cloister and entered the corridor leading to his spiral stair, with Benedict calling out and Dominic and Ludo in pursuit.

"You must stop this. It is a sacrilege and a mortal sin."

Abbot Clementine said nothing, his voice locked behind clenched teeth. He was breathing harshly, and his muscles had knotted like those of a man in battle. He was implacable, ruthless, and strong. He spun into the tower and took the first three steps of the spiral stair, almost running.

A screaming, hissing growl occupied the tower, its unearthly resonance amplified by the sympathetic acoustics. Clementine stopped with a lurch, his eyes wide, staring at where the steps above him disappeared into the spiral's curve. There on the uppermost step was the mongoose Filthling, but it was not the impudent and mischievous creature he had met before. It had grown to twice its previous size, its back was arched, and its eyes were crimson. Its wide-open mouth—the maw that spat the hissing scream—was jeweled with long, fanglike incisors and rows of dagger teeth. The fingers of the yellow humanlike hands had peeled back to reveal curved black talons, razor claws.

This was neither the jovial nor the eerie prankster that had shouted here before. This creature was ferocious and fearless, a killer of cobras. Its hatred for the man shone through every inch of its bristling body. Clementine knew all this instantly: it was a sixth of his size, but without weapons or protective armor, he was no match for the speed and absolute determination of its impending attack. Its vicious, unblinking eyes were focused on his face and throat. There was only one thing to do.

Slowly and with great care, he held the Oracle up between himself and the predator and retreated, walking backward down the tight curve.

The three outraged monks were waiting at the base of the tower, blocking his retreat into the rest of the abbey. On the last step, he turned to face them, not wanting to look up and see if that creature had followed him.

"Give the Blessing to me," demanded Benedict, and the moment the words were in the air, the Oracle started to come out of its torpor.

With tears in his eyes, the abbot shook the Oracle in the old monk's face. "I need to have time alone with this—a few days, a week at the most."

The anger of defeat possessed the man, and all who saw it knew it would lead to a dangerous and violent conclusion.

"That's all I will take," he said, and it no longer sounded like an explanation or a plea.

Then the Oracle sang a weak tune: *"But you already have it. What you have been seeking awaits you."*

Sudden knocking came from the door behind the abbot, the door he had made that led to the fields of the Gland. Everybody trembled. The knocking came again. They could hear Dominic's teeth chattering.

Ludo said, "Something is trying to get in."

"No, it isn't," said Benedict.

"It is the Quiet Testiyont. He has been guarding it for you. Your achievement awaits for eternity," pronounced the Oracle as the knocking increased.

"The Quiet told me that you would bring the gift and that my fortitude would be so rewarded," said the abbot, his voice elated.

He then gave the Oracle up to Benedict's gnarled hands and, looking him straight in the eyes, asked, "It is achieved?"

The old man crossed himself and gently replied, "Yes, my son."

The next knock broke the spell, and Abbot Clementine fumbled about his neck, pulling out a key on a long cord. He rushed to the door, undid its lock, and, opening the door, fell laughing into the dismal field beyond.

The monks tried to look out, but the door slammed in their faces, its lock turning like breaking teeth.

"You know your next task?" questioned the Oracle, and Benedict nodded and gave the bruised fragile body to Friar Ludo.

"Soothe the Blessing so that it may be taken to its new home."

Friar Ludo took his precious cargo and hurried back the way he had come. Benedict made his way to the nearest stone bench in the cloister. The sun was casting even shadows between the low arches.

"I am getting too old for so much work. Will you help me?" He reached out and patted his acolyte's hand.

"Yes, of course, Master."

The old monk had never spoken to him like this before, and Dominic felt the change deep in his heart.

"Please give my respects to Friar Cecil, the abbey's mason, and the blacksmith, and ask them to come to me. We must seal this door and the iron gate. I will be in the library; I have so much work to do."

With caution, Dominic asked, "What work, Master?"

"I . . . I have to find the correct words to ask Rome and Toledo for a new edict about the Glandula Misericordia. I have to find the perfect reason and the perfect words to ask that entrance to the Gland be forbidden and that it remains sealed forever—without arousing inquiry, doubt, or suspicion."

They sat in the warm silence for a long time.

Then the old man said, "I know you have many questions, but I must ask you to forget all that happened today and never to speak of it again. Abbot Clementine achieved his wicked ambition, and if that were known outside these walls, the consequences would be catastrophic."

"Are we sealing the gates so that he does not come back?"

"No, my son, we are closing that horrifying place so that no one will ever see or find him in there."

"But I saw him in there many years ago."

"You have seen many things, Dominic. I believe you are blessed with extra sight. But you did not see the abbot as he is now, and I hope in God's name that no one ever will."

He looked at the puzzled boy and put a hand on his shoulder.

"I can't even imagine what such a tortured soul would look like: A living man set amid that active vision and the enactment of carnage and terror for eternity. In there alone now, without the wraith of the sacred Testiyont that he so sinfully buried secretly in those grounds. He cannot join in with the slaughter and the perpetual rage. He cannot transform into some other being. Nothing in there can see him, but he has to watch, taste, and hear it all forever. He will not even be allowed boredom, because each new day it will begin again as if he had never been there before. He received exactly what he asked for. I can't imagine what he looks like now, let alone in a million years' time, and neither should you."

Unexpectedly, the old man half chortled, "Even Jerome of Bosch could not picture that."

THE LAST WONDER

Meg and her followers crossed the bridge, marching through Alvarez's blood and leaving scuffed trails in the process. When the women finally reached the bastion of the Caballistas del Camino, three rows of pikemen blocked the little army's way. Cavalrymen flanked them, their horses steaming and pawing the ground, anxious for battle after months of boredom and sour oats.

Meg stopped when she smelled their sobriety, a rare, almost exotic scent in these lands. She knew what it meant and that the outcome was totally predictable. She had been marching forward when it cut the air and made her stop. The women behind her slowed to see what happened. Meg raised the long black sword she had taken from Alvarez and held it sideways to make a gate beyond which nobody should pass, holding her withering ground. The ranks of pikemen parted to let a horseman and a guard come through to parlay.

"What do thee want, gentle Mother, on this unkind day so close to Lent?"

His voice was of a primness she had never heard before, and it made her shrink in her long-worn-out boots. She gathered the tatters of her own voice and tried to push it out, but the rectitude of this new force shredded her courage. She faltered and murmured about stolen goods, the brutality of the Camino, and the disappearance of her son. The officer spoke down to his guard, who scurried off as the officer sat back in his high, upright saddle.

"Very well. I hear your complaint."

The women behind her were all talking, a muddy lumpen murmur arising. It was hushed by three men who pushed a handcart from their barracks through the ranks of pikemen and set it before them. The cart contained a pile of items stolen from their homes and farms, mainly poorer-quality tat that got shoveled up with the treasures.

"Take it and be gone," shouted the officer.

The women pushed forward behind Meg in a throng that had changed shape and purpose.

"But what of our sons and daughters? Where are they now? When will you bring them out?" begged Meg.

The officer's horse whinnied, also being a thoroughbred, and the officer laughed.

"There is no parlay for criminals and heretics. They are beyond your voice, woman. Be gone in the grace I give you."

Meg's eyes filled with burning tears and she lowered the black sword. The movement was seen by the women as a sign to come forth, and by the soldiers as a posture of battle. The officer was swallowed back into the ranks of men who now set their pikes at a different angle.

Meg was just about to speak again when the first three women pushed forward to investigate the cart of compromise. They grabbed dented vases and doglegged candlesticks. One recognized a chipped plaster angel and called back over Meg's head to her neighbor, who tottered forward to retrieve her beloved possession.

The three guards who had brought the cart stood back from the fray and grinned at one another. One turned and stared at Meg, calling out, "I knows you, don't I?"

She wavered for a moment, holding back her fury while she

tried to recognize this man. They all looked the same in their uniforms. She knew only the one who she had just triumphantly gutted by his rich green helmet. They were all the same. She had killed one. Why not another? As she raised the heavy sword, a sudden black light filled her eyes, blocking her view. An odd spinning moon of a thing with the guard's words bellowed behind it.

"Here, hag, have a bit of treesoor. It's worth more than the corpse of your stupid kid."

He had thrown a small black iron skillet that hit her full in the face. The soldier enjoyed the sight of the pan bouncing off her so much that he began to guffaw. It was the funniest thing he had seen all week, and it made him roll about in uncontrollable laughter.

Dazed and furious, Meg swung forward with the full weight of the long sword, dizzying the air before her, but her swing coincided with the guard grabbing his knees, and the whistling blade passed clean over his head. Meg saw what would happen next and tried to brake the arc of the steel, but her reflexes were not enough to stop it before it embedded into the back of Willeke Dijkstra's head.

"*Ooh!*" Willeke yelled, turning one of her short arms backward to rub at what seemed to be a minor blow and finding the cold thickness of the blade lodged in her skull. "Ooh . . ." she said, and lifted her other arm to trace the full length of the injury, tottering around to find Meg on the other end of the sword.

"Wat is dat, Meg?"

Meg had nothing to say; she only wanted the mistake to go away. Without thinking, she grabbed Willeke's head with one hand in a motion akin to lifting a frozen turnip but being surprised by its lopsided weight. With her other hand still gripping the hilt of the sword, she began levering the blade out of the tight wound in a series of back-and-forth agitations. Meg was now crying in full and apologizing to her dear friend while trying to soothe the malicious injury. The guard and his two comrades were on their knees in hysterics. Everyone else seemed blissfully unaware of the predicament until the blade snicked out, taking a sliver of bone and a bright spurt of blood with it. Meg snatched a small china vase from the cart and quickly put it in Willeke's hand, pushing the lip of the vase to the lip of the wound in a grotesque kiss.

Meg put her arms around her confused friend. "Quick now, go home," she said, pointing away from the bubbling hoard. "Hold it tight and go home."

Willeke nodded and moved away without knowing exactly what had happened. The truth was that she had been thinking about claiming the vase for herself before Meg's rude actions overtook all. It was the delicate blue pattern against the bright white shine of the china that had so taken her: A filigree motif of leaves and flowers framed a tiny scene of rural farmlands, and a windmill stood boldly amid the bushy trees and flying clouds, so delicately set in motion by the small flocks of birds gracing the distant sky. A river or a pond in the foreground captured the reflection of the windmill and trees with great authority. Willeke could not see it now, held in such an odd position, but she hoped she might keep the pretty thing when she finally reached home and the terrible pain in her head stopped.

Unfortunately, the spurt of blood had hit one of the laughing soldiers mid-tunic, and he assumed he had been stabbed, so he pulled his sword and waved it above his head. This was the real sign that a battle had begun. The pikes were lowered to a horizontal position, and the ranks walked forward: inevitable, mechanical, and ruthless.

Meg saw the bristling wave approaching and screamed at the top of her lungs. Most of the women understood and ran, clutching all manner of worthless and broken goods to their once-kind, ample, and fast-beating hearts. A few of the duller ones dithered over the diminished contents of the cart. Meg screamed again, and they turned to look about themselves, saw the marching horror, and ran.

Just before the humpbacked bridge, the women dispersed, some dropping the goods they had deemed so worthy. Meg picked up a stained sack of cups and a smashed basket of dented plates and cutlery. They were the only tokens of her bold affray, and she decided there and then to keep them all. As she plodded across the bridge, she thought of her lost son and of her stupid husband, who would be telling her for days about the glories of his battle in the town square and exactly how long he had managed to stay upright on the fat barrel on its fat wheels. She did not know how many hours or days she would have to wait for the door to be kicked in, to be dragged out to face the justice of the caballistas. She considered running, but it was a waste of time. She had only her duties to hide behind; only drudgery to suffocate the horrors she imagined and the horrors that were inevitable. The swollen oafishness of the man she had once loved would be her only companion as she waited, and the thought of that made it worse.

She looked over the bridge into the sluggish water and envied all that lived in it. She would not cross this way again. One of the metal cups fell out of the basket and landed with the dull clatter of an impoverished bell. She could not even be bothered to pick it up. Maybe one of the imps that frequented this place could use it. The thought amused her, but none of the wondrous array of muscles that lived in her face could respond. Instead she wiped her bruised, dripping nose with the back of her hand, swallowed what was left of her pride with a great sniff of phlegmy remorse, and turned her head toward home.

As she did so, she felt something move beneath her hand. Something in the small, shabby sack of loot. She stopped and peered down the beak of her face to an equally pointed snout looking up at her from its hiding place.

"Gef," she said, and he grinned at her. The Filthling managed to free one of his tiny, yellow, almost-human hands from the tight mouth of the sack and waved at her. Instinctively her face ignited and she grinned back.

"'Tain't the end, Mother. 'Tain't the beginnings. We are in the middles."

His voice was pure and light.

"Mother Willeke will get better and forgive you. The guards will be too busy to remember you because the man you opened up on the bridge was not one of them. He was an impostor wearing a stolen hat. Your son still lives, and when we complete our business, I will bring him home to you. We can find our ways into and out of any man-made hollows; we have many shapes and sizes.

"Also soon your husband will die, but he will not sleep with the angels and will not haunt his house, which will be yours."

His grin was now even bigger.

"How do you know these things?"

"Because I am the Eighth Wonder of the world. Next time we cross the bridge, we will all be together."

"Together?"

"It will be the last days of my kind in these lands, and we'll join you and the other mothers to punish these cruel men for their cruel words and deeds."

Gef's words filled Meg with a great warmth, and their truth tasted of deliverance and honey. She took a full, involuntary breath of new air, and the hollow bell-like space inside her breastplate opened, giving enough room for the Eighth Wonder to swivel up and nestle in her bosom as she marched home.

RIM

"Didst thou understand why we had to come this way?" asked Pearlbinder as they walked the flinty road.

"No, but it must be where the payment lies, farther in that direction," Follett answered. He waved a vague hand before him.

"We must have been walking for hours now in this desolate way, and we have not seen a single living soul."

"Aye, but it's a well-trodden path. We hath done our duty like those who went before us . . . a prodigious line of men, all delivering similar creatures to that monastery."

"But what will they do with it?" asked Pearlbinder, stopping as his exasperation at the question seemed to flatten his lungs and render him breathless.

Follett also stopped and slowly turned his lance so he could lean on its verticality. "I don't know, but it must have led to this place in some way. We might be given a sense of it with our payment hither." His eyes narrowed as he stared at the road ahead.

The weather was different here. A mild heat haze made the hardness of the landscape shimmer into an unrealistic stream or a sluggish river. Beyond the tree-lined banks, the distant clamor had focused slightly; the men's stillness on the road allowed them to hear the edge of the noise. Both men listened, turning their ears toward its meaning, and then, as it continued, they recognized it as familiar: it sounded like a battle, far off and enormous.

They had to drag their heads away from the sound to sever their growing attachment and wordless understanding. Follett looked about himself, at the trees of linden and oak that fringed the road on both sides. He turned to look back whence they had come, and it was identical to the perspective of the path before them. No sign of gates, mountains, or walls—all had been swallowed in the curvature of the Earth. Follett allowed the weight of his lance to swing it into a horizontal position, and the momentum of the act jarred him forward. Pearlbinder followed the motion, and they started to walk again.

The sun was dropping, but the road and the trees remained the same; only the sky thickened, and the smell of fire became more tangible. They had been walking two hours or so when Follett had the sudden impression that they were not walking on a flat road at all but on the rim of a gigantic wheel—one that turned with their pace, giving the illusion of travel, while the trees held them in the channel of its circumference. He stopped again.

Was this the rotation of Earth, a constant bland orbit? He was just about to speak when Pearlbinder said, "Thou sees it?" and raised a weary arm to point ahead.

Follett had seen nothing and now found it difficult to focus his eyes on the distant horizon, the vanishing point, where a blur now stood.

"What is it?" he asked as Pearlbinder pulled out his brass telescope to answer the question.

Pearlbinder put the tube to his eye and allowed the compressed distance to swallow all sound.

"Well?" Follett asked, becoming anxious in his static seclusion from knowledge.

"It looks like . . . a sack . . . or a flag, planted in the middle of the way."

"It might be the point of no return."

Pearlbinder made a guttural sound and slowly closed his telescope.

"Whatever it is, I think it's moving"—Follett glared at his companion—"this way."

Its approach was broken and ragged. The movement of a thing uncertain, as though propelled by wayward breezes or purposeless uneven slopes in advance of its footfall. Or, more alarmingly, perhaps, it was traveling on a reverse rotation of the wheel. Follett was caught in the unease of that idea as the thing slowly wandered into focus. The rippling haze from the road eventually gave way to a recognizable profile.

"My God!" Follett exclaimed. "It's a horse."

"Was a horse," stated Pearlbinder as the staggering ghost of empty skin and rancid, scaffolded bones drifted into their presence.

Follett unsheathed the blade of his lance and seated the end of the shaft in a notch in the road, a standard defensive counter to a cavalry charge. Pearlbinder spat a gob of sound into the bristling air. The utterance was intended as laughter—a jest at the impropriety of what stood before them—but what emerged instead was instinctive: something between a scream and a sob. Because what was approaching on a trajectory of hopeless loss was the withered carcass of a once-huge horse, one that looked as though it had been dead and buried for months. All the flesh, all the muscle was gone from inside the teetering sack of bones. Great gashes in its dry hide let the wind pass through it and across the lips of its desiccated wounds, making a shrill whistle that emphasized the unnatural quiet of its hooves on the hard road. It stopped four spear lengths before them and lifted its long, hollow head, as if to acknowledge them; their dread doubled.

Pearlbinder blanched, his arms and his voice sinking to nothing, his eyes staring from his bloodless face.

"My God, it's Sophia," whispered Follett.

The physical apparition turned slightly, as if in recognition of its distant name. The stink from its blackened teeth and rotten joints was overwhelming, and both men wanted to run back to the towns, villages, and landscapes they knew, back into their previous existence. Back into life.

What had been Sophia moved forward, and both men shrank

back. Follett dropped his lance, which fell against the ridges of spine that pierced her scrawny haunches. Although not heavy, the lance dug solidly into the horse's hide and bone and shed pieces of skin onto the road. She slowly spun, the lance dangling alongside her plodding gait. Sophia shivered in the way that living horses do, but not with the adjusting tics of nervous tension. Her movements were sullen and disgusting, having no place in a body so bereft of vitality. She continued to walk away, turning her head to glance back at the spear that she dragged behind her and at the two men who did nothing to retrieve it.

The sound of the tip dragging against the flinty road traveled up the shaft and through the blade and snapped the lance into the empty ribbed interior. There it amplified, sounding like the clawing of fingernails on a blackboard in a deep, dry well.

Pearlbinder tried to vomit, but only dry membranes came forth. Follett covered his ears with trembling hands. This was the point of no return, and the great wheel started turning again in their direction. The lurch made them fall against each other before they were able to walk again, framed by the lindens and oaks that no longer efficiently filtered out the screams and the fire. Soon they would be passing into the vale of *The Triumph of Death*, and both automatically unsheathed their swords and daggers.

The soft organs of their bodies shrank inward, away from the contours of who they had once been. A sliver of space was left between the shell and the core, just enough for the memory of exactly where and when they had died to bloom and quickly fade.

A∫K NICELY

The day was dimming as Meg approached her house from the back field, not wanting anybody to see her come home in her armor, splattered with blood—not that bloodstained clothing was unusual for a butcher's wife. But mostly she did not want her neighbors to see her in conversation with the creature that darted and chattered at her side. She had stopped once after leaving the disastrous rout and told the Eighth Wonder of the World that he should now vacate the warmth of her bosom and keep out of sight elsewhere until they reached the fields. This he did reluctantly, which she found faintly touching. They stopped by the willow trees that fenced the boundaries of her back garden. She looked over toward the house that was obviously empty. The creature that called himself Gef scurried up the fence and struck a pose, ready to speak atop the gatepost.

"Can we all meet together here tomorrow?" he asked.

"You have grown. You are much bigger."

" 'Tis something I can do, Mistress."

"I have never seen anything like that."

"You have never seen anything like me. Sometimes some parts of me gets bigger than your husband's." He tilted his head in a rakish manner.

"That wouldn't be difficult," she riposted, and they both laughed.

"Anyways, as I said before, can we all meet together here tomorrow?"

"Who do you mean, all?"

"Me and my kind."

"No, no, my husband will be here."

"No, Mistress, he will not."

"Why not? Is he sick or hurt?"

"No, he sleeps in pleasure."

"What pleasure?"

"He is in copulation with one of my kind and Mistress Van Keulen."

"That whore! That's unnatural."

"Yes, she is very old, but safe from begetting and her husband is away."

"I didn't mean Mewdriss, I meant your . . . eh . . ."

"V'wuuk, it is V'wuuk, and he was wearing a mask. 'Tis my understanding that everyone does this in Carnival."

Meg nodded in troubled agreement.

"And yous thinks they all be human, ha ha ha."

Gef was enjoying himself, and Meg suddenly came back on track. "Did you just say *he*? Is my husband breeding with another man?"

"Not exactly. I have never seen him unclad, but 'twas told he hath no pillicock. Neither does he sport any vulvas, but does have a considerable quantity of paps and uddickeries."

Meg was silent.

"V'wuuk will keep him busy and away from us for as long as you want."

"Forever would be nice," Meg snarled.

"If that's what you want, Mistress."

Meg looked at the Filthling and realized he was taking her

very seriously. The toothy grin had certainly disappeared from his mischievous face.

"No, I don't mean that . . . that I don't want him back."

Only the first part of that sentence had conviction; it almost entirely petered out around the word *want*. Gef opened his eyes wider and Meg felt the litmus-paper hollow behind them waiting for her next doubt or lie.

"If your fellow can keep him away, then yes, come to my house. I will leave the garden gate unlatched."

"We will be there early next morning."

Meg was pleased to be home, dropping the heavy clanking basket and sack of spoils just inside the door and stepping over them. They meant nothing now, just tokens of a failed conflict. She went straight to the sink, where she made herself a strong drink of gin and sugar. She dumped her breastplate, helmet, and sword on the kitchen table and floor. Hastily she found bread, cheese, and cooked sausage, which she earnestly devoured while unbuttoning her stiff pinafore dress. She pulled off her stiff boots and released the unwashed butcher's knife in the passage.

The day had been a nightmare; all had gone wrong. She had gutted the man who had so grievously insulted her. She had stupidly injured her best friend. And now she was in fear of her life, while her lazy, drunken husband was fornicating with a slut and vermin. Then she remembered that her son was still alive. She had been told that he would escape and that all things would be well and bonny. And she believed it. Against all odds, she felt it would be true. Meg fell into her groaning bed, which was gloriously empty, still wearing her stained petticoat, trusting in the radiant optimism of a talking polecat.

In seconds she rolled into the innocent depth of an all-embracing sleep. Its purring warmth seemed to last for years—right up until Cluvmux tapped her shoulder with a very bony finger.

"All right, all right, I know it's breakfast time."

She automatically reached for the flint and taper. But just before she lit the candle, she remembered that Cluvmux didn't have a bony finger. He didn't have a bony anything, and he wasn't there.

When the flame swallowed half the darkness, she saw that she was not alone. The bedroom was packed with a mass of moving shadows of all shapes and sizes. She could see the details of those closest to the light, the ones that sat or stood around her bed, staring at her . . . and none of them were human. Every conceivable and even more inconceivable creature and monster had been watching her, waiting for her to wake. She did the only two things possible: she screamed and pissed the bed, in tandem.

Gef was in a quandary. He was shocked by Meg's reaction, and for a moment or two, he did not understand why she was screeching so. Then he looked at the faces and semi-faces of all those in the room and guessed that she might have found their overall appearance unusual.

This was an important meeting and he didn't want it to go wrong. Some of the visitors had already left the bedroom. The tall deer-headed one in the long red cloak, who never spoke and who he thought was called Dommi, clasped her feathered hands over her velvety pointed ears. Behind her clattered Kreypex, looking sour-faced and annoyed. His crossbill beak clicked in time with the glass ball tapping against his hat. The ball hung from a twig that sprouted from the large green metal funnel he wore on his head.

Gef thought it prudent to open all the curtains and extinguish the troublesome light. In that way, the hesitant dawn would reveal the party slowly. He told the ones closest to the windows to open the shutters while he went to comfort Meg.

Snuffing the candle out with his yellow fingers and speaking at the same time, he said, "Good morning, Mistress, it's only us, come for the meeting that we planned."

Meg could hear his voice and recognized who was speaking but still had the bedsheet over her head.

"You can come out nows, nobody will hurt you."

The damp sheet was being pulled gently by the three strong fingers of the branch-like arm of a hollow tree being. Its miserable blue face peered out from the thin dried trunk. Of all the creatures in the room, it most resembled a human. In its other arm, it held a baby wrapped tight in a swaddling of shiny white bark. Thinking a strong odor might be difficult for Meg, the tree being had considerately left its steed—a giant rat—outside; unfortunately it had no way of knowing that its own stench of rotting, mildewed wood was substantially worse. It had slithered up onto Meg's bed to occupy one corner, its scaled, sluglike body tapering out of its trunk and dangling down to the floor.

"We have come to help you regain yours son."

Meg shifted the sheet on her head so that she could look through its aperture at Gef, who had become more distinct in the early light timidly soaking the room. He beamed at her pale face.

"There yous are, no need to hide. We will not be afraid."

There was some movement in the throng that indicated his assertion might not be true for all in the company.

"Why are you all here?"

"Like we agreed, to meet today."

"Not in the middle of the night and not in here."

Gef looked perplexed.

"I expected later, much later, and in the garden or the yard," said Meg, finally taking off the sheet in the growing brightness. She did not look about her, staying fixed on Gef. But occasionally she allowed her eyes to look past him, to what dwelt behind. There were things sitting among her clothes and possessions that she would not let near her midden, let alone her bedroom.

Then, in a hushed voice, she said, "Get them all out of here. I want to get up, wash, and get dressed."

"You just go ahead. We don't mind staying."

"Out, out now."

"But I don't think that—"

"I don't care what you think. I will not be given orders by a weasel."

"Weasel?! I . . . I am a mongoose."

"I don't care what you are. Get them out, then we will talk."

She put the sheet back over her head and snuggled under the blanket.

Gef put his fingers to his lips, whistled, and then pointed at the door.

By the time he returned and knocked, Meg had cleansed herself, dressed, and stripped the bed.

"Come in," she called.

Gef entered to find her trying to shovel up some sticky droppings that had been trodden into a small carpet by the window. They both seemed irritated with each other, and it took some time before the conversation became fluid. It was the mention of her son that made her sit down and stop fussing with the housework.

"Yes, like I said before, we can get him out if the guards are not there."

"And how will we do that? You know what happened last time. They will be expecting us."

"They are too strong in their days times, Mistress, we must conquer thems in their nights."

Meg looked hard at the diminutive figure speaking to her. How could a polecat or weasel or mongoose have so much understanding?

"You must do thems in the way yous knows best."

Meg snorted a sour laugh and said, "But I know no ways."

Gef cocked his head and grinned. " 'Tain't true, Mistress, I bin a-diggin' on yours plot."

He then made a grandiose gesture of preening its whiskers, one tiny yellow hand twitching his mustache-like bristles. It took a few moments for the weight of those words to tally, and when it did, the color drained from her long face.

"Those add-mensturations could also be given to the soldier folks."

Meg was speechless.

" 'Twas it with 'shrooms or nightshades?"

" 'Shrooms," she said in a small voice.

"Did you grow them or forage for them?"

"A bit of both. Grietje taught me about them and many others. She had a great wisdom about such things. But I guess you know that?"

"Aye, I does. 'Twas I who showed her the poison arts."

Meg's long, impassive face changed, respect giving it a new rigidity.

"Did you ever think about slipping some juice to the police guards you hate so much?"

"How could I ever do that? They would never let me get that close. And there are so many of them."

"Duff'rence now is you ain't doing it lonesomes. Yous got us on yours sides."

"You would do that?"

"Likes I said before, we are near the end of our time in this realm. It took a long time for us to believe in the malice and spite that drive yous people. We learnt it the hards ways. So let's give some back in a farewell gift."

"How shall we do it?"

"Am I not right in thinking it's your good folk who supply vittels, wine, and beer for the garrison?"

"Eh, yes."

"There you have it. We simply doctor all."

"We will need gallons of poison, especially for those big tuns of beer."

"The beer will be our speciality. We have things you could not dream of."

He turned toward the door, which he had left open, and whistled loudly. Meg started to ask questions, but he held a finger to his mouth, stopping her.

"Come in," he called, and a few moments later something ran across the floor.

A mouse, she thought, until Gef picked it up. He walked over and climbed up on a chair close to Meg and extended his hand to show her a smooth, maroon-colored soft lozenge. It reminded her instantly of a slice of fresh liver.

"Mistress Meg, meet Judy. Judy, meet Mistress Meg," said Gef, and the thing squirmed in his hand, appearing to take a curt bow.

"It 'as no mouth nor ears and understands little but is gifted with a unique property."

To Meg's horror, Gef dug one of his long dirty fingernails into the thing and tore off a tiny sliver, holding it up before her eyes. It was the size of her little fingernail, only much cleaner. The sliver also moved and took a miniature bow. Meg opened her hand, expecting to receive it, but the mongoose pulled it away sharply.

"You must never touch a Judy. There is enough toxic venom in that small scrape to kill a score of your sort."

With that, he gave the scrape to Judy, who absorbed it back into itself. He then gently returned it to the floor, flicked it hard with the tip of his yellow finger, and pointed toward the door.

"Split," he said, and it cartwheeled and slithered to the doorway, where it stopped, turned toward them, and divided vertically in two. Both halves bowed before they left.

"One Judy per tun makes two hundred and fifty gallons of lethal merriment."

"How will it get in the barrel?"

"They can get in anywhere they choose."

"And how will we make it choose?"

"Ask it nicely. But there will be a price."

"What price?"

"Best not to know."

"Then why tell me of it?"

"Because it will pay for the life of your boy."

"Then it is worth it, no matter what!"

"No matter what."

THE BLIND

Cluvmux fell out of the tangled mass of bedsheets and woke up without any idea of where he was. He stumbled about the unknown room seeking a vessel to relieve himself in. This he eventually found in the kitchen of the strange house. On his way back to the bed, he foolishly opened the heavy curtain to look outside for a memory of place, time, or identity. The bright sunlight made him groan and cover his eyes. It also exposed the naked occupants of the bed he had been living in for the past three days. He approached the bed, hoping it was just a nightmare.

The sight of Mewdriss van Keulen was bad enough, but the sight of his other playmate made him lurch back, fall over his own feet, and grab the bedpost for support. Lying faceup, spread-eagled like a starfish, was a person, a thing whose green body was beyond belief. Its face was that of a smiling trout, and its lipstick was the same color as Mewdriss's big toe, which it held gently in its warty three-fingered hand. Cluvmux hoped it was just a grotesque costume, but he knew it wasn't. Memories of their couplings crawled into his stomach. The threat of more recollections was enough to evict him from this nightmare. He found scraps of his, and some of her, Carnival costume to cover himself as he tiptoed, stumbled, and crawled out of the Van Keulen house at the fastest speed he could muster. His head was pounding, his mouth felt scratchy, wanting a release—he needed a drink.

The streets were quiet, and the bright morning air was singed with the smell of distant fires. The nearest tavern was a large and noisy establishment, the Caballistas del Camino's favorite watering hole. Since the guards were not allowed alcohol inside the walls of the garrison, the tavern was always open, night and day. Cluvmux knew where it was; he and Meg had been there once or twice.

The building was in sight when he fell over the first corpse. Smoke was rising from the back of the building, and crows were squawking and gathering on its roof. He walked inside like a somnambulist, not believing what he was seeing. They were all dead. Sitting at the table, lying on the floor, one standing at the bar, locked in a bizarre rigor mortis.

"Plague," Cluvmux muttered. He grabbed up an untouched mug of beer and staggered out, wanting to find his way back home. The only traces left of Carnival were a few bits of torn bunting being carried away by the wind, and a couple of false noses in the cleaned gutter. All the laughter, songs, and parties had been shelved; the costumes of impropriety exchanged for sober gray work clothes. Lent had arrived, and his ugly wife would be even more of a nagging nuisance than before.

He supped his beer as he turned onto the wide street that ended at the garrison. Its brutal gates were open wide and smoke poured from its rooftops. He peeped inside, expecting to be challenged and abused at any moment. Something, everything here had changed; it was almost silent inside the high walls. One of the features of the stronghold was its constant noise, not just due to the loud men but also because of the machinery they used night and day. The machines, powered by treadmills, had stopped for the first time since their installation. Only the sounds of crackling could be heard coming from the vast prison, where the two wheels were continually powered by slave labor. But the wheels were in flames now, and their smoke-filled house would soon collapse in the hungry heat.

Cluvmux was in a daze. So he sat himself down on an upturned cart and held his hands over his face. Sadly, this meant he didn't see the Woebegot and the Filthling walking hastily out of the prison, holding a weak, emaciated man between them. The trio joined the few other people on the streets, who were all going in the same direction. Cluvmux wiped his eyes, staggered to his feet, and started to follow them. A crowd had amassed outside the monastery, whose doors were resolutely shut. He saw one of his cronies and was told how the monks had announced that the demise of the Inquisition's soldiers was none of their business. Then they'd closed the monastery doors, saying they would remain closed until Lent was over. Cluvmux took his last swig of beer and threw the clay mug at the doors, shouting, "Fuck 'em!"

As the day dimmed around Cluvmux, the faltering trio reached the back of Meg's garden, where she was hanging the washing on a long rope line. She heard someone struggling to open the gate and spun around, ready to defend herself against anything . . . except the return of her prodigal son.

Inside the abbey, no one heard the pathetic beer mug break against the solid doors. They were all far too busy. Benedict had taken command without any discussion or dissension. Even Friar Cecil had remained silent and mostly absent since the abbot's disappearance. There had been much speculation about what the new Oracle might bring and how its power would establish a more robust control of the Gland. The Lenten isolation had worked both ways. No guidance or wisdom was arriving from the church outside. It seemed that the most important thing now was the Oracle's internment ceremony. It did not take long to discover that Benedict was the only one of the brothers who had sufficient knowledge of the ritual and its language. To be sure, the Oracle itself had to be consulted, but only Benedict had had any dealings with it—and all the information about its requirements and day-to-day needs had died in the bloody conflict between the two men who brought it to the abbey gates.

It was necessary that someone speak to the Oracle to gain its opinion or its vision about what should happen next. But no one volunteered after what they'd learned from Pittancer Johbert, who'd been sent to ascertain knowledge of the Blessed One's nourishment. And Johbert had reported back dutifully. It was becoming clear that this Oracle was quite different from the Quiet Testiyont and that it possessed nothing of its predecessor's gentle personality.

Finally, it was agreed that Cecil and Ludo must take on the task. Cecil was chosen for his seniority, and Ludo for the popularity of his innocent nature. Neither monk was excited by the prospect. However, duty was duty, and they both rehearsed their approach and the questions they dared bring to the Blessing's cell.

As the bold brothers neared its door, a volley of rude and gaseous noises could be heard, followed by chunks of giggles. It sounded much like adolescent boys imitating the passing of wind by blowing into their elbows, thus instigating hours of merriment.

The brothers stopped and looked at each other, trying to find strength and comfort. They coughed and knocked to announce their presence. The Oracle did the same, mimicking them exactly. There was a moment of silent chill.

At last Ludo spluttered, "Blessing, we must consult with you on the question of your guardian, the next abbot of this abbey."

Cecil quickly joined in. "It is a matter that must be decided before your internment. May we come in?"

"Inturdment, stinks in here, pray enter."

This announcement was followed by another round of fart noises and giggles, which may not have been a problem had it not been delivered in Ludo's voice.

Benedict's authority was given on the eighth day of Lent, just before the internment ceremony. The Oracle had made it clear that it would not enter the Cyst until it had been agreed that the old man would be the next abbot. Just before entering the Cyst, the Oracle announced his name as Loxias the Blind.

When all had departed, Benedict was summoned to the hole in the wall.

"Tomorrow twilight, come hither. We have much to say and write down. Bring the boy; he will be our scribe."

"Yes, Divine One. May I ask you something?" There was no answer, so Benedict went ahead. "Are you blind?"

"Not yet," answered Loxias. "But this day, at the distant end of the Middle Sea, I have seen an island erupt, casting fire and brimstone into the heavens and turning the sky to ash. I have also taken all the tendrils and roots of your Gland and realigned their commitment. And I have put in the minds of those in Rome that you must run this significant house."

Benedict was overcome by the magnitude of the Blessing's achievements and by its statement.

"Now you must be given a new name," the Oracle pronounced.

Benedict bowed slightly and placed a modest hand on his modest chest.

"Abbot Twisted Lip the Ugly."

The next evening Benedict and Dominic slowly approached the Cyst. An overpowering scent of honey and ammonia laced the air, and the old man's brain changed shape in his skull. As night fell, the Oracle began to sing, promising to tell of great and wondrous things.

"Now we shall be silent before we start the important work."

The vigil lasted all night long, with no words spoken. Dominic sat with paper, a quill, and ink as instructed, awaiting the promised words of erudition. Excitement and trepidation pulled through their exhaustion to create a condition without name.

Just after dawn, as the scruffy skylark embroidered the waking air and the sleepy bittern hollowed out its first boom, the Oracle, in a voice they did not know, told them to write down everything.

"Saint Christopher is a dog-headed man," it began.

Acknowledgments

Great thanks again to Tim O'Connell for his faith, wisdom, skill, and determination in getting *Hollow* commissioned and edited, and to the team at Vintage. Endless gratitude to Caroline Ullman for her encouragement, intelligence, and commitment to me and to the transmutation of the original manuscript into English. To my steadfast agent, Millie Hoskins, at United Agents, and also to Jon Elek, who got the ball rolling. And to the redoubtable Seth Fishman at the Gernert Company. Respectful gratitude to all my readers and for those who went out of their way to support my ravings: Rebecca Hind, Geoff Cox, Alan Moore, Iain Sinclair, Michael Moorcock, Stuart Kelly, Philip Pullman, William Driscoll, and my pals at the Ruskin School of Art and the Royal Academy of Arts.

To the legends of Hieronymus Bosch and Pieter Bruegel the Elder, whoever and whatever they were—demigods to any of us who dwell and farm in the landscape of the imagination. Painters beyond comprehension in the breath of their invention and the divinity of their skill. Constructing windows into humanity and magic, with all their shadows intact and talking.

PROFUNDISSIMA CUM HUMILITATE
SUPPLEX VOS ADORAMUS

ALSO BY

B. CATLING

THE VORRH
The Vorrh Trilogy, Book One

Next to the colonial town of Essenwald sits the Vorrh, a vast—perhaps endless—forest. It is a place of demons and angels, of warriors and priests. Sentient and magical, the Vorrh bends time and wipes memory. Legend has it that the Garden of Eden still exists at its heart. Now a renegade English soldier aims to be the first human to traverse its expanse. Armed with only a strange bow, he begins his journey, but some fear the consequences of his mission, and a native marksman has been chosen to stop him. Around them swirl a remarkable cast of characters, including a Cyclops raised by robots and a young girl with tragic curiosity, as well as historical figures, such as writer Raymond Roussel and photographer Edward Muybridge. While fact and fiction blend, the hunter will become the hunted, and everyone's fate hangs in the balance under the will of the Vorrh.

Fiction

THE ERSTWHILE
The Vorrh Trilogy, Book Two

In London and Germany, strange beings are reanimating. They are the Erstwhile, the angels that failed to protect the Tree of Knowledge, and their reawakening will have major consequences. In Africa, Essenwald falls into disarray after its timber workforce disappears into the Vorrh; now a team of specialists must find them. Blending the real and the imagined, *The Erstwhile* brings historical figures and places, as well as ingenious creations, together to create an unforgettable novel of births and burials, excavations and disappearances.

Fiction

THE CLOVEN
The Vorrh Trilogy, Book Three

In the stunning conclusion to this endlessly imaginative saga, the young Afrikaner socialite Cyrena Lohr is mourning the death of her lover, the Cyclops Ishmael, when she rekindles a relationship with famed naturalist Eugène Marais. Before departing down his own dark path, Marais presents her with a gift: an object of great power that grants her visions of a new world. Meanwhile, the threat of Germany's Blitz looms over London, and only Nicholas the Erstwhile senses the danger to come. Will he be able to save the man who saved him? And as Nazi forces descend upon Africa, will the Vorrh finally succeed in enacting its revenge against those who have invaded and defiled it? *The Cloven* is a book of battles and betrayals, in which Catling's incredible creations all fulfill their destinies and lead us to an epic conflagration with the fate of mankind hanging in the balance.

Fiction

VINTAGE BOOKS
Available wherever books are sold.
www.vintagebooks.com